Dear A

I hope . . . "Ghost
story i've included

SINGAPORE
KILLER

in case you want
red book #4 first.

Best wishes

Murray.

Also by Murray Bailey

Singapore 52
Singapore Girl
Singapore Boxer
Singapore Ghost

Map of the Dead
Sign of the Dead*

The Lost Pharaoh

Black Creek White Lies

I Dare You
Dare You Twice

* Previously entitled Secrets of the Dead

SINGAPORE KILLER

Murray Bailey

Heritage Books

First published in Great Britain in 2020 by Heritage Books

167976112

copyright © Murray Bailey 2020

ISBN 978-1-9997954-0-5

Heritage Books, Truro, Cornwall

For Mum and Dad

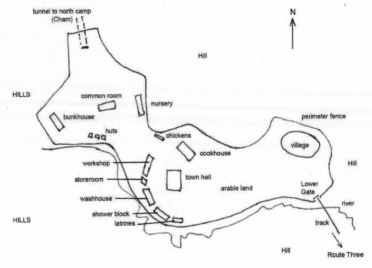

Map of Jeremiah's Shangri-La

ONE

Outside, the *whump whump whump* made people look and point with excitement or surprise. Helicopters were new and thrilling. Unless you were in the back with the doors open and the air rushing in.

The Search and Rescue pilot wore ear defenders and was totally focused ahead. He hadn't turned and looked or tried to make conversation the whole time they'd been in the air. He just sat at the front, his head and neck poking above the rear backrest. Inches away from the seats in the open section.

The man in the rear looked down and watched the treetops swirl and sway like random eddies in a stream. What was it about heights? Why the urge to jump?

Fear, the man knew. Both fear and excitement. Because a fall from here would be certain suicide.

Or murder.

The man glanced at the person beside him, of a very similar age and height and yet so different. A quick shove and the other man would be off the seat and out into the choppy air. Or at least he would be if they weren't handcuffed together.

The handcuffs looped above an overhead bar on a long chain. Some kind of safety arrangement, he figured.

Not long now. And then he saw it: a break in the jungle. They weren't going directly over it, but that didn't matter. He subconsciously began to nod as he worked out the pace and timing.

God, this was risky, but he felt the first tingle of adrenaline. He played out the moves and started counting.

Five.

He surreptitiously unclipped his seat belt. The man beside him moved his cuffed hand.

They looked at one another and the first man smiled encouragingly.

Four.

With his free hand, he chopped into the other's neck, unclipped his seat belt and pushed him to the opening.

The other man flailed and went over the edge. Unbalanced, the copter swayed and the first man held onto the straps.

Three.

Then he yelled as loud as he could. "He's out! My God, he's falling out!"

The pilot snapped his head back, saw the man dangling out of the door, saw the panic and snapped his head away again. Immediately, the helicopter descended.

"Clearing!" the pilot shouted. "Trying to land."

Two.

The first man fought with the straps, got himself into the second man's seat, and buckled up. All the time, he had the other arm jerking, the handcuffs tearing into his wrist.

They were coming down fast, canted to the right, swaying. Treetops swirled. Something thumped the fuselage.

One.

Retrieving the gun was easy. He aimed at the pilot's head and fired. It exploded, a satisfying burst of red, a moment to savour before the chaos.

The man hadn't been in an out-of-control helicopter before. He hadn't expected the spin and lurch. The world became a blur. His right arm felt like it would come out of the socket as the body on the other end thrashed and bashed into the fuselage. He felt contact and juddering. Something, maybe a branch, flashed in front of him and he pressed himself back against the seat.

He was spinning and falling and laughing.

And then he blacked out.

TWO

I climbed out of the military police Land Rover and stood with my friend Captain Robshaw. He was in uniform. I was not.

A Gurkha soldier beckoned to us and we headed through the trees in his direction.

My first view of the crash site was of broken branches, torn limbs like a giant had rampaged through the jungle. Then I saw the trees thinning and an opening and burnt undergrowth.

We stopped when we reached the edge of the clearing in which a helicopter lay canted nose down. There should have been three rotor blades but two had gone completely and the third had been snapped in half and pointed at an odd angle.

The Sikorsky S-51, nicknamed the Dragonfly, was an ungainly beast at the best of times.

The front wheel was missing, as was the sliding door. I changed position and saw that both doors were missing. Both stanchions for the left rear wheel were snapped and embedded in the ground, probably with the wheel still attached. The right wheel floated two feet off the ground due to the angle of the fuselage.

Originally, the helicopter had been silver grey. I could still see patches of the paint below the broken blade and

4

on the tail. The rest of the carcass had been blackened by fire.

I could see the tail and its blades embedded in the ground about thirty feet away.

Robshaw looked up at the bright but cloudy sky, shielding his eyes while sweeping back his straw-coloured hair. "The pilot saw a gap in the trees and tried to land it."

"Why?" I asked.

Robshaw shrugged and pointed to the stricken helicopter. "Shall we?"

I nodded and we walked forward and passed a shard of rotor blade. When we came to where the undergrowth was burnt, we stopped again. I could see footprints through the blackened ground. Too many.

"A shame about the scene," I said, referring to the lack of preservation.

"If it was more than an accident." He looked at me. "Tell me what you see, Ash."

I'd been a military investigator and now I was providing my services to the army in Singapore. Captain Robshaw was based in Gillman Barracks and a plane or helicopter crash should have been covered by SIB—the Special Investigations Branch of the military police—but there were only two SIB officers operating out here and they were both on assignment. I was ex-SIB, so Lieutenant Colonel Ambrose, CO of 200 Provost at Gillman, had asked for my assistance.

"I see a crashed helicopter that I suspect came pretty much straight down after clipping the trees."

"No wings," he said, shaking his head. "You wouldn't get me in one of those death buckets."

I said, "They're much more controllable than an airplane."

"Most of the time."

"The copter is fairly intact, which tells me it didn't fall far. Spun around a bit, hitting trees, breaking off the tail and rotors. The nose is gone, but the rest is pretty good."

"You'd think it was survivable."

"Where are the bodies?" I asked.

"Two men, on their way to Alexandra Hospital—the morgue." That was the main army hospital in Singapore, so we'd probably passed them on the drive here.

I said, "Burnt?"

"To a cinder."

I said, "Let's get closer."

We walked five paces and I crouched down and looked into the cockpit. Robshaw mimicked me.

There was more glass in here than in a plane's cockpit. All-round vision. Well almost, apart from the narrow footwell and directly behind. It reminded me of a gun turret on a bomber—without the guns.

I put gloves on and climbed in through the opening. The helicopter groaned and moved under my weight, and I let it settle before carefully climbing around the cockpit's single seat. I'm six two but slim. Even so, I couldn't help squeezing against the blackened metal. I figured it explained why I'd never seen a large helicopter pilot.

Up front, there was a steering column and an oval display directly ahead. Below were two foot pedals and a couple of levers. There was a hole where the nose had been. I figured it had taken most of the impact.

Everything was coated in soot. Most of the seat had been destroyed by the fire, although I could see the remains of the pilot's seat belt.

I touched the instrument panel and smeared the soot. Most came off, but some was baked on and blacker.

Two glass panels were missing, both on the left—one at eye level, one higher up. The remaining panels were all cracked.

I climbed back over the pilot's seat to where the door would have been. The helicopter creaked as it adjusted under my weight again.

"Have they found the doors?" I asked.

Robshaw called to the Gurkha, who walked over shaking his head.

I checked the runner where the door would have slid from front to back and saw no damage.

"The door was removed," I said. "Before the crash."

"And there's no rack," Robshaw added, and indicated where he was standing. There should be a rack here for carrying a stretcher. He turned to the Gurkha, who shook his head again.

"Why would it have been modified?" Robshaw asked rhetorically.

I was looking at the hold, which wasn't very big. There was a bench at the back where two men could sit, and space for one, maybe two where I was standing. I knew the pilots sometimes didn't land, preferring to hover and winch items through the door. I saw no sign of a winch. However, I did see scratch marks above the door. They weren't totally black, and running my finger over a metal bar confirmed my thinking that something had been attached. Something that could slide backwards and forwards.

The rear bench had gone, reduced to a metal frame and melted material. I carefully moved back and perched over the seat, not caring that my clothes would get covered in soot.

I looked up and around, touched the fuselage and noted the marks I'd left behind. Straight ahead was the pilot's seat, and I studied it long and hard.

"What are you thinking?" Robshaw asked, his head and shoulders through the doorway.

"How many bodies?"

"Two men. The pilot and a man in the back."

"Although the man in the back was thrown out. He didn't die here, did he?" I had seen evidence of where the pilot had sat but there were no similar burn patches in the back or scuff marks where a body might have been removed.

"That's right. The second man was thrown out. I guess it wouldn't have happened if the doors had been on."

"Helicopters may be new, but the pilots are damned good. I've seen men being trained at Tebrau Airfield in JB." JB stood for Johor Bahru, just over the causeway from Singapore. I'd been there a few times, as well as the Base Vehicle Depot sited on the same land.

"Right. That's where this one came from," Robshaw said. "They called it in as missing."

"This clearing is plenty big enough for them to land safely."

"But we're assuming there was a problem."

"There was a problem all right."

"The pilot lost control. Mechanical failure, most likely."

I was no mechanic, and a specialist would examine the components to establish whether anything had failed, but I knew the pilot had been dead before the helicopter struck the ground.

"You saw the windscreen," I said. "Glass discolours with heat. With extreme heat, it even melts."

He nodded.

"It didn't melt, but the blackening on the glass isn't just from the heat. And it's also on the instrument panel."

8

"What then?"

"Blood. That's burnt blood right in front of where the pilot sat."

"Banged his head, I guess. I heard he was quite a mess."

"The restraints should prevent that, no matter how hard the impact."

"If he was wearing them."

I knew airmen could be cavalier. Maybe they thought bravado made them sexier. The pilot might not have been wearing a seat belt, but I shook my head anyway.

"The burn pattern," I said, climbing out. "On the ground. Where's the fuel?"

We walked around the fuselage and found the fuel intake on the far side. The flap was missing, but I noted this side of the fuselage showed less burning than the other.

"What does it tell you?" I said.

"The fuel didn't ignite."

"Correct." I stepped back and surveyed the scene. "This burn pattern isn't from the helicopter's fuel."

"A spark then."

"I presume an RAF investigator will be looking for mechanical failure?"

"There's a mechanic on the way."

I nodded. "He can confirm, but because the burn is lower than up high, I'm sure the burn wasn't from the rotor engine. And there's the other thing."

Robshaw waited as I walked him back to the pilot's seat.

"I'm pretty sure the fire was most intense in two places. Here"—I tapped the glass, indicating the seat—"and by the doorway. The second body was found there, wasn't it?"

We looked at the Gurkha, who nodded.

I saw something in the burnt grass, picked it up, weighed it in my hand and dropped it into my pocket.

Robshaw raised his eyebrows.

"It's bad news, I'm afraid," I said. "This was no accident. Someone set fire to this helicopter—to the bodies in particular. And one more thing: I'm pretty sure the pilot was shot."

THREE

Captain Robshaw and I waited outside the morgue at BMH Alexandra in Singapore.

Doctor Kishan Thobhani grinned when he spotted me waiting. He was an unusual and quirky man, but I liked him a lot.

"Captain Carter, you are well I see."

"And you, Doc, have trimmed your beard."

Thobhani stroked his chin. "Ah, yes. Do you like it?"

"Very smart."

"Attractive was the word you were looking for, perhaps?" He shook his head with mock seriousness. "Now you've put me in a bad mood." He opened the double doors to the morgue and we followed him into the harshly lit room. Two bodies lay on tables supervised by the doctor's assistant.

Thobhani took a pair of rubber gloves from the other man and slipped them on. Robshaw and I stood at the foot of the tables, two paces back, while the doctor did a circuit of each. "Let's see what you've brought me today," he said, and the assistant picked up a clipboard, holding a pen at the ready.

"First body: male, aged in his twenties. Five foot eight. Extensive burns with charring to the hands, arms and head. Died at least forty-eight hours ago"—he shook his head as he thought—"Rigor's gone and decomposition has just about started. Always hard to judge in this hot climate, but I'd say less than sixty hours." He glanced at us and Robshaw nodded.

Now the doctor was at the man's head. "From the burn pattern I'd say that the first body was sitting: flames rising and burning his exposed skin on his arms, hands and head." He lifted a flap of what looked like skin on the side of the head and then traced his hand over the cranium. "This isn't skin, it's a cap. A leather cap."

"Pilot," Robshaw said, but this received a disapproving scowl from the doctor. Thobhani didn't mind nods, but speaking was strictly not allowed. He said it disturbed his focus.

Robshaw mouthed, "Sorry."

Thobhani took a pen and poked the lower face. "Lower jaw partially gone with severe charring inside the mouth. I can't judge whether he was still alive at the time of ignition because of the exposure. I'll know that once I get a look at his airways." He moved down to the shoulders and attempted to cut away at fabric. "Wearing a jacket that below the neck looks to have protected the torso from the flames. Two indentations—something else melted into the shoulder areas, which could have been straps. Seated and strapped in," he added.

I was keen for the man to be turned over but had to wait patiently for the doctor as he worked his way over the body. He used scissors and parted what remained of the jacket.

"An item in the pocket," he said, as he cut and used tweezers to remove a charred lump.

The doctor glanced at me. "We'll get this analysed but it may be too melted and burnt." He worked his way down and cut into the trouser pockets. "Again something in here. A packet, severely burnt. A penknife and possibly a pen."

He stepped back, put the items in a bag and looked at me. Then he nodded to his assistant and said, "All right, let's get this chap rolled over, shall we?"

Together they carefully flipped the dead man and my fears were immediately confirmed. Despite the charring, I could see a clear hole, the size of a sixpence, in the back of the skull. Only this was black rather than silver.

Doctor Thobhani worked his way up the body, concluding again that the man had been sitting with flames rising. When he got to the head he poked his pen into the hole. "Cavity in the occipital bone, likely to be an entry wound. Lines up with the jaw, which is likely the exit and explains the damage there. Could have been caused by shrapnel." He glanced at me. "More likely a bullet. This is our cause of death: a single shot to the back of the head." He must have read the question on my face because he added: "Impossible to tell the distance or calibre. Gunpowder residue normally tells us how close the barrel was. Obviously, we can't see that now, but from experience, I'd judge a nine millimetre from fairly close range."

I held out the small black item that I'd picked up from the ground beside the helicopter. He looked at it and nodded, weighed it in his hand like I had before bagging it. "Cartridge," he said. "We'll get it checked."

The doctor moved around to the next table and nodded to check his assistant was ready. "Second body: male, aged in his twenties. Maybe older, but not much older than mid-thirties. Five foot eleven, give or take. Burns worse than body one in places. Extensive charring to the head and neck, clothes largely burned away except for his left side. Hands in a pugilistic posture with extensive charring. Died between forty-eight and sixty

13

hours ago." He poked his pen into the man's mouth and opened it. "Soot present in— correction, burns in the mouth suggesting that he was still breathing."

"Burned alive?" Robshaw said, and received a scowl from Thobhani.

The doctor continued: "A COHb test will confirm, but it is likely that death occurred after he caught fire."

He moved to the left shoulder, cut away some material, and I saw discoloured white skin.

"Severe ligament damage to the left shoulder," Thobhani said. "And dislocation of the joint. The left side was protected from the worst of the heat and both lividity of the skin and less burning suggests he died lying on his side."

He worked his way down the body and finally cut away the remnant of the man's trousers. "Severe damage to the legs, and the right tibia looks broken." He picked up the trousers, felt them and inserted tweezers into the material. "There appears to be something in the left trouser pocket. Some burning but mostly intact. Again protected from the brunt of the fire by his posture."

He dropped the item in a bag, pulled off the glove and rubbed his hands together. "Right, gentlemen, the show's over for now. Some more work to be done and I'll have a full report within two hours."

I shook his hand and we walked out of the hospital.

"What now?" Robshaw asked.

"Now we visit Tebrau Airfield."

14

FOUR

The airfield was ten miles north-east of Johor Bahru on Route Three. After a break in the tall elephant grass, Robshaw turned left at a double signpost. The first sign said: Base Vehicle Depot. The second: Tebrau Airfield and FTC, which stood for Flight Training Corps.

After a short incline, the road split and we went right towards the airfield, which looked disused. Weeds grew through the runway and the pre-war hangars appeared old and tired.

We drove along the runway towards buildings with RAF written above the door of the largest one. Next to it was the squadron leader's office.

Robshaw parked outside and I knocked on the open door. Squadron Leader Alex Kennedy beckoned us inside.

We sat and he leaned against his desk. Kennedy's normally weary eyes seemed more exhausted than usual, and when he spoke I heard the strain in his voice.

"He's dead, isn't he?"

I nodded and introduced Robshaw.

Kennedy breathed, forced a smile, and shook the captain's hand. "Welcome to 656 Squadron."

"What was the pilot's name?" I asked.

"Flight Lieutenant Tony Billings. My best helicopter instructor. Nice guy, terrible poker player." He shook his head. "What can you tell me?"

"Not much," I said. "We've seen the bodies in the morgue. Preliminary PM has taken place with further analysis underway."

Robshaw said, "Tell us about the S-51."

"The Dragonfly."

"It had no doors and no rack for casualties."

Kennedy tilted his head. "That's right. It was a training helicopter, not intended for use in the field.

"So, what was Billings doing up north?" I asked.

"I don't know."

"You don't know?" I said. "But you keep records of all the flights in and out." On a different investigation, I'd previously been through these so I knew Kennedy ran an efficient operation despite this being a training centre.

He blinked and shook his head and I could see that the loss of his man had affected him deeply. Maybe his mind wasn't quite functioning.

"Yes," he said, "Billings logged the Dragonfly out the day before yesterday after we received a call. He knew where he was going but had been told it was sensitive."

"Sensitive?"

Kennedy shook his head. "If I'd known I would have challenged him. He was making a pickup."

"Of another man," I said.

"Right."

"From where?"

"The flight records say... Kahang."

That was about forty miles due north as the crow flies. The crash site had been slightly west of a direct route. We'd taken Route One and then cut east to reach it.

16

"Why not fly directly back?" I asked. "Why go westwards?"

Kennedy shook his head. "Maybe he detoured to Kluang. I don't know. We heard nothing from Billings after he left. Could it be relevant?"

"I don't know," I said.

"Who made the call? Who was the pickup?" Robshaw asked.

"The records don't say," Kennedy said.

"Is that normal?"

"No."

"So you don't know who or why?" Robshaw asked.

"No."

"I know 848 Squadron are the official helicopter support for the army," I said. "Why call here?"

"I don't know that either. We reported the copter missing two nights ago when Billings didn't return. Took them a day to find it."

We asked a few more questions but got nothing of use out of the old squadron leader.

Before leaving, I said, "Have you seen the crash report yet?"

"No. The investigator has just been and given me a verbal report before he writes it up. If you want him he's over at the BVD."

The Base Vehicle Depot had been on the left as we came in. Robshaw drove us back and we turned into the large fenced area with a sign on the gate: BVD 221. Two guards watched us drive by with nothing but a casual glance.

We passed rows of army vehicles, some of which appeared in good condition and here for storage and distribution. Others were in various stages of repair. We

17

passed a long cavernous garage with many people working inside and headed for offices at the far end.

I'd been here before and knew the unit was run by Major Chris Broom, although I'd never met the guy. Yet again, he wasn't in the office, but we weren't looking for him, we were looking for the crash investigator. We found him chatting in an office, and he greeted us with a casual smile and nod when we did introductions.

"Not done the report yet," he said.

"Would you mind giving us a verbal update," I asked, "like you gave the squadron leader?"

"Not a problem. I can give you a quick summary."

I nodded.

He said a bunch of technical stuff before clarifying: "No sign of mechanical failure," he said. "The engine looks fine. The rotor mechanics are fine."

"Fuel?"

"I detected no problem with the ignition or fuel system, although one thing was odd…"

We waited expectantly.

He continued: "The fuel cap wasn't there."

"We noticed it wasn't on. Why is that odd?"

"It had been forced off."

I said, "Conclusion?"

He shrugged.

"What about an overall conclusion about the cause of the crash?"

"Supposition," he said, raising his eyebrows. "The tail and rear rotor were snapped off, so I can't say for certain, but it's possible that the tail controls failed, putting the bird in a spin. This would have forced the pilot to attempt an out-of-control landing and hence the damage and loss of the blades."

There was something in his tone. I said, "But that's not your theory, is it?"

"No. My theory is that someone caused that Dragonfly to come down. They forced the fuel cap for access to an accelerant and then set fire to the helicopter."

"The burn pattern," I said.

"Right. But what I don't get is, why do it like that? Why wouldn't they just ignite the fuel? They could have burned the helicopter easier that way—blown it up."

"Thanks," I said. "That's my theory too."

"Which means there was a third man," Robshaw said. "The pilot, the other dead guy and someone who burned the helicopter."

The investigator said, "Who was the second man?"

"We don't know yet. The pilot died in his seat. The second man died outside by the hatch."

I said, "The pilot was shot."

"Jeez!" The crash investigator visibly paled. "Murdered?"

"Back of the head."

"After the crash?"

"As you say, unless the rear rotor failed, I don't see why the helicopter would crash otherwise."

The other guy nodded. "A bullet to the back of the pilot's head would certainly do it. Crazy. Sick."

"Let's hope we're wrong," I said. However, I thought that was unlikely. We were dealing with a crazy man who had brought down a helicopter.

"Why do it?"

"That's the big question," Robshaw said.

"I think there's a bigger question," I said as we drove back to Singapore. "It's not just why do it, but why didn't this third man just blow up the helicopter?"

FIVE

I had a small office on Carpenter Street. When I'd left Penang a few months ago, I was unsure of my future. I'd decided to stay in Singapore and use my experience and contacts. I worked with the army and military police. I also had contacts in the Singapore and Malayan police and I had dealings with Andrew Yipp. He was a major businessman and philanthropist in Singapore—on the surface. Beneath this veneer, he was the head of the largest Chinese secret society in the country. Of course, such gangs were illegal, but Yipp had so far eluded conviction.

I'd been employed by the Singapore government, for the secretary responsible for internal security, and he'd wanted me to help fabricate a case against Yipp. I'd eventually resigned and been rudderless for almost a year.

Now I was back, I'd set myself up as an independent investigator and recruited Madam Chau as my secretary. She was as wily as a fox and as bad-tempered as a baited bear—but only when annoyed, thankfully. Unsurprisingly, I did my best to avoid annoying her. In return, she was excellent at dealing with time-wasters and was a first-class translator.

I'd had trouble with a beautiful translator when I'd first arrived in Singapore, perhaps that's why I'd chosen the most unappealing one I could find this time. Madam Chau's face was so flat that it looked like she'd been struck with a frying pan. This, plus a miserable demeanour, reminded me of a basset hound—an ugly one. It was hard to judge, but I figured she was aged between forty and fifty. I didn't dare ask since she would have probably taken offence.

Why Madam and not Mrs Chau? Well, when I offered her the job, she insisted on the title. She said that it gave her an air of authority. It meant she was more than just a receptionist. Whatever made her happy.

After an early morning session at the YMCA Boxing Club, I climbed the staircase to my office and greeted my non-receptionist.

"Where have you been?" she said gruffly in response.

I hadn't been in the office for a couple of days and I figured she wasn't asking about my session in the boxing gym, so I said, "Working with the MPs."

She cleared her throat as though disapproving.

I smiled. "I'll have a cup of tea, please, Madam Chau."

"Lots of letters," she said after grumbling, then stood up and started fussing with a kettle that sat on one of two filing cabinets. One had crockery inside. The other had hanging files ready for the copious reports I was yet to write. Apart from that, Madam Chau kept the bills in there.

I crossed the spacious room and sat at my desk. The office was government-owned but had been empty for many years. We had spent the first week cleaning the place, including getting thick grime off the windows.

The sun was rising over Singapore and would be glinting off the Singapore River by now. Only I wouldn't

21

see it for a few more hours. I faced east but had a view of bricks and windows: an office building full of clerks and typists—all four floors of it. Occasionally people would glance across, and I wondered what they thought of the wide empty room and the two people in it: me and one craggy old Chinese lady. An odd couple, but it was a work in progress.

"Anything interesting?" I asked when Madam Chau placed my steaming cup of tea in front of me.

"Hold on!" she said, and she plodded back to her desk. Once there, she collected a bundle of letters and plodded back.

She stood over me and I detected the distinct smell of boiled cabbage, probably what she'd eaten last night.

"Yes?" I prompted.

She put a bundle of letters in front of me. "Five requests for assistance," she said, "and one marriage proposal."

"Let's deal with the five requests, shall we?"

"Two of them are from young ladies asking for help finding young gentlemen. Only they weren't such gentlemen otherwise these girls wouldn't be so burdened now, would they?"

Madam Chau was referring to soldiers who had made girls pregnant and disappeared—or at least that's what was claimed. While I realized it was a real problem, I'd also heard of local girls claiming that a number of different men were responsible for their single child.

If they had proof of a relationship, and the soldier was a regular, they could get compensation. Most of the time they lacked proof or the soldier was on National Service. I'd been operating for six weeks and had so far received a dozen such letters.

"I don't do that sort of work, Madam Chau," I said.

"I know." She gave me a grin. "I tell them you don't do it, but they still write. There is one letter about a lost dog, asking if you could find it. There is one complaining about a leaky roof and asking for you to deal with the landlord."

"You said five letters. What's the last one about?" I asked.

"Ah, a proper job for a man with your talent." The way she said it made it sound sarcastic, although I think she was being genuine.

She handed me an envelope and I removed the letter inside, written in Chinese.

"What does it say?"

"It's from a man whose son died of a snake bite."

"OK."

"The father thinks it's suspicious but the police won't investigate."

"Is it a reasonable case?"

"Judge for yourself; the father will be here in"—she checked her watch—"thirty-three minutes."

I knew Madam Chau was a stickler for timekeeping. She arrived at eight in the morning and left on the stroke of seven in the evening. She never spoke of her private life, although I knew there was a Mr Chau at home and he expected dinner at a certain time every day. I wondered if he called himself *Master* Chau.

Madam Chau grumbled when I was late or unreliable and I knew that any visitor would be read the riot act. She would have told this man what time to arrive or he would have his request rejected—like most of the letters I received. I'm sure she knew I was desperate for interesting cases, but she still persisted with her ruthless attitude.

It worked, however, and minutes before his allotted time, a nervous Chinese man stood at my door. He wore a dark blue suit and a hat, which he removed, and ran a comb through his thinning hair.

My receptionist barked at him as though he'd been late and ushered him into the hard-backed seat opposite my desk. Before he sat, he gave me a deferential bow and blinked rapidly. Madam Chau stood behind him and I figured she was about to translate.

I introduced myself and the poor man half stood and bowed again. He tried to speak but his words came out as a stutter.

I raised a hand, stopping him. "Please would you make him a cup of tea, Madam Chau?"

She glared at me, and I waited while she boiled the kettle and made excessive noise preparing three drinks.

By the time she returned, my visitor had relaxed slightly, enough to speak anyway.

"My name is Wu Jun Fan," he began, speaking through Madam Chau. He told me where he lived and that he used to run a greengrocer's shop. He had stopped due to ill health and his son had taken over the job four months ago. His son—Alan Wu—worked hard but the income had declined because of competition. To maintain margins, the son worked harder. He would regularly travel to the mainland and buy fruit and vegetables cheaper.

"That's when the trouble occurred."

"What do you mean?" I asked.

"The man I used to buy everything from did not like it. He said that if my son buys his wares in Malaya then others will follow suit and his business will suffer."

"That's business."

"Of course, but this man was not happy. He sent someone to the shop who smashed things up."

"You told the police, Mr Wu?" I asked.

"My son told them."

"What was the man like?"

"Tall, Chinese, maybe thirty."

"Anything more specific?"

"He had a snake tattoo."

"And your son died of a snake bite?"

The old guy blinked tears before getting his emotions under control. "Yes, two months ago."

"It happens."

The man shook his head firmly after Madam Chau translated.

"It happens in the jungle," he said. "My son hated the jungle. He would never go there. He would never take the risk. The man put a poisonous snake in my son's truck so that he wouldn't see it in the dark."

I wrote down the details: the name of the supplier, the date of the incident, and a timeline leading up to the alleged murder. However, Mr Wu couldn't tell me the name or anything more about the snake-tattoo man.

"I will talk to the police," I said when he'd finished.

"You cannot trust the police."

This was undoubtedly true, to a degree. Some police were corrupt, but then you could say that about any organization. I didn't think the police were any more corrupt than, say, the Singapore government or Customs.

"Leave it with me," I said. "I'll do my best to find the truth."

The man gave me a weak smile and nod before scuttling out. He hadn't touched his cup.

"What do you think?" Madam Chau said, sipping her now cold tea and screwing up her face in disgust.

I shrugged. "I don't know, but I'll certainly ask questions and see what turns up."

SIX

A driver appeared at my office door and said I was needed at the hospital. I left a few moments after Mr Wu, and our military police jeep passed him, a sorry figure, walking with a limp towards the docks.

Captain Robshaw greeted me when I arrived at Alexandra Hospital and we waited for Doctor Thobhani. It wasn't his job to report the findings of the analysis but he did us a favour by shortcutting official channels.

"Body one—the pilot—definitely died before the fire," Thobhani said without preamble when he arrived. "Bullet to the back of the head. In terms of identity, the items in his pocket weren't decipherable. No chance of fingerprinting, but we could resort to dental records for identity."

"No need," I said. "He was Flight Lieutenant Tony Billings. 656 Squadron."

Thobhani grunted. "One piece of good news: the cartridge you gave me. Cleaned up, it's clearly a TT-33—a Tokarev cartridge. You know what that means?"

"I know the implication. What about body two?"

"As suspected, he was alive when he caught alight and the fire was the cause of death. However, in addition to the torn shoulder, he had severe internal injuries, like he'd been badly beaten down the left side, although there

26

were signs of damage all over. I confirmed the broken right tibia, but he also had a broken left wrist. Weirdest thing I've seen—like the bones were pulled apart."

Torn left shoulder and broken wrist, my brain processed.

Thobhani continued: "Again, no fingerprints for identification. The item recovered from the man's pocket was in better condition than the pilot's. Identity papers," he said, and paused. "No name distinguishable but it's clearly a warrant card."

"Warrant card?"

"Military police, I'm afraid, Ash."

I said nothing and exchanged glances with Robshaw, who had gone pale.

"Can I see it?" the captain said quietly.

"I'll have it sent over."

We stood in silence, each in our own thoughts, before I said, "Doc, the broken wrist and damaged shoulder... could body two have been dangling by his wrist."

"For that degree of damage, it would have to be more than dangling. Thrashing about maybe."

I was looking at Robshaw again and nodding. "Handcuff," I said. "Could that have caused the kind of break you were looking at?"

"Dangling from a metal ring around the wrist? That's possible if combined with extra force."

I shook Thobhani's hand.

Outside, I said, "I think there was a handcuff on a chain. It ran over a rod by the missing door hatch."

"And our man dangled outside the helicopter by the handcuff." Robshaw winced as he must have imagined the image: a body thrashing backwards and forwards against the fuselage, causing damage like he was being beaten.

I said, "He was barely alive when the copter came down. The handcuff was removed and he was set alight. Burned alive."

"One of our own," Robshaw said quietly.

Of course, I'd been thinking the same thing but hadn't vocalized it. He'd been a military cop wearing a handcuff, which could only mean one thing: there had been a man handcuffed on the other end; the man who had shot the pilot, caused the crash and burned them.

"We need to update Colonel Ambrose," Robshaw said, waving for his driver to pick us up.

A short drive later and we were in the CO's office.

"The helicopter crash," he said, reading the look on our faces. "Bad news?"

Robshaw and I ran through what we knew, and I concluded with: "The second man had a military police warrant card in his pocket."

"God!"

"It looks like our man had a prisoner. He telephoned Tebrau Airfield and got Flight Lieutenant Billings to fly out and pick him up." I paused, delaying the obvious question. When I saw Ambrose nod, it was like he was giving me permission to ask.

"Who are you missing?"

"No one that I know of," he said.

"But..."

"The special investigators..."

I'd been in SIB Three Company. There were two guys in Malaya, working out of Singapore, from Two Company. I'd recently met Lieutenant Joe Jenkins in Penang when I handed over to him on a job up there.

"Jenkins and Harwood," Ambrose said.

"When did they last check in?" I knew the SIB guys could be out in the field for days, often weeks at a time. Occasionally, if on a dangerous mission, they would schedule a check-in so that Command would know whether there was a problem or not. However, most of the time, they reported in when they had information.

Ambrose made a phone call, waited and then relayed the information to us. "Jenkins checked in two days ago, Harwood three."

"What were they working on?"

Ambrose raised his eyebrows. "Classified."

I nodded. That wasn't unusual, and when I'd met Jenkins a few months ago, he'd implied as much.

Ambrose said, "What else can you tell me?"

"We found a TT-33 cartridge. The doc initially suspected a 9mm but it was smaller. As you know, Tokarevs are commonly used in Soviet and Eastern Bloc weapons."

"And the weapons used by the Chinese terrorists." He was referring to the MNLA, the Malayan National Liberation Army—the ones we unofficially called bandits. "Working hypothesis?" he asked.

"One of our men requested extraction," Robshaw said. "He had a prisoner handcuffed to him but the bandit either had a weapon or got hold of a weapon and shot the pilot. He probably threw our man outside beforehand, but they were still connected. After the crash, our bandit unlocks the handcuffs. Easy enough to get our man's key at this stage."

Ambrose nodded. "Removes the handcuffs and sets fire to the helicopter."

"The men specifically," I said. "He burned the men more than the copter."

"Why do that?"

"Out of bullets?" Robshaw suggested.

I thought differently. "Could have been, or he wanted our man to suffer. The MP survived hanging outside a crashing helicopter. There aren't many worse ways to go than burning alive. Maybe these guys had history or maybe the prisoner was just an evil piece of work."

No one spoke for a moment. I'd dealt with a few evil men in my career, but that wasn't typical for the standard MP. I suspected neither Robshaw nor Ambrose had seen atrocities like I'd witnessed in Palestine. Occasionally they gave me nightmares, but most of the time I locked the images away in the dark recesses of my mind.

Ambrose took a drink of water. "So what did he do next, our bandit?"

"Just walked out of the jungle?" Robshaw suggested.

"Did he have transport? Did he hitch? Did anyone see him?" Ambrose was looking at Robshaw. "Take five men and get on it. I'll find out what Jenkins and Harwood are working on—see if we can make contact with them."

"What can I do?" I asked.

"Nothing for the moment, Ash," Ambrose said.

"I'd like to help. If it is one of our men…"

"I know. I know. Thanks, but leave this to us for now. If I need your help with SIB, I'll let you know."

SEVEN

I contacted the police about the greengrocer and was told minimal details. They had a name, the cause of death and dates. They had filed the death of Mr Wu's son as accidental. Case closed.

Then I went to find the grocer's shop. It was in Kallang district on the eastern fringe of the city. A shophouse: stalls downstairs and living accommodation upstairs. Madam Chau told me what the name written in Chinese meant: Fresh Garden. The name remained despite the change in ownership, and Mr Wu didn't live upstairs anymore. He'd moved out after his son had died as he could no longer run the shop.

I spent the rest of the morning with Madam Chau in tow, asking questions. I interviewed the new shopkeeper and Madam Chau translated when necessary. He was small and wore light-brown overalls. At first, I thought he was just an assistant and asked for his father.

"I am the owner," he said through my translator.

"And you bought the business off—?"

"Mr Wu."

I nodded. "How old are you?"

"Twenty, sir."

"Where did you get the money from?"

"I raised it."

"From?"

"By working hard all my life."

"Did you know Alan Wu?"

"No, sir."

Most people would ask who Alan was and would guess a relation to the old owner, but not this kid. He served a customer and then I caught up with him again.

"He was Mr Wu's son. He died of a snake bite. Do you know anything about that?"

"No, sir."

"Who do you buy your produce from?"

He looked surprised by the change of direction. In fact, I read it in his eyes before Madam Chau translated. Then he gave me the name of the man who had supplied Wu.

"And how are his prices?" I asked.

"His prices are good."

"Does he put any pressure on you?"

"I don't understand."

"You could buy cheaper in Malaya. Does he make you buy from him?"

"No, sir."

I asked again about the money but he refused to say where it had come from. When he turned his back on me to serve a customer, I noticed the name of the shop, written in green on his overalls.

Realizing I wouldn't get anything more from the young man, I left the shop and started talking to his neighbours. It didn't take long to confirm that he wasn't the owner. His age and intelligence made me suspect he was just a manager. He hadn't wanted to talk to me but he liked to brag to his neighbours. He'd told them he had a rich benefactor who owned half of the business. Although he'd let slip to one neighbour that his half would come later. He owned nothing but a promise.

Another beady-eyed neighbour said they suspected the supplier. He acted like he owned the place when he occasionally turned up.

So the supplier had been angry that Alan Wu had switched to a cheaper source. Then he'd bought the business and inserted a manager.

"Occasionally?" I asked. "Doesn't he deliver every day?"

"Not anymore. He has people who work for him. They deliver the fruit and vegetables."

I asked where the supplier lived, but none of the neighbours could tell me. Neither did they recognize the poor description of the snake-tattooed man.

When I returned to the greengrocers, I accused the man of killing Alan Wu. He panicked and ran. Not an intelligent man on two counts. I didn't have any evidence so he should have played ignorant. Secondly, he shouldn't have run.

As well as being an amateur boxer, I'm a runner. So I gave him a head start before giving chase. Of course, Madam Chau grumbled and made no attempt to follow.

The shopkeeper went north-west, and after his initial dash, he jogged comfortably, not realizing I wasn't far behind. After a mile, he stopped outside a detached house which was clearly way beyond his means.

I sprinted and caught up with him as he was about to ring a doorbell. With my hand on his collar, I jerked him back, away from the door.

"He lives here, doesn't he?"

The guy looked at me with wide eyes.

I said, "Does he have a snake tattoo?"

"Y-yes," he stammered. Of course, he spoke English.

"Did he do it? Did he kill Alan Wu?"

The man's lips clamped shut but his eyes told me the truth. I let him go.

"Run and keep on running," I said, and let go of his shirt.

As soon as he was out of sight, I rang the doorbell.

The Chinese guy who answered had the cocky look of someone who thinks he's smarter than everyone else and the dice will always fall in his favour.

I tried to look non-threatening and a little sheepish despite my size.

"Hello," I said, sounding nervous.

"Uh he?" he said noncommittally.

"I'm looking for someone who keeps unusual pets— snakes and lizards."

His eyes narrowed. "What do you mean?"

"I need a… a snake for something."

"Something?"

I looked around nervously. "For a job. I mean, I can pay you good money." With that, I pulled out my wallet.

"Come in," he said.

He took me along a hallway to the back of the building. I could smell something harsh and acrid, and heard the buzz of crickets. We went through a door and came into a room full of glass cases. Some held buzzing insects, but most contained reptiles. Most were snakes, but a large one held a Komodo dragon.

"What is your taste and budget?" he asked.

"Something that bites."

"With permanent effect?"

"For the job…"

"Of course."

He took the lid off a case and with a pair of tongs lifted a sand-coloured snake with V's along its back.

"A pit viper," he said. "Will do a good— permanent job."

I blew out air. "What if it bites me by mistake?"

"They have anti-venom at Tan Tock Seng Hospital."

"None here?"

"I can sell you some."

"Let me see."

He dropped the snake back into the case, then opened a cool cabinet and pulled out a vial. With a grin, he gave me an exorbitant price for the snake and anti-venom.

"How do I know it'll work?"

"It'll work. I get it directly from the hospital." He grinned again and I held out my hand for the vial. "I have contacts."

As I took the vial, I swept his legs from under him. Even as he was landing, I was grabbing the tongs and fishing out the snake.

He squirmed to get away and I dropped my knee onto his chest. Almost two hundred pounds pressing down on him. At the same time, I pushed my right forearm under his chin and he must have thought I'd make the snake bite his neck then.

Now I used my normal voice. "Tell me the truth. I'll ask you only once."

He nodded.

"Did a snake bite Alan Wu?"

His eyes flared and he tried to squirm away but I held him fast.

"You had one chance," I said.

I figured a bite to the neck would mean a quicker death. Instead, I let it bite him on the leg.

He screamed and writhed like the venom had turned him into a snake as well.

I got up and dropped the snake back into its case. He was up on his feet and scrabbling for the cool cabinet. Before he had it open, I grabbed his outstretched arm, twisted it and pulled it up his back.

"You have about thirty minutes," I said into his ear. "Unless you run, of course, in which case you'll have about half that time."

He tried to pull free, but I lifted his arm until the pain stopped him.

"But I have another plan," I said. "Remember, I have the antidote, so you're coming with me."

If the trishaw driver thought it was odd that I strong-armed the guy into the seat, he said nothing. Then I gave him the Hill Street address of the police HQ and he nodded with relief.

Five minutes later, we were walking through the halls of the station and I called out for Inspector Singh. His round face always held a smile, and I suspected that a predilection for boiled sweets added to his wide girth.

After a quick explanation, I handed over my prisoner and the vial.

"When he tells you the truth about killing Alan Wu for his grocery business, let him have the antidote."

I returned via Kallang and collected Madam Chau from outside Fresh Garden, the grocers.

We heard the telephone ringing before we got back into my office. Madam Chau answered.

"Crash investigator?" she said, like it didn't mean anything. Of course, I realized it was the guy who I'd spoken to at the BVD unit beside the airfield. I scooted over and took the handset from my receptionist.

"Ash Carter," I said. "You have some news?"

"The full report is complete," the investigator said. "Nothing extra to report except technical stuff."

"So no need to read it?"

"Not really."

"OK, thanks for letting me know." I thought it was an odd thing to call about, but then he said something that made me curious.

"There's one thing. One odd thing."

"What?"

"Well you know I thought the fuel cap was odd?"

"Yes."

"Well, in the fuel pipe there was a rag. Blocking it. Burnt like it had been a fuse to blow the tank but then gone out because it was too tightly packed in."

"And that's odd?" I asked.

"Well it explains why the helicopter didn't explode, but no, that's not the odd thing. The odd thing is the dog tag wrapped inside."

"You found a dog tag?" I said, barely able to breathe. "A soldier's tag?"

"Yes and no. Yes, it looks like a US Army dog tag— you know, the metal kind. No, because I'm not sure it's a soldier. There's no detail, no blood type, and the name is odd."

I said nothing, waiting for him to explain.

"Just one word," he said, his voice sounding loud down the line. "BlackJack. Capital B but also a capital J, and all one word like the card game."

EIGHT

The man who had walked away from the helicopter crash—the man who had caused the crash—called himself BlackJack. It wasn't particularly inventive or original. But it amused him because life was a game. A game of risk. A game of chance. However, it was also inspired by his hero, Jack the Ripper, the Victorian killer who had never been caught.

And BlackJack knew why the man had never been caught. Jack the Ripper was too clever. He was close to the operation, so close that no one suspected. All he needed to do was cover his tracks.

And BlackJack was also a master at covering his tracks. Like he'd done with the helicopter crash. He'd killed them and just walked away like nothing had happened, and the people who knew his identity were dead.

Jack the Ripper was originally known as the Whitechapel Murderer, although the police were unable to connect his eleven murders in the area. Jack had used different techniques, deliberately misleading the police. They finally realized the link because of the brutality of the murders: deep abdominal and throat slashes, genital mutilation, facial mutilation and removal of internal organs. They connected them because of their dissimilarity. But that didn't help them catch him. And he wasn't even called Jack. That was also part of the misdirection.

BlackJack knew who Jack the Ripper was. He'd studied lots of murders and murderers but Jack was the one who really appealed. At first, BlackJack had thought Jack had been a coward because he'd left so-called clues that didn't lead to him.

The first clue had been a tanner's apron, and the police finally got it and arrested a man. John Pizer was a gangster known as "Leather Apron". However, an inquest found him not guilty since he had solid alibis for two of the murders. Missing Jack's other clues, Abberline—the detective inspector—focused his attention on a Polish barber who was charged with killing three former partners. However, the man was a poisoner. He didn't disembowel his victims.

Despite his obsession with the barber, Abberline finally picked up on the clue that pointed at a member of royalty: the Duke of Clarence. However, through incompetence or deference, he never pursued it.

Instead, the attention turned to two doctors, since the brutal murders were judged to have been carried out by someone with medical skills. One was found dead, floating in the River Thames *before* the final murder. Clearly, Jack the Ripper's greatest joke.

And the other doctor? Dr Thomas Cream was eventually convicted of murder—but again the method was all wrong. He was yet another poisoner.

Before he was hanged he allegedly said, "I am Jack."

Of course, he hadn't really confessed, and he was in prison at the time of some of the murders, but Abberline was satisfied for a while.

As for the real Jack the Ripper, he hadn't been caught. In a sense, he'd run away. But he wasn't a coward. The genius of the man was to plan the conclusion. Plan to stop and pursue something else.

He had probably dabbled in murder again, but it would have been so random and unconnected that he could sate his hunger for death and resume his ordinary life.

That's what BlackJack planned too. A few more kills and his mission—this part of the game at least—would be complete.

NINE

The following day, I was looking through my notes, considering whether any of the rejected cases deserved investigation, when Madam Chau answered the ringing phone.

"A call from the Perak Protection Force?" she said looking at me.

I grinned and jumped out of my chair. "Accept the call." Then, taking the phone from my receptionist, I said, "Hello."

"Could I speak to the special investigator, please?" said a voice that I recognized.

"Slugger!" It was Scott Stevenson, head of the private security firm, my one-time opponent in the boxing ring and now my friend.

"How are you doing, Carter?" Despite our friendship, I'd given up trying to get him to call me Ash—since he thought Ashley was a girl's name—and his alternative names for me were less than flattering. "Making ends meet?"

"Keeping busy—or at least keeping out of trouble." I paused. "This isn't a social call, is it? What's up?"

"Something I thought you'd be interested in—if you aren't *too* busy."

"Tell me more."

"We found a body."

"And the police aren't handling it correctly?" I prompted after he didn't elaborate.

"They're doing fine," he said. "It's just that it's an unusual case."

"Murder?"

"Definitely."

I listened to the hum of wires for a few seconds. "Come on, Scott, you're being very circumspect."

"If you mean I'm not saying much, it's because I'd like you to come and see for yourself."

"It's a long way just to see a dead body."

He still didn't elaborate, and I checked my watch and considered timings. If I left now and pushed hard, I could do it in eight hours, which would mean arriving around 10 pm. Alternatively, I could take my time and stay overnight in Kuala Lumpur. Up early in the morning…

"How about 10 am tomorrow?" I asked.

"Perfect," he said. "Pick me up at the bunkhouse in BG and we'll head up to the morgue."

When I handed the phone back to Madam Chau she had a questioning look on her face.

"I don't know the details," I said.

"But you'll be out of the office for at least a day." She was then speaking to the operator and asking for a hotel in Kuala Lumpur. She may be difficult, but she was nothing if not efficient, and she promptly booked me a room for the night.

As I left, she said, "Let me know if you're going to be more than a day."

"Of course," I said, and she scowled in response.

Returning to my apartment on Beach Road, I packed an overnight bag and jumped into my Land Rover. With the hood down and the wind in my hair, I trundled north out of the city towards Woodlands Crossing.

There was a long queue at the crossing, with goods vehicles being checked by Customs and the army. I got a nod from an MP on the barrier and jumped four vehicles and got onto the causeway that connected the island with Malaya. There were more checks on the far side, but again I was waved through.

Route One cut up the country from Johor Bahru by the crossing all the way to Thailand. The road was good, with a lane on both sides, and providing there wasn't a tractor or animal cart on the road, it was pretty fast.

Initially, I was slowed by trucks, but once beyond the most southerly town I began overtaking and managed to put my foot down. For long stretches the jungle flashed by on both sides. Occasionally there would be a break in the monotony, with a kampong by the road. Twice I had to stop because vehicles in front had pulled over to buy something from a vendor. Only they hadn't pulled right off the road and my lane had become blocked.

I appreciated that villagers needed to sell fruit and vegetables and handmade goods to survive, but the roads weren't built for such custom.

Torrential rain also made me stop and attach the roof, and for twenty minutes I made slow progress as my wipers did very little against the flood on the windscreen.

Because of the delays, I was glad I'd chosen to layover in Kuala Lumpur, and it was already dark by the time I joined the queue of traffic into the centre.

The first thing I did when I arrived at my hotel was to arrange dinner. I asked the operator to connect me to the police HQ, and once through I asked for Captain George McNaughton, who I knew had been transferred up from Johor Bahru recently.

"Chief inspector now," he said when he came on the line. I told him I was local and he immediately asked me to join him for dinner and met me an hour later outside the Jockey Club.

Although not as grand as the Singapore Club, it overlooked the *Padang* and so provided an excellent view of sporting events. Anyone of any status in the capital had to be a member.

"When I heard you'd been transferred, I guessed you'd join the club," I said as we approached the single-storey mock Tudor building.

"Had to. Just had to."

We mounted the steps and passed by the doormen who'd barred my entry when I'd been here six months ago tracking someone down.

I congratulated McNaughton on his promotion and he wanted to know about my adventures. I explained that in my new role I needed to maintain my contacts in the police and he didn't mind.

"I was worried you had another case like last time," he said. "I should thank you, because my promotion was down to handling that case, but too many of those"—he laughed—"well, let's just say I enjoy life. Police work is dangerous enough with this Emergency going on."

"Police work is dangerous anyway."

"There are degrees and I'm certainly not looking for trouble." He studied me closely and rubbed his chin. "You really don't have anything for me?"

"Honestly. I'm just staying in touch, and if I should need help from another police force...?"

He smiled. "Of course, I'll introduce you." He signalled for the waiter to bring him another bottle of wine. "Now tell me about that trouble you had up in Penang, and make it juicy because I like a good story. I like danger providing it's not my own."

44

He polished off most of the two bottles of wine before we finished and said goodnight. I was glad to call him a friend despite needing him as a contact.

My relationship with Scott "Slugger" Stevenson was very different. He wasn't someone plugged into a large organization. Yes, he had some contacts through running his small protection unit, but he was really someone I could rely on. If I needed help, I knew he'd be there. Likewise, I hoped that he knew I'd have his back. That was really why I travelled north. I was interested in what he had to show me, but I was mostly here because he'd asked.

I left before the sunrise and found the roads clear for the first hour. I'd driven this stretch many times, out of the city and through the jungle. The railway followed the same line as Route One and the Highlands were to my right. Most of the time I saw nothing but dense forest on either side.

The first sign of industry I saw was a logging truck. Then the jungle ended for a while as I crossed Slim River where giant sawmills and warehouses appeared on my left. I was now in Perak and very soon met with rubber plantations on the right-hand side. Kinta Valley was on the left and I knew hundreds of tin mines were being worked out there in the wetlands. I started hearing the grunt of gravel pumps and then spotted the giant mining dredgers.

I knew them well because I'd lived out here for a few months at the start of the year, and I felt a twinge of something—regret perhaps? It wasn't like the attraction of Singapore. That was a paradise island, whereas this strange mining area with its frequent thunderstorms and muddy roads was both familiar and comfortable.

45

I drove through Kampar, where the rail line veered north-west towards the Malim Nawar power station and then through Batu Gajah, my destination. However, in a car I couldn't take this direct route and continued on up Route One through the rubber plantations until my road appeared on the left.

I had to drive through the little town, cross the Kinta River and then the train line before taking a spur road that took me to an old sawmill with Perak Protection Force on the side and jeeps lined up in the yard.

Slugger Stevenson must have been looking out for me because he opened the door as I pulled up.

He climbed in beside me, pumped my hand and said, "Have you had breakfast?"

"No."

I knew he enjoyed his full English breakfasts and I had been looking forward to enjoying one with him this morning. However, he disappointed me.

"Good," he said, "and let's keep it that way. When you see what I have to show you, I don't want you making a mess on the floor."

TEN

Slugger Stevenson directed me to Ipoh Hospital and from there walked me to the morgue. A junior doctor met us and led the way to a covered gurney before leaving us alone.

Slugger pulled back the cover and revealed a body. Even though it had been in a cooler, I still covered my nose as the stench of decay hit me.

I saw a naked white male, and despite exsanguination, I could see tan lines on his thighs from wearing shorts down to his shins where his socks would have come up. His chest was bleached white, and again there were tan lines midway on his biceps due to a short-sleeved shirt. His neck was also tanned.

All of that was normal, but above the neck was where it got interesting. The guy had no face except for lidless eyes that bulged out.

Slugger was looking at me. "I thought you'd be sick."

"It's an unpleasant sight, but I've seen worse."

He nodded. "We're calling him Joe Bloggs because we have no identification."

"Found naked?"

"Yes. Except for a gold chain around his neck."

I wondered about that before saying, "The skin on his face looks like it was cut off."

"The face was removed after death. Cause of death is this puncture wound on the left of his neck."

I circled the gurney and studied the small hole made, I suspected, by a stiletto blade. "Into the carotid artery."

Slugger nodded. "He's estimated to be between thirty-five and thirty-eight. Marginally over six foot, and you can see the remaining hair on his head is fair to ginger. Eyes are blue. He'd been dead about three days hence the decomposition and some insect infestation—that's why it smells. Bloody flies didn't waste any time."

I studied the staring eyes, and despite their milky coating, I could see they'd once been blue. Then I pointed to gouges on his arms and legs. "Post-mortem?"

"Definitely. Small rodents most likely. We're lucky a larger animal didn't find him or we could be looking at a pile of bones right now."

I stepped away from the body.

"So, how can I help?"

"I'm hoping you can identify him. Someone's missing this chap."

"Let's get a copy of his file and get me that late breakfast."

Within fifteen minutes we were in a bar on the outskirts of Ipoh waiting for that full English I'd looked forward to. Despite having eaten breakfast already, Slugger was happy to eat an early lunch.

"I really didn't think you'd be able to eat," my friend said. "You're such a pussy."

"Thanks. Tell me about Joe Bloggs. Why are you involved?"

"One of my men found him out on patrol."

"In the open?"

"No, he was beside the road under a bush. You remember Cranfield, right? He stopped off to take a piss and it was pure chance he saw the body."

"Blood at the scene?"

"You're wondering whether Joe was murdered there. The coroner says no. He was killed, bled out and then dumped."

The food arrived and we tucked in.

"He was still wearing his clothes when he was killed," I said, reading the file between eating. "Otherwise there would have been more blood on the body."

I studied a photograph of the gold chain around the man's neck. It had no pendant, so no additional clue there, but the chain itself might be a clue.

"Why strip the man but leave the chain?" I asked.

"Rushed and forgot?"

I shook my head. "This doesn't feel rushed. And how well hidden did Cranfield say the body was?"

"Not very."

"Almost like he was meant to be found." Although I said this aloud, I was really just thinking.

"Maybe, but why?"

"Why indeed. And why leave the chain?"

"He looks distinctive," Slugger said. "Tallish white chap with light ginger hair. My assumption is army or police."

"Not an estate worker?"

"No one in Perak. We've asked all the plantations. Same with the tin mines. Either no one knows him or they aren't telling."

"What about the power station?"

"Yes, I personally asked in Malim Nawar and at their offices in Kampar. No joy."

I looked at the picture again. The face had been peeled from the upper lip all the way to the crown of the head. The ears hadn't been touched. I could see neat cuts on either cheek.

He said, "You're looking at the cuts. The coroner thinks it was a razor blade—shallow and precise."

"This was premeditated," I said. "Our murderer met Joe with his stiletto blade. If he was right-handed, he stabbed Joe from the front. Left-handed it was from the back." I mimed it using my cutlery, knife in my left hand since I'm left-handed. "Easier from behind. Stab, hold and wait until the victim dies."

"Carotid artery would have been quick."

I nodded. "Then he took out his razor blade and sliced off the man's face."

"Why?"

"So that we don't know who Joe really is."

Slugger nodded, but I could see that he had his own answer. "Maybe he didn't care if we knew him or not. It's unlikely Joe is from around here since no one recognizes his description."

Now I nodded.

"Maybe this was a trophy." He waited for the implication to sink in.

I shook my head.

"Iban," he said, and widened his one good eye.

Ibans, also known as Dayaks, were from Borneo, specifically the region of Sarawak. They were excellent trackers and as such were used by the British Army against the communist terrorists. However, there was a downside. The Ibans were headhunters. The army had to turn a blind eye to their practice of scalping the enemy. I'd seen it first-hand. It was both shocking and horrific, especially since I'd heard stories of them scalping wounded bandits rather than wait for them to die.

"God, I hope you're wrong," I said.

He voiced what I was thinking. "It means they've killed one of us. No way Joe was a bandit. If we have a rogue Iban, then none of us are safe."

After breakfast/lunch, we returned to the protection force bunkhouse and I used Slugger's phone to call Fort Canning in Singapore. It was home of the Commander-in-Chief for the Far East, and General Gaskill was a very useful contact of mine. I rarely spoke to him, although I always got a good response.

After introducing myself, I said I needed to speak with Captain Thorpe of 22nd SAS. The clerk explained that the captain wasn't directly contactable, however, a message would be sent to him. That was what I expected. I'd bumped into the SAS unit in northern Malaya before I returned to Singapore. I knew they were active in the field, a law unto themselves, rather like the SIB military police guys. I provided my contact details in Singapore and ended the call.

We shot the breeze for a while and chatted about the plantations and various tin mining operations. There were lots of characters out here and Slugger had stories about them all.

I asked how he was getting along with his girlfriend, Cindy, and although he didn't say much, I could see he was still in love.

"Serious then," I said.

"Might just have to marry her." He grinned and changed the subject, asking me to stay over and join the team at a drinking club for the evening. He also suggested that we have a boxing match when all the boys were back to watch. I knew he was fit from the little weights area and punch bag in the bunkhouse. I regularly worked out at the YMCA boxing gym and my ring experience was fresher than his. However, I made weak excuses and he called me a pussy again but then pumped my hand and wished me a safe journey home.

I knew I wouldn't reach the crossing before it closed for the night, no matter how fast I drove. So I took it steady and stopped for thirty minutes at a roadside café when a thunderstorm struck.

When I reached Johor Bahru, the sun had set hours before and I had the choice of sleeping in the jeep at the front of the queue to cross the strait in the morning or find a hotel. The choice was easy, despite money being tight. I'd had a long day of driving and splashed out on the European and Oriental, the best hotel in the town.

After a night in such a sumptuous old British colonial hotel, I was fully refreshed. My early start from Kuala Lumpur yesterday had meant that I'd missed my morning regime, so before breakfast, I went for a run.

I used the hill in the gardens of the Grand Palace of Johor as a guide and headed for it. The giant concrete entrance arch welcomed me, although it seemed incongruous. On either side was grass and trees, so it was like the entrance to a fort without the rest of the fortification.

With the sun coming up and the birds in full song, I enjoyed looping around the grounds before stopping close to the istana, beside the strait. I'd seen very few people in the gardens until now but this spot attracted dozens of martial artists. I found my own area and went through my standard exercise routine. No doubt I looked as peculiar to the martial artists as their programme appeared to me.

Washed and breakfasted afterwards, I was ready to cross the causeway and get back to Singapore. However, I wasn't prepared for what I would find when I reached my office.

ELEVEN

"Oh, Master Carter," Madam Chau said as I arrived. Her cheeks were smeared with grey tears. She was hunched on the steps outside the office building, and besides crying, I saw her hands shake.

I'd not done it before, but instinct took over and I put an arm around her. I had the sense that she avoided any contact, but for a moment I felt her relax against me. Then she straightened her back and stood up.

"I'm sorry," she said.

"For what?" My thought now was that she'd done something wrong, but she hadn't.

"For what has happened." She pointed at the entrance, took a breath and then led me inside.

I immediately smelled wood smoke and something more acrid. As I mounted the stairs, I realized the wood smell was also damp, and it didn't take a genius to work out what had happened. My office door was open and burnt. I say open, but the door was just a chunk of blackened wood dangling from the hinges. Dirty water pooled along the landing and inside.

I stepped through the doorway expecting the worst. However, the fire hadn't gone very far. The walls and ceiling on either side of the door were covered in soot and the floor was a black and glutinous mess. The

53

linoleum flooring had melted in a semicircle and was undoubtedly the source of the acrid smell.

"If I'd arrived earlier it wouldn't have happened," Madam Chau said behind me.

"It looks like the firemen got here in time," I said. "We're lucky there's so little damage."

"But if I'd arrived sooner..." She walked around me and started opening the windows.

"What time did you arrive?"

"Just before eight. The fire had barely got going. I saw rags stuffed under the door. That's what caused the fire."

I didn't bother explaining that someone had set fire to the rags. "Did you see anyone leaving the building when you arrived—anyone suspicious?"

"No." She put the kettle on and picked up the teapot. "Tea?"

"Madam Chau, you've had a shock. Take the day off."

She scowled at me. "What do you think I am, Master Carter? A lazy bones?"

"No. I—" I smiled, because my receptionist, the tough old Chinese lady, was back.

"Good, because we have work to do," she said. "While the tea is brewing, I am going to clean up. Then it's on with the work. First of all, you can go across the road and talk to the people who were here before me. Someone may have seen something."

I'd thought the same thing and was already looking at the people opposite. I noticed a handful kept glancing this way, checking on the situation. Maybe they had seen the arsonist.

"Good plan," I said, "and I'll have my tea when I return."

I went out, crossed the road and entered the building opposite. I discovered that this was occupied by a shipping company where the main job appeared to be the recording and filing of bills of lading. I located the general manager, who was happy to accompany me to each department and ask for anyone who had been in the office before eight.

On the ground floor, they had started at eight and no one had seen anything except the firemen arrive. It was a similar story on the first floor, although the manager and a secretary had been in earlier but had been too busy to notice anything until they heard the fire bells.

On the second floor, I was more fortunate. Two young ladies had arrived very early and watched others arrive. They mentioned seeing the manager and secretary from the first floor and one of the girls smirked. She couldn't speak for a moment, and I suspected their early arrival was partly about spying on the other two.

The second girl said that she'd seen someone suspicious outside the office before seven thirty.

"Why suspicious?"

"He walked past and then back again. And you know how it is—he were glancing about as though checking the coast was clear. That's when I called for Doris."

This was the other girl, the one who had smirked. Now Doris nodded. "But when I came, there was no sign of him."

"Until he came out," the first one said. "He looked up and down again and then ran."

"Which way?" I asked.

The first girl pointed left, in the direction of the docks. "That way."

"Can you describe this man?"

The girl closed her eyes as she tried to locate the memory. I knew witnesses could be very unreliable especially when it was a fleeting image.

"I thought he was a boy," she said, opening her eyes again. "He was small. Had a flat cap on. Brown. And his clothes were lighter brown."

"Like this?" I asked, pointing to a brown dot on the other girl's dress.

"Lighter."

"Yes, lighter. Tan-coloured," Doris confirmed. "But he wasn't a boy, was he, Marie?"

"No. When he came down the steps, I saw he was wider. You know, chunkier. A man, not a boy."

"Age?"

Both girls shrugged and exchanged glances. "Hard to tell," Marie said after a moment, and then: "He had a funny run, so I wonder now if he had arthritis in his hips."

"Oh," Doris said. "Did we mention he had something under his arm at first. I thought it was a holdall. But then later thought it was a rolled-up thing, like a carpet only smaller."

"And when he came out of the building again, he didn't," the other girl added.

So he'd been in the building and probably taken in whatever it was he'd set light to. They'd seen him come out, down the steps and run off in the direction of the docks. "Anything else you can add?" I asked.

"His suit had something on the back," Marie said. "Green. Perhaps a logo of some kind."

"A suit with a logo? That'd be unusual," I said.

"Maybe it wasn't a suit. No, come to think of it maybe they were overalls."

Doris blinked. "Oh, and he wasn't white. Did we say that already?"

"What was he?"

"Not Indian—not a dark one anyway. Maybe Chinese?"

"Chinese, I thought," Marie said. "We didn't get a good look at his face. Looking down"—she leaned towards the window to demonstrate—"we don't get to see faces much."

I asked them more questions before establishing that they couldn't tell me anything more. However, I already had a good idea of who it was.

TWELVE

A police officer was standing at the top of the stairs waiting for me when I got back to the office.

"Inspector Singh," I said, shaking his hand.

"I warned you about this," he said. Despite the smile, his voice was serious.

We walked into the acrid-smelling office, although the open windows had allowed most of the smoke to escape.

"About what?" I asked.

"Andrew Yipp. You play with fire, you get burned."

Singh was referring to my contact with Singapore's alleged underworld. He'd warned me about sharing information with Yipp. He also knew about my run-in with him a few months back.

"Yipp has a long memory," Singh said as I shook my head. "Months, even years can go by and"—he slapped his hand on my desk—"bam! It's all over."

I laughed. "This wasn't Yipp."

"It was a warning."

"If Yipp did this, it wouldn't have just been the door that burned. And he doesn't need to warn me. If he wanted me dead, I'd be dead."

Singh nodded sagely. If I hadn't known him well, I might have assumed his smile was now mocking me.

I said, "You're right. It was meant as a warning of sorts. And it was amateurish. The arsonist was seen coming into this building and leaving again."

"Witnesses?"

I pointed across the way, where Marie, Doris and a group of other women watched us discreetly from their desks. "Two ladies saw a suspicious man with a roll of something under his arm. This was probably what he burned under the door."

"I'll send men to interview them."

"No need. I got a description." I went on to repeat what they'd told me.

He rolled his eyes. "That could be anyone."

"The light-brown suit was in fact overalls. There was a name on the back. It will have been Chinese for Fresh Garden, the grocer's shop."

Singh shook his head, not comprehending.

I said, "It's too obvious. I'm supposed to think it was the young grocer who now manages Wu's old business."

"Alan Wu—the murdered man?"

"The cap was a disguise. But he should have committed the crime earlier. If he'd truly wanted to be anonymous then he'd have done it before the workers across the road arrived. I think he waited until they were watching. Being seen was part of the plan."

"So who do you suspect?"

"Someone with access to Fresh Garden's overall's. Someone with a motive."

"The owner?"

"The old owner. Mr Wu."

Singh blinked his surprise. "The old man? Alan Wu's father? But you found the man who'd killed him—and he has confessed by the way. What possible motive...?"

"I'll leave that to you to find out."

59

I heard Madam Chau tutting and assumed she disagreed with my conclusion, but she wasn't. When I looked in her direction I realized she was holding the telephone out for me and looking impatient.

I took the receiver and recognized his voice as soon as Captain Thorpe started speaking.

"I got your message," the SAS man said.

I shook Singh's hand and watched him leave before turning my attention to Thorpe.

"Can I ask where you are?"

"No." He laughed lightly. "Well you can ask but I can't tell."

"Successful?"

"Of course!" He laughed again. "Now, how can I help you, Captain?"

"When we met, you'll recall that the young lady with me was shocked. We saw your tracker scalping the bandits."

"And as *you'll* recall, I explained that he's an Iban from North Borneo. It's like a rite of passage for them as warriors to take the heads of their enemy. They're bloodhounds, damn good at tracking the bandits through the most impenetrable jungle. We're winning this damn war and a good part of that is down to them."

I let him finish his justification before I said, "I've no doubt, but I wanted to talk about the scalping."

"Right?"

"Are you aware of them scalping any white folk?"

"Well, back when the first British settlers went to Borneo, they were terrified. I don't know for certain, but there are plenty of stories about settlers being killed and decapitated. An enemy is an enemy, you see?"

"One second," I said. Madam Chau handed me a piece of paper. It had the price of repairs written on it and there was a workman standing by the burnt door.

The price seemed high and I was about to agree when Madam Chau shook her head. She crossed out the number and wrote a figure half the size of the first. Then she marched back to the workman and started berating him in Chinese.

"Sorry about the shouting in the background," I said. "Just had a spot of trouble here this morning. You were saying an enemy is an enemy. So, in theory, a white man could be scalped."

"Correct."

"What about your man. Has he scalped a white man?"

"Not so far as I'm aware. What's this about, Carter?"

So I told him about the body that Slugger Stevenson's unit had found.

"The face, you say?" Thorpe said when I finished.

"From the upper lip to the crown of the head."

Thorpe said nothing for a few beats, possibly considering the situation.

"I've never seen anything like it," he said. "However, I've never seen an Iban cut off a man's head and we know they do that. So just because I haven't witnessed it doesn't mean it doesn't happen."

"And your tracker?"

"Only cuts across the top of the head and takes a chunk of hair... and skin. It's a trophy. You know, they have been known to use faces as decoration, especially on their swords."

"The cuts were shallow, like they'd been done with a razor."

"You'll have seen my chap's *mandau*. The sword's blade is close to two feet long and sharp as a razor. Scalps easily and it'll take a man's head off in one clean stroke—like I said, I've never seen it happen," he added quickly, and I started to suspect he had.

61

He had paused, and I started to tell him about my case when he continued.

"From what you describe, it sounds too delicate," he said. "However, they all have a small whittling knife called a *pisau raut* that dangles from the hilt of the *mandau*. It's a vicious-looking thing for fine cutting. If an Iban wanted to remove a face, I'm sure he'd use a *pisau*. Wouldn't surprise me if it'd look like a razor cut."

"Thanks," I said. "One more question. Are you aware of any Ibans operating outside of the army? Could this be a lone wolf?"

"Definitely possible. But we pay very well, so it'd surprise me."

"Unless his tastes aren't catered for by the army."

Thorpe grunted, which I took as either confirmation or that the army's blind eye included more than simple scalping.

"I seem to recall that you owe me and my men a beer or two," he said after I thanked him for his help.

"I'll happily buy the beers if you tell me where you are."

He laughed and used the phrase I'd heard him say before: "Don't forget to tell everyone that the SAS saved the day!" And then he was gone.

I had Joe Blogg's file open at the photograph of the head. Despite the gruesome face, I had a sense of familiarity. I'd had a twinge of it the moment I'd seen the body, although I'd put the thought aside. Perhaps it had been my subconscious working when I spotted the necklace. Did I know a man around six foot with light ginger hair who wore a necklace?

I shook my head. I couldn't place him, but it didn't help that the workman had been banging around the old burnt frame to remove it. Now he was sawing wood.

I got up, deciding to visit Gillman. Perhaps the men at 200 Provost would know.

Fifteen minutes later I was in the CO's office with my file.

"Good God!" he said, looking at the photographs.

"Do you recognize him, sir?"

"No. It's just awful." He put the file down and took a breath. "And you think he's a soldier?"

"I don't know. It's a possibility."

"God, I hope not!"

He looked like he was going to say something. I sensed it was bothering him.

"Colonel?"

He clenched his fist and placed it in front of his mouth. When he breathed, the air blew loudly over his knuckles.

"Sir?" I prompted.

"The helicopter crash. Body two."

I nodded. "The man with the warrant card."

Ambrose breathed out noisily. "There's a good chance he's Captain Harwood."

"The SIB man."

"Jenkins has checked in, Harwood hasn't. Five foot eleven. God!"—he snorted over his knuckles—"Burned alive. It doesn't bear thinking about."

I nodded and waited a minute. Ambrose relaxed and removed his fist from his face.

"What case was he working on?"

"The disappearance of men." His lips twitched and I could see he was holding back.

I said, "When I met Lieutenant Jenkins, he told me he was tracking someone—thought it was a killer."

Ambrose looked relieved. "It's on a need-to-know basis. No one else knows this."

I waited for more.

"Someone is killing our men, only it's a bit more complicated than that. This isn't about communist terrorists picking off men in the jungle. It's men who are on R and R or AWOL."

"Any of them scalped?"

"I don't know. I'm still waiting for the details." He nodded, processing the thought. "Your man in the file might be one of them."

"Just a consideration..." I then told him what I knew about Iban trackers from the SAS captain.

"A rogue Iban?"

"Possible. Great at tracking people down and known killers."

He sighed. "Do me a favour. Captain Robshaw is going back over to Tebrau today. Join him and also visit the JTC at Kota Tinggi. They use an Iban tracker in the training team. Maybe he can help."

I knew JTC stood for Jungle Training Corps, and I'd visited them once before, last year. What I didn't know was that they used an Iban.

Driving up to Woodlands Crossing, Robshaw explained that since Ferret Force had been disbanded, the trackers had been reassigned, some to Federation Police Jungle Squads, others here and there, including the SAS and JTC.

I knew about Ferret Force. It had been a special unit of volunteers from British, Gurkha and Malay battalions and the Malayan police. There had been sixteen infantry sections, and they were largely responsible for Johor being virtually free of the MNLA.

In the MP Land Rover, we were waved through at both ends of the crossing and were soon on Route Three, the main road that went north-east from Johor Bahru.

The road twisted and turned, with elephant grass taller than a man on either side. After eight miles we came to the road to the airfield and the BVD unit. We turned and drove alongside the runway just as an Auster rumbled over the uneven surface and then took off to the east.

The squadron leader was outside his office watching the little plane and then gazing at us as we pulled up in front of him.

"Gentlemen?" he said, half a question, half concerned.

We shook hands and followed him into the building.

"Not more bad news, please. Every time you come here," he said, looking at me, "something bad happens or is about to happen."

Robshaw handed Kennedy a photograph of John Harwood. "Do you recognize this man?"

Without hesitation, the squadron leader shook his head. "Who is he?"

"We think he's the man your Flight Lieutenant Tony Billings picked up," I said.

"The second body?"

I nodded.

Kennedy thought for a moment and looked from me to Robshaw and back. "He was an MP, wasn't he?"

"Special Investigations Branch," I said.

"Undercover, so no uniform?"

"Right."

Kennedy shook his head again but then called to a man in the next room. A second later we heard a bell ringing outside: a summons.

We stepped outside and saw men flowing out of the hangars and other buildings. Within a couple of minutes, we had a semicircle of airfield crew, mechanics and pilots all looking expectant. If this had been an army unit we would have seen scowls and heard mutters of discontent. Foot soldiers hated MPs, but the RAF had no such concerns about our presence.

The squadron leader said, "You all know about Tony. But what you might not know is that another man died in the crash." He held up the photograph. "We think this is the chap and I'd like you to each look at his photograph." Now he passed it to the nearest man. "If you recognize him, anything you can tell us would be beneficial."

We waited and watched as the picture was passed around, men clustering, breaking away with shrugs or shakes of their heads.

And then one man stepped forward. A pilot.

"I remember him," he said.

THIRTEEN

Everyone was dismissed and the pilot joined us in the squadron leader's office.

"What can you tell us, Tom?" Kennedy said.

"I recognize him, that's all, sir."

"From where?" Robshaw asked.

"Here."

"He came here?"

"Yes. About two months ago. I can't be sure when, but I remember the face."

"Anything else you remember?" I asked.

"He spent time talking to Tony. I remember now. At the time I wondered what he wanted and Tony was a bit evasive."

"In what way?"

"Said he didn't know the man. Said he wanted directions to Kota Tinggi—the camp."

"And that was evasive?" Robshaw asked.

"Well, it took a few questions to get that out of him. And you see it was a bit odd because they'd been talking for a while."

Robshaw had a notebook out and scribbled something down. "How long is a while?"

The pilot shrugged, thinking hard. "Oh, I don't know. Longer than asking for directions. Maybe five, maybe ten minutes. And they'd gone into hangar two. Why do that if you're just giving directions?"

Kennedy said, "Why didn't you say anything, Tom?"

"Didn't seem important—sorry, sir. It was only when I saw the picture that I remembered Tony's strange behaviour."

"Do you think they knew each other?" I asked.

"That's the impression I got."

We let the pilot go and there was a clerk waiting at the door. Kennedy waved him in.

"Alan?"

The clerk came in and gave us nervous nods. "Sir, I think I might recognize the photograph. The face seems familiar. I can't be sure, but I think he was a visitor who asked for Tony Billings a while back. He had a Brummie accent."

"From Birmingham?"

"Can't say for certain, but... well, the Black Country at least."

I looked at Robshaw, who said "yes" with his eyebrows.

The clerk continued: "And I think it was the same voice who called for an extraction the day Tony..." He swallowed. "The day of the crash."

I'd not seen the squadron leader annoyed before, but his voice was full of barbs. "Why the hell didn't you say before, Corporal?"

The clerk flushed. "Sir, sorry, sir. I didn't think."

"What did he say when he called?"

"It was unusual. He said to let the Flight Lieutenant know that the pickup from Kahang was required immediately."

We knew Kahang had been the location but not who'd placed the call. I said, "Definitely *the* pickup?"

"Yes."

Robshaw said, "And now you think it was this man?"

"Just putting two and two together."

"Why didn't you say something, man?" Kennedy said, still annoyed.

"Because Tony said it was off the record. He said I had to keep it secret."

"Even though he died. You still thought to say nothing?"

The clerk nodded sheepishly.

"Dismissed," Kennedy barked. "You've not heard the last of this."

When the three of us were alone again, Kennedy asked, "Was your man a Brummie?"

"Captain John Harwood," Robshaw said. "He was from Sutton Coldfield in the Midlands and had a bit of an accent. It doesn't surprise me that he'd be called a Brummie."

I said, "And *off the record* makes sense. If Harwood didn't want anyone else to know who he'd picked up... Limiting the number of people you tell about an operation is a wise precaution. I would have done the same thing."

Robshaw nodded. "He briefed Billings in advance and, when the time came, called for a pickup. He had his man."

"Who?" Kennedy asked.

"I wish we knew, but we may have another lead." I hadn't intended to show the other photo to the squadron leader but handed him the one of the body from Perak.

"Jesus!" Kennedy spluttered. "What in God's name...?"

"I won't ask if you recognize him," I said, "but he was about six foot with fair to ginger hair."

"RAF?"

"Possibly army."

69

"Could be anyone," he said with a shake of the head. "I mean, lots of men would fit that description."

I thanked him and asked that he let us know if he heard of anyone missing who could match the brief description.

We drove out of Tebrau, past the BVD unit and then left onto the main road.

Men at both of these sites stayed in a huge open base called Camp Kota Tinggi. Ironically, it wasn't anywhere near the town of the same name. It was actually just outside a village called Ulu Tiram. Either the people who named the camp made a mistake or they found Ulu Tiram too difficult to pronounce. I figured a mistake was more likely.

The long grass petered out, replaced by trees and hillocks. Eight miles from the airfield we passed a World War Two pillbox, half consumed by undergrowth. Then, around a bend, we were suddenly on the edge of the village, which was a strip of shops and bars that were modern and no doubt thriving because of the camp nearby.

Less than a mile later a hand-painted sign took us left and then we came to a boom barrier and a guardhouse.

A guard jumped up and raised the boom as soon as he saw the military police Land Rover. We left the smooth road and hit compacted sand. Years of heavy trucks coming up the rise had created ridges that made the jeep bounce and rattle.

Camp Kota Tinggi was a vast multipurpose area and the bumpy road took us to central buildings, all white, all standard for a base, including a NAAFI and cinema.

To the left was an area that looked like a scout camp but was, in fact, the base of a humanitarian aid unit. Scott "Slugger" Stevenson and a few of his men had worked there before ditching the army in favour of the Perak Protection Force.

Ahead and right were scattered buildings that looked like it may have originally been a Malay village: rows of huts with attap roofs. These were the billets for all of the units around here, including the RAF at Tebrau and the BVD unit. It was a huge concentration of support units all in one place—and with limited protection. Since there was no perimeter wall, it would make for an ideal terrorist target. Thank goodness the bandits had never thought of it.

Our target wasn't the humanitarian aid guys nor was it the accommodation section. We wanted to speak to the Jungle Training Corps. Their base was at the far northern end. From the road, all we could see were the Nissen huts, their curved metal roofs glinting in the sunshine.

We could have driven across the rough ground to the JTC unit, but I preferred to walk than be shaken apart by the lumps and bumps.

It took a good few minutes to cross the wasteland and reach the six metal huts. I could see soldiers sitting in one of the training rooms. There was also a common room for instructors, an armoury and a communications room.

We reported to Comms and asked for the CO. A lieutenant greeted us, glanced at me and stared at Robshaw, suspicion in his eyes. I was in civvies, but of course, Robshaw wore his military police uniform.

"You have an Iban here?" I said.

"Yes," he said, his voice betraying his concern. "Is there a problem?"

"No problem," Robshaw said. "We're hoping he can help us."

The lieutenant relaxed and pointed to the training room full of men. "He's in there, talking to the latest batch of jungle virgins," he said. "I'll send him over as soon as we're done."

"How long?"

He looked at his watch. "About half an hour. Why don't you wait in the canteen? I'll send Koda over."

Robshaw could have pulled rank and position but there was no rush, so we trekked back to the buildings and queued with a bunch of men getting dinner: sausages, over-boiled vegetables, and watery mash potato.

As I picked at my meal, I was reminded of how awful army food could be, and these guys had to suffer it day in and day out.

Forty minutes later, a shirtless native came in and stood by the entrance. An Iban. He looked around, fixed his eyes on us and raised his chin.

About five-five with black hair tied back in a ponytail, he had black rings in his earlobes and smoked a cigarette. He wore loose-fitting green trousers and nothing on his feet. A large sword hung down his left side, held there by string that looped over his shoulder and around his waist. It was like the equivalent of a policeman's Sam Brown, only thin string instead of thick leather. I noticed the tassels that dangled from the sword's hilt.

Rather than approach us, as I anticipated, the Iban turned and walked out of the canteen.

Robshaw and I exchanged baffled looks before getting up and heading for the exit.

We found him right outside, leaning against the wall, smoking his cigarette.

His eyes watched us approach, his face showing nothing. No curiosity, no animosity, no friendliness either.

"Koda Joo," he said in good but flat English. "And I didn't do it."

FOURTEEN

"Didn't do what?" Captain Robshaw asked the Iban.

"Whatever you think I've done," the man from Borneo said, his voice as cold as his dark eyes.

"We don't think you've done anything."

"Are you both MPs?" he asked, turning those dead eyes on me.

"Yes," I said, not bothering to explain my position, "and we just need your help."

"I'm already assigned to the JTC."

I pointed to his sword and the tassels. "Are those scalps?"

For the first time, Koda showed his teeth. It was a proud smile, although his eyes didn't show it. "Five kills."

"That's not many."

Now the smile vanished. "No, it's not. I would have a lot more based up north. There aren't many bandits in the south anymore."

"And the Jungle Training Corps doesn't go looking for the enemy," Robshaw said.

"No. So what do you want?"

"Given the lack of bandits, would an Iban possibly look for alternative enemy?" I asked.

"Alternative enemy?"

"Other than bandits."

His eyes narrowed as he looked at me hard. "There is no other enemy."

"But you are in Malaya to hunt heads, no?"

Koda said nothing and lit another cigarette.

I noticed his body was on the relaxed side. His ancestors, I'm sure, would have been fit and wiry. Being part of the British Army had made this man soft. His body at least.

"More scalps, more honour," I said. "Isn't that right?"

"Yes."

"So, in theory, someone might look for other ways to collect scalps."

The hard eyes again. "In theory."

Robshaw said, "Why work here? Why not join a force where the action is?"

"There are about two hundred Iban operating in the country. Finding the right job is getting harder these days. And because I like my cigarettes," he said, finishing his second. "You can't smoke and track."

So Koda had weighed up the comfort of being at Kota Tinggi and the JTC versus the pride of facing and scalping the enemy. And comfort had won.

I pulled out the photograph of the man with no face.

Koda looked at it briefly but said nothing.

"Who did this?"

"Not one of my people if that's what you mean."

"You don't seem sure," Robshaw said, picking up on the man's monotone response.

"I'm sure."

"Why?"

He waved for me to show him the photograph again and pointed to the nose where I'd noticed skin.

"That."

"The skin on his nose?" I asked.

"This face was pulled up from the bottom. An Iban would never do that. We cut from the top and pull down if we want the face."

"So you do take faces?" Robshaw asked.

"Sometimes for decoration. You see the skin on the nose? This was a poor job." He seemed to be enjoying himself now that he was illustrating our ignorance. "And the ears. If I did this, I would take the whole face including the ears. Much better for decoration."

I said, "Have you ever seen a face removed like this before?"

He lit another cigarette. "No. Never."

Robshaw drove us away, and once we were off the bumpy track I looked at the photograph.

"Frustrating," he said.

"Did you think it might be him?"

"You never know, and he was suspicious. And those damn eyes. They're the closest thing to evil I've ever seen. He could have been lying."

"I don't think so. I think we learned that the dead man wasn't scalped by an Iban."

I carried on looking at the face. Something niggled. Was he familiar? It was so hard to imagine skin and ignore the bulging eyes.

We went past the turning to Tebrau Airfield. After another hundred yards of elephant grass I said, "Turn around."

"Back to the JTC?"

"No, back to the airfield."

Robshaw swept the jeep in a loop, bumping off the road before heading back the way we'd come. A minute later he turned left at the sign, but then where the side road forked, I told him to go left. To BVD 221 rather than the airfield.

"The crash investigator?" Robshaw asked me as we went through the gates.

"I don't know," I said.

We parked outside the office and a sergeant came out and snapped off a salute. This was the chief clerk of the unit: Sergeant Des Styles.

"You were the man looking for Gary Bender, weren't you?" he said to me, referring to my visit last year. "Still working with the Red Caps? How can I help this time?"

I pointed to the office door. "Can we go in?"

He glanced towards the garage, where I guess he'd been heading, and then nodded. "Of course."

He took us into the office and we passed two rooms. The first had a young clerk in a turban, working behind a desk. He nodded a greeting. The second was empty, and it had been where we'd met the crash investigator.

The sergeant took us into the third room and sat behind his desk. He had a nervous tic in his eye. I recognized it from the last time I'd met him—when he'd been responsible for losing a Bedford truck.

"I heard you confirmed one of the helicopter crash victims was Tony Billings. Nice chap," he said. "Who was the other one?"

"Captain John Harwood," Robshaw said.

Sergeant Styles shook his head, and I noted that the tick in his eye had stopped. "Not a name I know," he said. "Which unit?"

"One of ours."

A slight smile played on the sergeant's lips before he masked it. "Sorry to hear that. Now, how can I help?"

I produced the photograph of the man with no face.

"Oh, Jesus!"

77

I thought Styles's reaction a little strong since he was looking at a black and white image rather than real life. Then he said, "Sorry, I've never seen a dead body before. RAOC doesn't really prepare you for such things."

I nodded. "He was about six foot tall with fair to ginger hair."

"Where was he found?"

"In Perak—the jungle east of Ipoh."

"Bad," Styles said, nodding to himself. "Poor bugger. But I'm not sure how I can help you."

"Do you recognize him?"

"No. Do you think he was army? There isn't a barracks close by Ipoh."

I said nothing and looked around the room.

Styles said, "We've got a rush job on. A Scammell is broken and a tank needs moving from Terendak Barracks over in Malacca."

My eyes alighted on a photograph, a similar one to the one in the second office, where we'd met the crash investigator. Major Chris Broom.

"Where is the major today?" I asked.

Styles pursed his lips and shook his head. "He's the boss. I don't keep tabs on him."

There was something in Styles's tone. I kept looking at the photograph. Major Broom in his RAOC uniform: smart, tall, fair hair.

I rushed out of the office, into the next, and grabbed the other photograph. The major in whites: shorts and a short-sleeved shirt. And around his neck was a gold chain.

FIFTEEN

Robshaw arrested Sergeant Styles and we took him back to Gillman Barracks for questioning.

We let him stew while we debriefed the CO.

"SIB were monitoring Major Broom," Ambrose said. "A couple of reports on him. Seems he had a tendency to be where he wasn't expected."

"Linked to either drugs or alcohol?" I asked, thinking of previous cases.

"Not linked to anything," Ambrose said. "Just unusual behaviour, otherwise we'd have picked him up. Maybe the sergeant will tell us more."

Robshaw left but Ambrose called me back.

"I've requested all of Harwood's and Jenkins's SIB reports for this year." He was about to say something but stopped himself.

"You had trouble getting them?"

"Very much so! But I persuaded them because of the helicopter crash. Because we're involved. Even so, they were reluctant. For Christ's sake, one of their men was probably murdered and they still needed persuading!"

I waited for him to calm down. He was talking about my old division. I knew how the SIB could be.

"So it's sensitive, but we knew that," I said. "More sensitive than usual."

"My eyes only."

And yet he was telling me. He'd called me back into the room and had told me. Me alone.

I nodded.

"I'll send you that package," he said as though the other conversation was over, "as soon as it arrives."

I nodded again, realizing he was talking about the SIB files. "I look forward to it."

Robshaw raised his eyebrows as I joined him. I shook my head and he didn't ask what Ambrose had wanted me for.

Styles was called from the cells and looked sick when he was brought into our interview room.

"It's the major isn't it?" he said.

"Seems that way," Robshaw said. "Why didn't you say something straight away, Sergeant?"

"I hoped it wasn't him."

I shook my head.

Styles breathed in and out. "I didn't want to admit it—even to myself. That's why I said nothing. You know, I hoped it was just a resemblance."

"Why was the major up in Perak?" Robshaw asked.

"He travelled around. Like I said, he's a law unto himself."

I shook my head. "You actually said you didn't keep tabs on him."

Styles shrugged. "He was often going off for a few days. Told us it was RAOC related but I don't think it was—not always. He once said he was going to a barracks in KL and I tried to reach him there. He never turned up."

"Did you challenge him afterwards?"

"I asked him and he said he was called away on another matter. Sir, he's a major. I don't know what business he has to attend to."

I banged the table, partly out of frustration with this guy and partly to make him jump. "Enough of the bullshit!" I shouted. "You know what he was up to."

"I don't," he said, but I wasn't convinced.

"Then you can spend some time in the clink until it jogs your memory," Robshaw said. "Guards!"

Two MPs came in, pulled Styles to his feet and marched him out. They'd take him to the main cells at the city office on Bras Basah Road. Hotel Bras Basah we affectionately called it, and I'd been held there myself when I first arrived on the island.

He knew something and 200 Provost would make him sweat in a cell until he talked.

When I arrived at my office the next morning, I was amazed to see that not only did the door look like new, but the hall smelled of paint and the flooring had been repaired.

Madam Chau looked up from her desk and scowled at me.

"Good morning," I said.

"You were out all yesterday again."

"Madam Chau, you need to get used to the fact that I won't tell you what I'm doing every minute of the day."

"Just one minute of the day would be nice."

"You're worse than my first sergeant," I said, joking.

"I'll take that as a compliment."

"My compliment is that you sorted the repair so quickly. It looks amazing—good as new. Thank you."

She looked at me through narrowed eyes but I was sure she was happy with the praise. Confirmation of this followed when she made me a cup of tea and stopped complaining.

She stood over my desk and went through the post with me, which included some bills.

"I can delay them," she said.

"No, I expect customers to pay me on time, and I do the same."

"Mr Wu won't be paying you now he's been arrested."

"No," I said. "I don't expect he will."

"Will the military pay you for what you've been doing for them?"

"I've not asked."

She shook her head with a look that told me I was insane. Then she held up a letter.

"Will you take the case of the missing dog?"

"It seems a bit beneath me, don't you think?"

"What else are you going to do, then?"

"I'm waiting for an important military police package."

"When will that arrive?" she asked, and I had to admit that I didn't know.

She slid the letter towards me. It was in English and I already knew the author. Her name was Margery Slone, married to Major Slone based at Tanglin Barracks on the island. Previously she'd offered a reward of five pounds to find her dog. Now she'd doubled it.

"It's beneath me," I said again.

"Finish your tea and go and find the lady's dog," Madam Chau said sternly. "You can't just sit here waiting for this mysterious package."

"But you don't like me out and about."

She tutted and huffed back to her desk. "No, I just want to know where you are. I worry about you."

That was the first time my receptionist had said anything of the sort and I scooted across the room and kissed her cheek.

She looked shocked. "No need for that!"

I smiled and waved and promised to be back before lunch.

Margery Slone's house was not far from the barracks. I drove the length of Orchard Road and then turned left, which took me onto Tanglin Road, then I took another right. Trees lined her street and I could see the Botanic Gardens close by.

When I rang the doorbell, a Malay servant answered and bowed and invited me into the drawing room.

I had no idea what to expect but double blinked when the lady of the house walked in. My first thought was about her pretty face. My second was to notice her slightly inappropriate attire for greeting a male visitor, especially since I had Madam Chau call ahead of my arrival.

Mrs Slone wore a loose silk kimono like a dressing gown. As she moved, I got a brief glimpse of skin and underwear.

She must have seen my downward glance because she tightened a belt and then smiled demurely. I placed her at about twenty or twenty-one, more a girl than a woman, with an impish face and short curly brown hair. Her eyes were dark and large.

"I could come back later," I suggested.

"Oh, no, Mr Carter. Thank you for coming—"

Her voice sounded off, and when she moved forward to shake my hand I realized why. She'd been drinking.

Her touch was smooth and cool, and I broke off the handshake after a second.

"Your dog," I said, looking out into her extensive rear garden. "Is he still missing?"

"Oh, yes, Rufus is missing." She pointed to a sofa and sat on it, expecting me to sit beside her.

"Mrs Slone…"

83

"Right," she said seriously, "first rule is that you call me Marge. Mrs Slone is my mother-in-law." She pulled a face and shook her head. "I'm not my mother-in-law."

I remained standing. "Marge, tell me what happened. When you say 'missing'—?"

"Disappeared."

"Could he have been taken?"

"You mean kidnapped?"

"It's possible if you have an unusual dog—something sought after."

She thought for a moment, raising an eyebrow as she did so, and seemed to be studying my eyes.

"Aren't you going to sit down, Mr Carter?"

I chose a chair opposite and perched on the edge of the seat. "Have you received a ransom note?"

She shook her head.

"When was the last time you saw Rufus?"

"The night before last, when I went to bed."

"Oh, but your letter was dated Monday."

For a moment I thought she looked awkward. Then she said, "He came back and went again."

"All right. What time, on Wednesday night?"

"About ten o'clock."

"Where?"

"In my bedroom." She giggled. "Oh, you mean Rufus! I last saw him in his room. We have a small room with his bed and food in."

"And when did you realize he'd *disappeared*?" I emphasized the word she'd used.

"Yesterday at 10 am."

I stood up. "Could you show me his room, please, Marge?"

She got up unsteadily and I smelled gin as she wafted past me and led me along a hall, through a parlour, through a kitchen, through a laundry, and into a small room. There was an external door with a key in its hole.

I turned the handle and confirmed the door was locked.

"How did he get out of the room?"

"I don't know."

"Did someone open the door?"

"Maybe Rufus did," she suggested seriously.

"May I?" I said, unlocking the door and stepping outside. Now I was in a rear garden. I could see a fence at the far end and scrubland beyond.

"Could Rufus jump the fence?" I asked, standing outside. She remained in the doorway, a hand on either side, maybe for support.

"I don't think so, but there's a gate."

"Was that open two days ago?"

"I don't know."

"Is it open now?"

"No."

I nodded, and she moved aside so I could come back in. Again I got the waft of gin.

She followed me back to the hallway. "What do you think, Mr Carter?"

I stopped and looked at the fine wood panelling. There were some quality, very English, watercolours but no photographs. I hadn't seen any in the other rooms either. Didn't dog owners normally have lots of photographs of their pets? I wasn't sure since I'd never had one, but it seemed likely.

"What does Rufus look like?"

"So you will look for him?"

"Yes," I said, but only because I had nothing better to do and I didn't want to face Madam Chau's wrath if I declined the job.

Mrs Slone touched my arm. "Thank you."

"You were about to tell me what Rufus looks like."

"Oh yes, he's an Irish Setter about six years old. And this high." She held her hand at about waist level. The movement parted her kimono slightly and she smiled.

I had a good idea what an Irish Setter looked like and knew I'd never seen a long-haired red dog on the island.

"Let's start by assuming he's run away again, Mrs Slone?"

"Marge."

"Marge," I corrected myself.

"It's possible."

"Where did he go last time and how did you get him back?"

"He was seen in the Botanic Gardens, which aren't far." She pointed back towards the rear of the house and I'd already realized you could get there by going through the back gate and across the scrubland.

"Then that's the way I'll go," I said. "If you don't mind?" And so we returned to Rufus's room and I went back outside.

I left her in the doorway, with her hands either side again, and glancing back I saw that it separated her dressing gown just above the knee.

After a plush lawn with a rose garden and small maple trees, there was an orchard and a pond before the back gate. It was indeed shut, and I went through from flat ground to coarse scrubland. I looked left and right, saw no dog and walked forward.

What the hell was I doing? Had it really come to this?

Maybe it was the search for a dog and the association with dog tag, but as I walked, I found myself thinking about the word BlackJack on the dog tag. Was that a clue? Then I thought about Major Broom's body. Why naked but leave a gold chain? It was a clue and yet I couldn't grasp its significance. BlackJack and gold chain.

Two dead bodies, two clues. So were the two murders linked?

SIXTEEN

Did anyone understand why people enjoyed killing other people? BlackJack had read that killers tended to start young, probably by experimenting on animals. Kill a neighbour's pet and realize the thrill as it died. Especially if that death was slow and painful.

Perhaps there were killers like that. Perhaps they had psychological problems caused by a dysfunctional upbringing. The police certainly seemed to think there was a *type*. But BlackJack knew it was nonsense. Certainly in his case anyway.

The first thing he'd killed was a bird. A collared dove had been wounded by a cat that he found pawing at its prey as though urging it to fly and be caught again— keep playing the game.

The bird had lain on its side, bleeding from the neck. Not much, but enough to show that it wouldn't survive. So young BlackJack had fetched his father's spade and considered the most merciful method of killing the creature. Hit it or chop off its head?

No choice. He thrust the spade down as hard as he could, but the blade was too blunt and the head didn't sever. So BlackJack pressed down harder.

The bird's eyes had been closed but the one he could see now opened. It seemed to be looking at him. The beak opened like it was gasping for air and a wing flapped twice. The legs kicked and the body went into spasm.

He had no idea how long it took for the bird to die. Maybe it had been seconds, although it felt like minutes. And the whole time, the cat watched him curiously.

When the creature was finally still, BlackJack shovelled it up and dumped it into the rubbish bin.

Had he felt anything? Had the apparently slow death given him the first thrill? No. He'd felt absolutely nothing.

And he hadn't killed anything else deliberately for many years. In fact, the first time he felt the tingling in his fingers and the flutter of his heart as he took another's life was only a few years ago. And it was by accident.

The other man had pulled a knife on him and they had struggled until BlackJack had the upper hand. The guy should have dropped the knife, but instead he was still holding it as it slid between his own ribs and pierced his heart. That was when BlackJack had felt the frisson of excitement, the power and the energy of taking another man's life.

There was something intimate about a blade. Killing a man up close and personal was what gave him the thrill. But there was something else too.

That first man had been a crook, and if he could have killed BlackJack, he would have. It seemed that the excitement of the kill only came to him when he was dealing out justice. The men he killed deserved to die.

He'd tried getting the same thrill from killing a random person. He felt nothing. It had been so easy to get away with that he killed two more before giving up the quest. He also tried a woman. Jack the Ripper had only killed women, presumably gaining some kind of

89

sexual pleasure from his deeds. Maybe he'd been sexually frustrated for some reason. That wasn't the case for BlackJack. He had a great sex life. No complaints there. Lots of young women—of legal age—and no desire to kill them.

The only thing that niggled was his increasing need to leave clues. Intellectually he knew it was risky, but then wasn't that the point? Jack had left a clue every time and he never hid a body.

Had the authorities picked up on his clues? Possibly, but then there was the Emergency. Maybe they were too preoccupied with the politics and the Chinese bandits. That's why so many soldiers were criminals. That's why he had to be judge and executioner.

And the greatest of all crimes was the gold pipeline, as they called it. BlackJack had stumbled on it by chance, found a small man at the end of the line, a man being paid off for his service and silence. Although he squealed like a pig when the knife went in.

So BlackJack had found Major Broom. A big fish and one who deserved a painful death. Admittedly he'd been dead before most of the face had been removed, but he got what he deserved. And his rank had provided BlackJack with his biggest kick yet.

For the first time, he'd hidden a body, but not because he didn't want it to be found. It was because he needed a few more days. His timing could have been better, but beggars can't be choosers, as his mother had always told him.

He'd been tempted to leave something else with his name, maybe engrave it across the corpse's chest, but that would have been too obvious. He needed to leave a clue that required intelligence. If there was going to be a chase, if someone was going to come after him, then he had better be smart.

The guy wouldn't win, of course, but it would add an extra layer of challenge, an extra adrenaline rush to the conclusion.

The gold chain was perfect. It connected everything.

SEVENTEEN

BlackJack. What did it mean? Twenty-one was a card game that Americans called blackjack. The metal dog tag implied American. But then the bullet had been Soviet. He could be Russian or Chinese.

That thinking led me nowhere so I returned to the card game. Could he be saying it's like a game of cards—a game of chance? Risk maybe? If it was a clue, then the killer was taking a big risk.

There seemed to be no connection to a gold chain. I couldn't think of a card game about gold. Was that too straightforward? Did that mean the two incidents weren't related? And yet the gold chain had been deliberately left like it was a message.

I had crossed the scrubland and reached a dry ditch with a long pipe about three feet in diameter. It ran the whole length of the common before disappearing below ground. A drain, I figured.

I followed the ditch and noticed it became a stream. Or maybe the water had leaked from the pipe.

Further on, I saw people walking dogs, and they all knew Rufus. They said he was often seen running around the fields and also in the Botanic Gardens.

By lunchtime I came out onto the main road and found some lunch and water, and carried on, looking and asking anyone I met. I crossed the road and went into the gardens. Another half an hour and I found Rufus lying in a hut, resting out of the heat. It appears that not all mad dogs go out in the noonday sun.

Holding onto his collar, I led him out of the gardens, across the road and across the field to the back of the Slone's house.

"Rufus!" she declared with delight, and she gave him a lot of fuss while I watched. She was dressed in a tight-fitting top and leggings that didn't leave much to the imagination. She had a great little figure.

Then she looked at me and smiled. "You are clever."

"Not really," I said, noting that she hadn't asked me where I'd found him.

"Tea and cake have just been served," she said, leading me almost like I'd led Rufus. She took me into the lounge, where tea and cakes were indeed set up.

She sat on the sofa and, like before, patted it.

"I should be getting back, Mrs Slone."

She gave me a coquettish smile. "You're supposed to call me Marge, remember?"

Despite her allure, I remained standing. "Something's been bothering me," I said.

"Oh?" She poured two cups of tea, and it struck me that she seemed to be prepared for my return.

"Why didn't your husband look for Rufus?"

"Oh I daren't tell him Rufus was out. You see he'd blame me. And if he had found our dog, well then I'd never have got to meet the dashing Ash Carter now would I?"

"Aren't you interested in where I found him?"

"Not really, I'm just grateful that you did. You've done me a huge favour and I'm ever so grateful." She batted her eyelashes.

"I'd better be going."

She stood up and used the sofa's arm to steady herself. "We could come to an arrangement," she said, and there was desperation in her voice. "He runs off all the time and I'm here alone. You could—"

"Goodbye, Mrs Slone," I said, and let myself out.

On my drive back, I wondered if this was what my job had come down to: soldier's pregnant girlfriends and desperate army housewives?

I shook the negative thoughts away and focused again on BlackJack. Maybe we'd missed something. Maybe there had been a BlackJack or similar clue where Major Broom's body had been found.

On Orchard Road, I came to the turning that would take me around Fort Canning towards the river and then my office. But instead, I went left.

I went to HQ on Bras Basah Road.

"How's Sergeant Styles doing?" I asked the young desk clerk as I walked into the foyer.

"Relaxed, sir."

"Relaxed? He does know this is a jail and not a hotel, right?"

The kid laughed.

And then it struck me.

"Call Captain Robshaw. Tell him to get down here pronto. We need to talk to Styles."

Within twenty minutes, Robshaw and I were sitting in an office.

"I think he's happy to be in jail," I said. "I think he feels safe."

"Safe?"

"Under your protection. His boss was mutilated. It wasn't just a murder, it was a message."

Robshaw nodded, and we talked some more before he called for the prisoner to be brought before us.

After Styles was frogmarched into the room he stood at ease in front of us.

I said, "We're going to let you go, Styles."

He looked from me to Robshaw, his eyes calculating.

"More than that," I said. "We're going to say you helped us."

"Told us everything about Major Broom," Robshaw said matter-of-factly.

I saw fear in Sergeant Styles's eyes.

"Talk," I said. "Who are you afraid of?"

He thought before speaking. "The person who killed the major."

"Who is that?"

"That's just it, I don't know!"

"Is he American?"

He shook his head. "I really know nothing."

We sat in silence, let him sweat until he spoke again. "Can you help me?"

Robshaw leaned forward. "How can we help you?"

"Protect me."

"Who from?"

He gulped. "I really don't know. That's the problem."

I said, "You can't stay in here forever."

"I realize that."

"Then talk."

"All I can tell you is what the major was up to... but not until you make guarantees."

Robshaw said, "If you aren't guilty, then I can get you transferred."

"I'm not guilty of anything apart from not speaking up." He took a nervous breath. "And I only did that because I was afraid."

"Then you have a deal. We protect the good guys."

He took another breath, preparing himself, and told us that he knew Broom was up to no good, going off on unscheduled trips. He would get a call from an unnamed person and then go at short notice. Frustratingly, Styles said he didn't know what Broom was doing, and I believed him. Styles assumed that his boss was doing some sort of trade with the other guy.

Robshaw shook his head. "Is that it? Is that all you have?"

The sergeant swallowed.

I said, "Tell me about the gold."

Bingo! Style's eyes went crazy, but he stayed quiet.

I said, "We'll let you go and make it known that you told us about the gold."

"I know nothing!"

"Not true," I said.

We let him sweat and eventually he broke.

"The major was trading in gold. I don't know what. I don't know details, but…"

"He was paying you off," I suggested. "He gave you some gold."

"Not much. It was like a reward."

"For turning a blind eye," Robshaw said.

"Yes."

"To what?"

"To his movements."

I shook my head. "We need more than that."

I looked at Robshaw and nodded. "Guards!" the captain shouted at the door.

It opened and two MPs stepped inside.

"Take Sergeant Styles back to his BVD."

"OK!" Styles shouted as hands were placed on his shoulders.

"OK what?" Robshaw said.

"I heard the term pipeline once or twice."

"And?"

"I think maybe Major Broom was part of a trade in gold that was called the pipeline. And yes, he was paid in gold and then paid me for my silence."

I said, "Who is BlackJack?"

His eyes narrowed as he shook his head. "It's not a name I know."

"Is BlackJack who you're afraid of?"

"I don't know any black Jack."

Robshaw said, "What about Jack Black?"

I looked at him, surprised. I hadn't thought about that. Could the man have switched his name around?

Styles was shaking his head. "I don't know him, I tell you!"

Robshaw raised his chin at the guards and the sergeant was marched out, leaving us frustrated.

"How did you guess about the gold?" he asked me when we were alone.

"The gold chain on Broom's body. I figured it was a clue of some kind."

"Bloody big one. Although—"

"It's not much to go on." I finished his sentence for him.

"Do you think Styles is really under threat?"

I shook my head. I couldn't really gauge the likelihood, but there was no indication that the killer knew Styles had overheard anything or had been suspicious.

"Send him back to the BVD," I said. "And leave one of your men there under some pretence. If Styles really is a target maybe it'll draw our killer out into the open. If he's holding something back, then maybe it'll make him talk."

I went back to the office. Madam Chau met me and complained that I'd said I'd be back before lunch. Then she handed me a brown paper package marked "Eyes

Only". It was the file from the SIB, and my life was about to get interesting.

EIGHTEEN

There were two files inside the package: the dictated reports by John Harwood and Joe Jenkins.

I picked up Harwood's file first. SIB HQ held a similar file from my time in the Middle East. I figured mine would be as sketchy as this one. There were many *no development* updates. Which didn't mean he hadn't been doing anything; on the contrary, it meant that he simply wasn't ready to provide a full report. And despite the fact these weren't formal, they were recorded for posterity.

I sifted through the sheets and found the interesting ones. They contained details of four dead men. The first man was killed eleven months ago. A corporal found hanged at a place called Takafuji Cliff. I had to check a map and located it about ten miles north-east of Kuala Lumpur before the Genting Highlands.

Harwood had tracked him thereafter, suspecting the corporal of black market trading. Harwood's notes asked the obvious questions: what was he doing out there and who was he meeting?

The cause of death was strangulation from the noose. There was no broken neck, and the coroner suggested the corporal had taken a long time to die in agony from a crushed windpipe. Stab wounds were also noted on either side of his abdomen.

Harwood's notes included interviews with the men in the deceased's unit, at the Kuala Lumpur base called Batu 10. He hadn't learned anything and neither did I.

I turned to the sheets on the second man and stared. This was a sergeant who'd been scalped. The scalping wasn't like that of the faceless Major Broom. This soldier was a Gurkha missing the top of his head—a traditional scalping, I thought.

He'd been based at Kluang although his body was found at the Batu Caves, just outside Kuala Lumpur. He'd been AWOL for three weeks and Harwood said he'd traced the man to the capital before finding him in the cave area. I looked at the picture again and couldn't help wonder about the Ibans. Could this man have been killed by a headhunter? He wasn't a white man, so Koda, who I'd spoken to at Camp Kota Tinggi, hadn't lied. Was it possible that an Iban mistook him for a bandit?

I filed the thought away and pulled out the next file. Another AWOL soldier. This one from Terendak Barracks in Malacca. He'd been missing for nine weeks before turning up dead in a lake ten miles east of the capital. However, he hadn't drowned. He'd been disembowelled "with brutal force" according to the coroner's report.

Harwood hadn't found this guy. A local man had fished the soldier out of the water and the police initially suspected it had been an accident—until the coroner saw the body.

Harwood had linked this to the previous two deaths based on the location. Now he was suspicious that there was a killer operating out of Kuala Lumpur.

However, the fourth body was way over on the east coast, near Pahang. A corporal who had been reported AWOL a week before.

The scalping of the Gurkha had been nasty. This fourth man had been flayed. He was found tied to a tree with the skin of his arms and legs stripped off.

Harwood thought the manner of the corporal's death suggested torture. Again, there were interviews with the man's colleagues, and I noted that his friend was surprised he'd gone AWOL.

The SIB man's notes started to question whether he'd been misguided. Maybe the cases weren't linked. The MO was different in every case. There was a note on file about the body I'd found—the ex-soldier who'd gone missing in the Kinta Valley. I knew his case was different, but Harwood had investigated it nonetheless.

There were also notes about Major Broom. Harwood had investigated him although he wasn't linked to any of the deaths. Harwood didn't know what Broom was doing but he figured it was suspicious and that's why Ambrose at 200 Provost had been asked to keep an eye out for him.

There was no mention of gold or anything like a pipeline or trade route.

I turned to Jenkins's file and went a long way through before finding information on a murder. A fifth body was found in Genting Highlands. Jenkins had been first on the scene after tracking the man for months.

This was another sergeant. Although not officially AWOL, he'd taken five days' leave. He'd been based at another Kuala Lumpur camp.

Jenkins had been following the sergeant, believing him to be involved in drug distribution. The body was left in a public place, naked, with the man's genitals removed and stuck in his mouth.

This had occurred almost four months ago. Jenkins had been withdrawn to tie up the loose ends of my investigation in Penang at that time. He'd virtually told me he was looking for a killer.

I skimmed through Jenkins's notes on my Penang case and learned nothing I didn't already know. Then Jenkins went back to the murder case and interviewed the man's colleagues. Two soldiers thought the sergeant had a predilection for children, which made sense of the genitals in the mouth.

Jenkins wondered whether the killer had been someone who'd found out about the man's sexual activities or whether it was the parent of a victim.

His investigations had drawn a blank.

Then he got a call from the Kuala Lumpur police about a gruesome case where a body had been found with his chest cavity smashed open and his heart removed.

He had ID and was a known black-market trader. The police had involved Jenkins because the guy was an ex-soldier. That had been ten days ago.

I went back to Harwood's file. Although he'd been focused on Major Broom's activities, he also compiled a list of other suspicious deaths. He started to be convinced that there was a prolific killer in Malaya, not just soldiers and ex-soldiers, but others—although it was always men.

He started calling them executions, and every single method was different. He found twenty cases, one before the first soldier was hanged and the rest in the past year.

I was wondering whether he'd gone too broad, whether this was about five or six soldiers, when I realized Madam Chau was talking.

"Telephone," she said, holding up the receiver. "You have an urgent call from a Lieutenant Jenkins."

NINETEEN

I dashed to her desk and took the receiver from her. "Hello?"

"Captain Carter." I recognized Lieutenant Jenkins's voice. He said, "I just checked in and the clerk put me through to you—a request from Colonel Ambrose. Is this about the Penang case?"

"No. It's about your case, Joe."

He said nothing, presumably wondering what I knew.

"When was the last time you spoke to Harwood?"

There was silence while I guess he was thinking. "A week ago."

"Exactly a week?"

Again the silence. "No, it must have been eight days. Why?"

"What was he doing in Kahang?"

"Kahang? I don't know. We last met in KL. Tell me what's happened? Something's happened to him, right?"

"Seven days ago he made a call for a helicopter pickup from Kahang. It looks like he had a prisoner with him."

"Looks like?"

"They never made it back. The helicopter crashed. The pilot and Harwood bought it."

"Bugger!"

"Right."

A second of silence and then: "So what? Has Ambrose assigned you to the investigation?"

"Yes."

"You said there may have been a prisoner…"

"It looks like a third man shot the pilot and set fire to everything."

"How did John die?"

"From the fire."

"Bugger!"

Neither of us said anything for a few seconds. I guessed he was processing it.

I said, "Does the name BlackJack mean anything to you?"

"Black Jack?" he said slowly, sounding it out like a first and second name.

"One word, like the card game."

"What?"

I started to repeat it but he interrupted. "Remember I said I had been working a case?"

"Yes, and I've seen your recent reports."

"You've seen the files?"

"I have."

He might have challenged me, asked under whose authority I'd received them, but he didn't. He just accepted it the way I would have accepted another SIB looking into my files if the roles were reversed.

"Right," he said, "so you know about my most recent case."

"The one with his heart cut out."

"Right." Jenkins took a breath. "He had a card in his pocket. The jack of spades."

"BlackJack."

"I didn't think anything of it until now. Why did you mention the name?"

"It was on a dog tag at the crash site. I think it was meant to be found."

"The prisoner..." Jenkins said, and I could almost hear the cogs in his head. "That means John had caught BlackJack. He'd caught the killer!"

"But he got away."

"Right."

"And Harwood didn't tell you anything?"

"No. This must have all happened after I met up with him in KL."

"Do you know about Major Broom?"

He hesitated. "Harwood was investigating the major. The guy is as bent as a nine bob note."

"He's dead too."

"Another murder? Did John find him?"

"Definitely murdered. The timeline suggests that Broom was killed two days after the helicopter crash."

There was a long silence and I figured Jenkins was thinking about his partner and how he'd burned to death after the crash.

I threw out a random comment to bring him back: "A lot of the activity you've both investigated was around KL."

Jenkins said, "I've been making progress out east."

"Where are you?"

He hesitated, probably questioning himself. Should he tell me?

"I have the files, Joe. I'm involved. Let me help."

"Jerteh."

"Where's that?"

"On the coast. Way up. North of Terengganu."

I waved for a map and Madam Chau passed one to me. I found Terengganu and traced my finger up about sixty miles.

"Tell me more," I said.

"I think I'm on the killer or killers' trail."

"Could there be more than one killer? You're saying they're connected?"

"At first we thought the murders weren't related. Now I think they were deliberately different, or it's a group of men."

I said, "If you just look at the seven plus Broom, they all involved a knife. Not the cause of death necessarily, but maybe a signature of some kind."

"Sounds reasonable."

"The second case last year"—I read the name from the file—"was a scalping. Major Broom had his face removed. So I wondered whether the killer was an Iban."

"John suggested that after we found the scalped Gurkha."

"But a tracker told me that he thought the technique was all wrong. Broom's face had been taken off the wrong way: lip to head and missing the nose."

"I think we're looking for at least one white man."

"Why?"

"Two possible sightings. Unconfirmed."

"Theory?" I asked.

"Ex-military. Someone with a grudge."

"Why target AWOLs and criminals?"

"Soldiers out where they shouldn't be, perhaps?"

I thought about Major Broom, out in the jungle near Ipoh. Alone. An easy target.

"Makes sense," I said.

I let the sound of the wires fill the silence before I spoke again. I think he anticipated what I would say next. "I'm coming out there."

"I can handle this."

"You're alone. Your partner is dead, probably killed by the same man. SIB HQ hasn't recognized Harwood's death yet. You're all alone."

"If the roles were reversed, would you like assistance?"

I thought for a moment. He was right. I would expect to finish a job myself. "No," I said. Then I thought of Slugger and added: "But I sometimes ask for help."

"And so do I. But now isn't the time."

I listened to noise for a few seconds again wondering how to change his mind.

He said, "I'll report in, so you know either way."

"Either way?"

"Well, you'll know straight away when I need you or if I'm in trouble."

"If you don't call in."

"Right."

I nodded, although he couldn't see me of course. "Call this office," I said. "Make it between six and seven each night."

I ended the call, feeling a little better. Each time we spoke he would give me an update and I'd find a way to get involved.

It was now late afternoon and I hadn't eaten, so I headed outside in search of a street vendor. I turned left and was only two paces from my door when I saw a soldier running.

"Stop thief," he yelled as he approached. "Someone stop him!"

I looked right and saw a man disappear around the corner, thirty yards ahead. A Chinese guy in a white shirt and grey pants, I registered. He'd ducked into an alley between the buildings.

The soldier passed me, still shouting.

Instinct kicked in. I started running the opposite way. Since I was close to the end of my building, I was soon in the alley running towards the same road as the thief. If he turned right at the end, he'd run into me.

I hit the road after the alley and swung left again. No sign of the Chinese guy. I ran fast towards the next alley, and just before I got there, the soldier appeared on the street. He stopped, put his hands on his knees, shook his head and turned back the way he'd come.

"Did you see a Chinky come out? Did you pass him?" he asked, breathing hard as I reached him.

"No."

"Then he didn't come out." The soldier pointed into the shadows. "He must be hiding down there."

The guy started back along the alleyway and I followed. There were doors on each side and wooden crates. We moved the crates in case he'd hidden under or behind them. Then we started checking doors.

Suddenly the other guy stopped and looked at me.

"You're Carter, aren't you?"

"Yes," I said, thrown by his focus. And less than a second later I realized why. He hadn't been looking at me. He'd been looking over my shoulder. Too late. Something whacked into the base of my skull and I went down onto all fours, dazed and sick with the pain.

"A message," a voice said behind me. "Stay away from Mrs Slone."

TWENTY

The sun was setting as I drove into Tanglin Barracks, asked for directions and walked into an office block. A clerk looked up from a desk. I saw his eyes flare with alarm, but he said nothing and I marched past him and down a corridor. Ten paces later I was standing outside an office. The name on the door was Major T Slone. A nice brass plate, calling for respect.

I kicked it and barged in.

Major Slone was sitting behind his desk. He had dark curly hair and a weak chin, but I could see he was reasonably large, and when he stood up, I gauged him to be about my height. But he wasn't fit, and when he came around his desk I could see he'd already gone to seed. I figured he was maybe ten years older than his pretty young wife.

"You got the message," he spat out between teeth that forced a smile.

"You bastard," I growled.

"You were seen at my house."

"So?"

"Having an affair with my wife."

I felt my hands twitch and my feet felt light, as though I was in a boxing ring.

"You idiot," I said. "I'm not seeing your wife."

Now I saw his hands ball up. He was still square on and looking big. It was a good intimidation tactic, which might work with another man. Maybe it had worked for him in the past, but it was foolish. He was exposed and a quick kick to the balls would teach him a lesson.

"You attacked me for no reason," I said.

"You deserved it. Stay away from my wife!"

I took a breath, resisting the urge to kick him. "I should deck you," I said.

"Try it." Now his hands came up but his genitals were still exposed.

"A year ago," I said, "I'd have had no hesitation. Five years ago, I would have slept with your wife—just for revenge."

He snarled and inched closer.

"But not today," I said. "Instead, I have a message for you: pay more attention to your wife, rather than the men you think are after her."

And with that, I spun and walked out.

I heard him shout "Coward", but it just made me shake my head. I felt a better man for not punching his lights out—or kicking him in the balls. And as I walked into the hallway, I saw two men standing in the reception area. Both sergeants. Ten paces down the corridor I confronted them.

One was the soldier who'd lured me into the alleyway. The other was a huge guy, maybe six six and solid. But that wasn't what I noticed first. He was leaning on a cricket bat like a man about to play.

I'd assumed Slone had been the man in the alley, the man who'd hit me from behind. Now I thought differently.

I also realized these guys had been waiting for trouble. The confrontation with Slone had been a set-up. They

110

expected me to hit him and would have come charging in to his rescue.

I nodded at the big guy. "What's your name, Sergeant?"

"Becks."

"You handy with a bat?"

He swung it up so that the blade slapped against his other hand. "I play," he said.

The first sergeant said, "So, Ash Carter is a coward."

I shook my head, still looking at the big guy. "Put the bat down and let's go one on one."

I saw him thinking about it, weighing up his chances.

After a moment I added: "But not here. Not now." I saw relief pass behind his eyes. "You want to see how I handle myself, come down to the YMCA boxing gym any morning. And if you have the guts, step into the ring with me."

He snarled. "I'll do that."

"Good, because if you don't then I'll come looking for you, Becks. No one hits me with a cricket bat and gets away with it."

He came out with some bravado bullshit but I was already walking away. It felt good and I was proud of myself.

Scott "Slugger" Stevenson stood on the edge of a disused opencast tin mine.

"Thanks for calling me," he said to the police officer beside him.

Down in the pit, a light flashed, and the officer turned and barked an order to another inside a pickup vehicle. Immediately, a winch groaned and whirred as a tow line took the strain.

It turned slowly and Stevenson saw the back of the stricken vehicle appear and inch towards him.

111

"No sign of the driver," the officer said.

"What are you thinking?"

"That it wasn't an accident."

They stood in silence and finally Stevenson could see the rear clearly. As he'd been told, it was a Land Rover: dark green with no markings. It didn't belong to a tin mining operation. All their vehicles had company names stencilled along their sides.

"How long's it been down there?"

The policeman shook his head. "Full of rainwater, but it wasn't there ten days ago. Best estimate is between nine and five days."

The Land Rover lurched over the edge and the winch stopped its grind.

Stevenson walked around the vehicle, playing his torch over the panels and bumpers.

"Nothing," he said.

"No registration plates."

"Right, but it was army."

"How do you know?"

Stevenson shook his head and directed the torchlight at the right-hand wing behind the rear wheel. Bare metal shone back.

"British Army vehicles have a number painted on there. Someone's deliberately removed it. I think we've found our faceless man's jeep."

When I woke up in the morning, I had a thumping headache and the lump on the back of my head was sore to the touch. Instead of my usual hard workout, I did some light exercise before going to the office on Carpenter Street.

Despite being Saturday, Madam Chau was there and she fussed over me in her grumpy yet likeable way. I'd seen her before my visit to Tanglin so she knew all about my injury, and this morning she had some weird Chinese poultice for my head.

She tied it on and I must have looked like an old washerwoman. When I saw the ladies across the way look over, I decided it was time to get some shutters for the windows.

This morning I had the usual nonsense requests and was relieved that Mrs Slone hadn't written. I had no doubt she would hear about what happened. The major would want her to know how her potential lovers got treated. Maybe that's what she wanted—her husband to fight for her. If she did, I bet he wouldn't tell her it was Becks who'd struck me with the cricket bat.

I put the Slones out of my mind and tried not to think about Jenkins's case and BlackJack. I'd been thinking all night and come up with nothing new.

I pulled out a letter that caught my attention. A woman said that her husband had been behaving out of character and she feared that he was involved in something illegal.

Mr Tharoor ran a small bakery in the east of the city. I left the office and found Mrs Tharoor at her home in Little India. She'd told me he was hardworking and a good man but had become nervous and wouldn't talk about whatever was bothering him.

She'd always fretted about people trading on the black market and had confronted him about it. He'd denied it but she knew he was up to something. Gambling perhaps, she now suspected.

With the Slones' situation fresh in my mind, I asked whether Mr Tharoor could be having an affair. Her response was that it was impossible, although he might cover for someone else like his brother, who was a rogue.

Then I found a bench from which I could watch his bakery.

I saw nothing suspicious happen all day, and at five o'clock he closed up and walked home. He didn't deviate, didn't stop to gamble anywhere. Mrs Tharoor had told me he'd eat his dinner and be in bed by six because he would be up at four in the morning to start baking again.

I returned to the office and waited for Lieutenant Jenkins to call.

"How's the head?" Madam Chau asked me.

I had stopped wearing the ridiculous headband and poultice as soon as I'd left the office this morning and the ache was still there. However, I said, "Perfect. You cured it."

She nodded and smiled—at least I think her grimace was a smile.

With a minute to go before seven, Madam Chau held up the phone and said, "It's him."

"Checking in," he said, and I detected a hint of mockery in his tone.

"Everything all right, Joe?"

He paused, and I imagined him weighing up how much to tell me. Finally, he said, "I've travelled up north. Now in Permaisuri."

I checked the map and saw he was less than fifteen miles south of where he'd been before.

"Why there?" I prompted.

"The man I was following has been picked up by another. Both ex-army."

"Two men," I said, thinking.

"Right."

"You said there could be more than one killer. Different methods, same motive."

"Right," he said. "I think I'm really onto something this time."

"It would be better if you had support."

"I'll let you know if I need you."

I wanted to tell him to be sensible, not to play the hero, but I knew it'd be patronizing. I also knew I was desperate to be involved rather than having to chase dogs, married women, and bakers.

"Call you again on Monday, Ash," he said.

"Tomorrow."

"It's Sunday."

"Are you taking a day off? Of course not. Call me tomorrow."

"I won't promise, but I'll call if I can find a telephone," he said. "Otherwise I'll call you on Monday no later than seven." Then he was gone.

TWENTY-ONE

Madam Chau had left for the evening when the phone rang again.

"Slugger! What a surprise," I said after hearing my friend's voice. I was the one who normally made contact. "Is everything all right?"

"I was just hoping for an update."

"An update?"

"On the case of Joe Bloggs, the faceless man."

I said nothing for a moment.

"Come on," he said. "What do you know, Carter?"

"Why do you think—?"

"Because I've just been told that the army collected the body. So he was a soldier, wasn't he?"

I took a breath. The body had been taken, but I knew the army wouldn't declare anything—not until they were sure about Major Broom's identity and what had happened. There had been all those other suspicious deaths I'd read about in the SIB files. People knew men had died but no one apart from the SIB saw the bigger picture. There was a killer out there and Broom may have been one of his victims. I wouldn't have known that if Slugger hadn't called me up to Ipoh last week.

"OK," I said, coming to a conclusion. "It looks like he's a major from BVD 221."

Slugger whistled. "I knew it."

"Knew he was RAOC?"

"No, I mean I knew he was important—an officer! Bloody hell."

I said, "It's sensitive."

I listened to dead air and wondered what he was thinking. Finally, he said, "I think we've found his jeep."

"Where?"

"A disused mine up near Sengat."

I pictured the area: east of Route One a few miles below the state capital, Ipoh. Outside the main Kinta Valley mining area.

He said, "Dumped with the plates removed and the reg number scraped off."

"I'll let the army know."

"Come on, Ash. Tell me what's going on. You owe me that much."

Slugger never called me Ash. To him, I was Carter or College Cop or Pussy.

"Ash?" he said again, like he knew he was getting to me. "I want to be involved."

"This stays between us, right?"

"Scout's honour."

"The faceless man was Major Chris Broom, and we think he was trading on the black market. You can keep an ear out for—"

"Ear out?" he interrupted me. "I'm blind in one eye, but I'm a big boy. You don't have to pussyfoot around it." He emphasized pussy and I heard a smile in his voice.

"Point taken. Keep an eye out for any army guys in the area who could be connected. Also if you come across the term pipeline."

"Pipeline, like a drainage pipe?"

"The trade is in gold. And there's some kind of pipeline involved. Probably not a physical thing."

"All right. It'd be better if I told the men." He was referring to the rest of his team in the Perak Protection Force.

"No! Strictly confidential."

"And if you hear anything else, you'll let me know?"

I promised I would and then hung up.

I thought nothing more of the conversation because I didn't expect Slugger to discover anything helpful. The next morning, I got up early because I wanted to follow Mr Tharoor on his way to work. My head still hurt so I figured another day of gentle exercise would do me good.

With two hours before sunrise, I watched the baker walk the half-mile to his shop. I saw him unlock and let in two workers, both boys.

I saw the smoke coming out of the chimney and figured the ovens were lit, and within half an hour I smelled the delicious aroma of fresh bread.

I saw two more men arrive. They knocked loudly and were let in. I assumed they were more workers, maybe helping with deliveries, but less than five minutes later they came out and walked smartly away.

Half an hour later a boy came out on a bicycle—one of those with a huge basket on the front. It was laden with what I assumed were loaves. He cycled off, and shortly after, the other boy came out and cycled away in a different direction. The first boy returned and went out again. Then the second returned but didn't reappear.

A long queue formed outside until the doors of the shop opened at seven and I saw people coming out with loaves of bread. Most of the customers were women.

With my stomach rumbling, I joined the queue and purchased a small wholemeal loaf. Tharoor served me and seemed fine except for the pressure of serving the demanding queue. I spotted the boy behind him using a peel, sliding baked loaves out and putting dough into the oven.

I sat outside and ate the warm bread. The second boy returned and the queue rapidly diminished.

At no time did Mr Tharoor come out, and whenever I stretched my legs with a walk past the shop, I saw him either at the counter or behind in the bakery.

After the initial rush, the queue disappeared and only occasional shoppers called in. The boys took deliveries throughout the morning and I guessed they were visiting hotels preparing for lunch.

Nothing much happened in the afternoon, and at five, Tharoor shut up shop. I followed him, but he went straight home.

His wife had told me he never went out again, so I decided surveillance was up for the day and returned to the office because I wanted to be there in case Jenkins called.

TWENTY-TWO

Spotting the SIB investigator was by pure chance. Darkness had fallen hours before but the moonlight cut through the trees. The man was creeping through the jungle and BlackJack saw him just in time as the pale light caught him.

The man was so close. BlackJack could have reached him within five or six paces. But he didn't. Instead, he slid back into the darkness and waited.

He wasn't concerned. In fact, seeing the investigator so close made BlackJack's heart race with anticipation. *Cat and mouse. How exciting!*

The investigator kept on going, moving from tree to tree, hidden from the road. He was careful and slow. He'd have a weapon, a service revolver, but must have had it holstered. BlackJack, on the other hand, took out his favoured paring knife and began to follow.

Each time the investigator took a step, BlackJack matched him, twenty paces back. When the investigator looked around, BlackJack hugged the shadows.

At first, he was heading for the gate at the end of the road but then he veered right and started a gentle climb. Then he switched and turned south.

What was he doing? He must know about the gate because he'd avoided that. Now he was going over the hill. The wrong way really. Nothing of interest out here.

BlackJack knew this region well. He knew the whole layout of what lay to their right. If the investigator had gone the other way at the gate he would have found an easier route and eventually found the track. Maybe he was filling in the blanks.

Had he found the fence? He must have. He was keeping in the trees rather than the open space by the perimeter fencing.

Then it was as though the other man answered BlackJack's question. He came out of the treeline and into the deliberate open space before the fence. A flashlight—thin and directed—came on. The investigator probably had tape over the head, limiting the beam.

BlackJack grinned. The investigator was checking the fence. He was looking for a way into the enclosure, hoping for a damaged section—or maybe he intended to cut the wire.

There was no weakness. BlackJack knew for sure. The investigator was wasting his time.

On they went, around the hill and over the tunnel—although the investigator wouldn't have known about any tunnels.

People became accustomed to the background click of cicadas. But it wasn't a steady sound. It fluctuated like waves fading in and out of resonance. The noise peaked and it could suddenly fall like all the waves were cancelling one another out.

That's what happened now, and there was sudden silence.

The investigator stopped and turned.

BlackJack swayed back, beside a tree. He gripped the knife, felt the hilt warm and keen in his fist.

The jungle sounds immediately returned but neither man moved for a long minute, the investigator looking into the gloom, BlackJack tensed and ready.

And then the SIB man started walking back. He was walking directly towards BlackJack. He got within two arms' reach.

BlackJack could hear the man's breathing, so loud. And maybe his last, the killer thought.

He raised the knife, felt its electricity, its lust for blood, and stepped forwards. The investigator was just there. He was a few feet away. A jump forward, a quick arm around the man's neck and the blade into his throat.

BlackJack felt the gush of warm blood over his stabbing hand. Felt the man's shock and desperation and his final fight for life.

But it was just in his head. BlackJack hadn't moved. He watched and let the man continue. Killing him now was too easy. It would be no fun. Cat and mouse, remember. That's what he wanted. More of a challenge, more excitement.

There were plenty of other men to kill first.

TWENTY-THREE

My one-time girlfriend, Su Ling had told me that Chinatown was called *Bu Ye Tian*—the place of the nightless days. That's because Chinatown never slept. I'd seen it—people working all hours of the day and night. The hustle and bustle and excitement of Singapore's Chinese sector.

The Indian sector wasn't the same and I walked through quiet streets. It was almost four thirty in the morning and I saw a couple of people and four stray dogs before Mr Tharoor came out of his house.

I'd slept well and my headache had gone. I'd also stopped thinking about BlackJack because when I got back last night I'd missed the call from Lieutenant Jenkins.

Madam Chau had been at the office and said Jenkins had called earlier than scheduled. She relayed the message that everything was fine. He was staying in the area following leads, and it wasn't convenient to call later. She had ended the call by making Jenkins promise to call on time tomorrow.

That made me smile. Madam Chau at her best.

Yesterday had been boring, but maybe that's what I needed for a while. Maybe I just needed to follow

Madam Chau's advice and raise a little cash doing these mindless jobs. For a few days at least.

I trailed Tharoor all the way to his bakery. He walked quickly without any unusual behaviour: no furtive glances or detours, just straight to his place of work.
Just before five o'clock, two boys arrived. Tharoor let them in and I soon smelled the bread baking.

It was still dark when the boys reappeared. They both had delivery bikes with bread piled up in the large basket at the front.

One returned and went out again. A queue started forming outside the shop, and when the second boy returned, the shop door was opened. I strolled up and queued and noticed the boy was now at the counter with Tharoor behind, juggling the baking and service.

I bought some fresh bread, returned to my bench and ate it as the sun crested the horizon.

The first boy returned and took out another large delivery. The queue waxed and waned and nothing of interest happened.

Every hour, I took a break, stretched my legs and got a drink of water. Before lunchtime, the frenetic activity of delivering bread began again with the boys haring off on their laden bikes.

After lunch, things began to quieten down. The only customers were occasional and the boys went home.

No one came or went for twenty minutes and then two Chinese men came down the street. I couldn't be sure but they reminded me of the two men I'd seen early the previous day. This time, one had a small blue holdall under his arm. From the way it folded, it clearly had nothing inside.

They went into the shop and came out again a few minutes later. The bag was no longer empty. A loaf perhaps?

124

I didn't think so.

I'd seen this sort of thing a hundred times before. They had confidence verging on arrogance and they didn't look like typical bread customers.

I watched them walk back the way they'd come and scooted after them. Keeping my distance, I saw the Chinese guys make turn after turn, although they never looked back.

Finally, after less than a mile, they went into a building and I noted its address. Then, returning to the shop, I confirmed my suspicion. Tharoor looked like he was wearing a mask, his face frozen with shock or fear.

Both of his hands were on the counter. Fixed like they were glued, his eyes staring blindly.

I said nothing, just stood there waiting.

Gradually his focus returned.

I said, "Those two men?"

He nodded.

"Extortion?"

His eyes said, "Yes."

"How long has it been going on?"

He tore his hand from the counter and showed me four fingers.

"Four weeks?"

Nod.

"It's got to stop," I said.

He nodded again and found his voice. "You can't tell the police."

"Because?"

"Because they will know and I will be punished."

I nodded. He was probably concerned about police involvement. Maybe he was right. I said, "Leave it with me."

"You can't do anything. Only one man…"

He was right. I was just one man. I could stop these two and get this week's money back but then more would come. I could react now but I would probably fail in the long run. I had no idea who was behind this, although I was sure who wasn't behind it.

I walked to the Cathay Building where Andrew Yipp had his office on the twelfth floor. As the head of the biggest gang in Singapore I was sure he'd want to know what was going on.

Yipp had told me that he wasn't into extortion. He was for the people, not about ripping them off. And I believed him.

He wasn't available. Su Ling was his stunning personal assistant, but I didn't get her either. Instead, I got a Chinese kid I'd never met before. He introduced himself as Tan, and I figured him to be no more than eighteen, but he had bright eyes, and as he spoke I guessed he had an equally sharp mind.

Tan explained that he would now be my liaison. Any information I had for Mr Yipp would be passed on through him. And should Mr Yipp have information for me then it would come via the same channel.

I was disappointed but wasn't too surprised. I had history with Yipp, his henchman and his assistant, and it wasn't all good. But I remained useful to them, being a bridge to the ruling class, the British elite. I had contacts and Yipp wanted to be accepted as a philanthropist and leading businessman rather than a potential threat and criminal.

So, I told young Tan about Mr Tharoor and the extortion racket that I'd witnessed.

Tan had his hands together, fingers pressed against his lips as I spoke. I figured he was memorizing my words to replay them to his boss.

When I finished with the address I'd seen the men go into, he nodded and said, "Thank you. Mr Yipp will ensure this criminal activity is stopped."

I returned to my office, satisfied that the problem would be dealt with swiftly, and was surprised to find Madam Chau there.

"You came in over the weekend. I told you to take Monday off," I said.

She shook her head. "There's too much paperwork. And I told Lieutenant Jenkins to call on time today. Someone needs to make sure he does... and answer the telephone for you."

I thought of explaining that I was capable of picking up a telephone, but looking at her scowling face, I decided against it.

"So?" Madam Chau prompted. "Tell me about the Tharoor case."

I gave her a quick summary of events.

When I finished she nodded. "Good. Shall I raise the bill now or wait until Mr Yipp has definitely stopped the extortion?"

"Neither," I said.

She scowled at me. "What are you saying?"

"That we won't be raising a bill. There's no charge to Mr and Mrs Tharoor. They can't afford it."

"And no bill for Mrs Slone?" She sighed and shook her head. "So you are a charity now. We can't live on banana money."

It was the first time I'd heard the expression. "What's banana money?"

"Money issued during the war—by the Japanese. *Banana* because there was a banana tree on the notes. Utterly worthless after the war. But that's not the point, Master Carter. Who is going to pay your bills?"

"We're OK," I said. "Don't worry about it." But she was right. Since I'd stopped being on the Singapore government's payroll, I was rapidly running through my savings. I sat and thought about options. I didn't have many, since the work wasn't banging on my door as I'd hoped. Seeking the work seemed the only reasonable alternative. Tomorrow, my first visit would be to Philip Norris, the new Secretary for Internal Security. We'd previously discussed how we could work together, and now seemed the time to revisit that option.

Madam Chau made me a cup of tea and I re-read the SIB file. The clock ticked round to 6 pm. Jenkins would call soon and distract me from my personal concerns.

Time seemed to elongate as I kept glancing up at the clock. Jenkins would probably leave it to the last minute. Keep me waiting.

The big hand reached the top of the hour. No phone call.

Jenkins didn't call.

In fact, Jenkins never called anyone again.

TWENTY-FOUR

I gave Jenkins another thirty minutes before calling the HQ on Bras Basah Road just in case they'd heard anything.

The SIB lieutenant hadn't called them either.

"You're going up there, aren't you?" Madam Chau said in her critical voice.

I picked up the files and headed for the door. "I am."

She sighed, looked at me sternly and raised a finger. "Then you call me every day. No excuses. You call between six and seven, just like you arranged with Lieutenant Jenkins. Agreed?"

"Agreed," I said.

"And before you disappear, you call the CO at Gillman Barracks so he knows where you're going."

She didn't wait for an answer and was already asking the operator to put her through.

I stood by her desk and she handed me the phone.

"Take Robshaw with you," Colonel Ambrose said after I told him I was heading for Jenkins's last-known location.

"No," I said. "This is an SIB matter."

Ambrose said nothing for a moment, and it surprised me that he didn't argue. He just said, "I'll make sure they're informed."

"Good idea."

"But, Ash, if there's any sign of trouble, I want you to promise me you'll call for help. I'll get the whole bloody army up there if need be."

I knew that was nonsense but said, "Thanks. In the meantime, could you keep the causeway open for me? I'm leaving soon, but just in case…"

"Consider it done. And, Ash… I want you to report in daily. I want to know what's going on."

I explained that I'd call Madam Chau and she'd relay messages. Ambrose pressed me to call the HQ, but I wasn't backing down. The more he got involved, the more likely this became an army issue in general rather than an SIB investigation. And my first loyalty was to my old unit.

After collecting an overnight bag my service revolver and the Beretta I wore in an ankle holster, I drove fast for Woodlands Crossing.

It closed at nine but I was there in plenty of time. Nevertheless, the MPs at the barrier were expecting me and I jumped the queue and was soon on the other side and taking Route Three out of Johor Bahru.

I knew the first section well because it took me past the airfield and then Camp Kota Tinggi. From there it was all new territory for me, although, in the dark, I saw little of the scenery. The traffic reduced dramatically after the army base and I drove fast until hills slowed me down. There was dense jungle and steep cliffs that shone in the moonlight and the road got narrower and bumpier. But I still drove hard. I was going to a place way up on the east coast and it would take all night.

Another hour later, I reached the large town of Mersing. I'd travelled less than a quarter of the distance and I was already tired. Of course, I'd been up since four thirty and was starting to think my mad dash north had been a foolhardy idea.

I stopped by the sea and found a café serving coffee. I got it black and strong and added cold water so I could drink it faster. Then, after a sugary pastry that perked me up, I set off north once more.

The road took me back through heavy jungle before emerging at another town on the coast. This was Endau, where the Allies had suffered significant losses both at sea and in the air as the Japanese invaded. I'm sure there was a big war memorial here, but I had tunnel vision and just kept on driving north.

The next stretch was monotonous, with the sea on my right and black jungle to my left. I had the roof off and the fresh wind from the sea helped me keep focus on the road.

A few lorries came the other way, but apart from those, the roads were quiet, and at times, I felt like I was alone in an alien world.

The moon descended and was gone and my weak headlights did little to illuminate the road ahead.

I was almost halfway when I reached Pekan on the Pahang River, and I could go no further. The strain of trying to keep on the road and tiredness took its toll. After failing to find somewhere to buy coffee, I pulled over and just closed my eyes.

Some time later, a truck rumbled past and woke me with a start. My watch said four in the morning, and I blinked away the sleepiness and began my hard journey north once more.

Most of the road hugged the coastline except for a detour around a hill just south of Kuala Dungun. I thought I was going to have to rest again but then the sky rapidly lightened and the sun came up and life felt good.

131

I had the sea air in my lungs and sunlight sparkling off an azure sea.

A glorious fifty minutes running alongside a golden beach took me to Kuala Terengganu. It came as a shock: a sprawling town after miles and miles of nothing but beaches, palm trees, and the occasional kampong.

The road veered away from the coast between two hills and I could see a wide estuary to my right. I noted an unattractive smell in the air and soon saw warehouses and hundreds of boats on the water. I figured this was a major port, probably *the* major port of the region. Minutes later, a mass of lorries clogged the streets, confirming my theory.

The warehouses included old godowns, but I also saw banks of modern buildings that suggested the town had grown rapidly since the war.

I stopped for breakfast and coffee after leaving the industrial sector behind and crossing the brown sluggish river. From there I could see that there was also a large fishing port, which explained the smell in the air.

My waiter was Malayan and so were the majority of inhabitants I saw, which was surprising since the architecture was distinctly Chinese.

I asked the waiter and he said it was because Terengganu had once been a major port for Chinese immigration. But things had changed and the growth of the town had pulled in more locals. He said that many of the Chinese had moved across country. I knew that Thailand had been known as Siam until the end of the 1930s. What I didn't know was this and the region to the north had been in Thailand during the war. He said that it had also been strongly anti-Chinese. That's why people had left.

Refreshed, I set off once more, only now the road went west, through the jungle and then hills. For ten miles it felt like I could have been almost anywhere in the country. Every mile or so I passed a kampong with peasants scratching a living from beside the road. Dogs ran out, chickens scattered, and children tried to flag me down, selling God only knows what. Trucks rumbled the other way, presumably heading for the port, and I wondered what they were carrying. This wasn't a region famous for logging, rubber or tin, not like Kinta Valley where I'd spent a few months.

Finally, just before 10 am, the jungle cleared and I entered the town of Permaisuri—although I learned that its name was really Bandar Permaisuri, which meant Queen's Town. I was told this when I stopped at a mosque on the outskirts. The elderly man I spoke to also proudly told me that it used to be the capital of the state, although I found that hard to comprehend. Terengganu was significantly larger and better positioned on the coast. However, I accepted his wisdom and asked where I would find the nearest hotel.

"Terengganu," he said.

"Nothing here?"

"No."

"Telephone?" I said. "Where can I find one of those?"

I half expected him to say Terengganu again, but he didn't. He told me there were three shops in the town with public telephones and described where I'd find them. Perhaps he imagined I wanted to ring a hotel. I didn't. I had another priority.

In the first shop, I pulled out a photograph of Lieutenant Jenkins.

"Have you seen this man?"

The shopkeeper shook his head.

In the second premises, the shopkeeper didn't speak English and called for a neighbour to translate. Both men

133

studied the photograph and frowned. They hadn't seen him either.

It was a small town and I was starting to wonder whether Jenkins had been totally honest. The last location he'd told me was here. He had made a phone call and so it was logical for me to assume he'd called from a public phone. If he hadn't, or he hadn't really been in this town, then I'd have no chance of finding him.

When the third shopkeeper shook his head, I thought it was all over.

"There are other telephones," the man told me. "Perhaps…"

"I've tried the other two."

"What about the one in the post office on the other side of town?" he said.

The building wasn't actually a post office, but it handled letters and they had a phone.

"Do you recognize this man?" I asked, handing the photograph to the first person I met.

The man's face screwed up and he stared at me. I got the sense that he understood but was reluctant to respond.

"I'm looking for this man. Please."

The shop worker called a woman and they huddled in deep conversation.

I took a step towards them and they both looked at me, their eyes full of uncertainty.

"What's wrong?" I asked.

The woman said, "We don't see many white people in this town."

I held up the photograph. "What about him?"

The man said, "Last week?" like he was unsure.

"I've spoken to him since then. I think he called me from here."

The man and woman conferred again. Then he said, "Ah, sorry. He was here three days ago. That was the first time. He then came in again more. Sorry, my mistake."

"So the last time you saw him was two days ago?"

"Yes. Sunday."

"About nightfall?"

The woman shook her head. "Earlier and we were closed. He banged on the door and insisted on using the telephone."

Great, that tallied with the call that Madam Chau had taken. Although she'd said everything was fine which didn't sound like a reason for making the call.

"Where did he go afterwards, do you know?"

"No," the woman said, "but he was probably staying at one of the lodgings because he was white and not from around here. The big hotels are too far away."

"Terengganu," I said, relaying the information from the man at the mosque.

"Yes."

Then she gave me directions to five places that offered rooms: two in the town, one north and two east. As I drove away, I couldn't help wondering about their reaction. Why so circumspect?

I found the right place along the river to the east. It was a café with rooms to rent.

"No vacancy," the Chinese landlord said when I appeared at his desk.

I held out the picture. "Has this man stayed here?"

The man's eyes narrowed. "Yes, and he owes me five days' rent."

I knew he was exaggerating, and he then said, "You can see his room if you pay his rent. Five days, yes?" He gave me a price and I dealt out the Malay dollars. Then he took me upstairs.

"When was the last time you saw him?"

"The night before last. He came in and went out again after about an hour. Maybe he met a young lady." The landlord scowled. "But he should still pay his rent, yes?"

He opened the bedroom door and gasped.

The whole room had been turned upside down.

TWENTY-FIVE

"This wasn't—" the landlord started to say as we stared at the mess.

"What?"

"I did not throw everything around like this."

I stepped into the small room and towards an open wardrobe. There was one shirt hanging from a rail. I saw another on the floor. It looked like clothes from the shelves had been swept onto the floor as well.

Behind the far wardrobe door, I found an upside-down rucksack and picked it up.

"Hey! What are you doing?" the guy asked me, pressing close behind.

"Looking."

"You only paid to see the room, not search it. I rented it out to the other man. What if he comes back?"

I turned and looked at him in disbelief. Three nights ago he'd rung me from Jerteh. Then he moved to Permaisuri.

"The man stayed here three nights ago," I said with authority. "He stayed for a night and went missing. Plus last night makes three nights. You just charged me for five. So I figure I have a right to search. Since he's clearly gone and I've paid, I reckon that this is now my room."

He tried to process this argument or maybe consider his own.

"What if he comes back?" he said again.

"Then you shouldn't have shown me into his room. And he's not coming back." I didn't know for sure, but Jenkins was army. No way would he have left the room in this state—and he hadn't reported in last night.

"When I leave in the morning, I'll leave it tidy." I waved my hand towards the door and the landlord backed up. He started to complain, but I added: "I'm sure you don't want to be implicated in his disappearance."

He hesitated, shrugged and nodded, one gesture straight after the other. Then he took another step back onto the landing.

As I shut the door he regained his composure. "If it's not tidy, I'll charge you for another night."

I stepped back to the wardrobe and lifted the bag out. There was nothing in it except for a map. Beside the bag lay a crumpled pile of clothes. I reckoned they'd been in the rucksack and dumped out. The map had been jammed at the bottom, probably stuck and missed by whoever had turned over the room.

The mattress was canted at an angle resting on the metal bed frame. I pulled it back, opened the map and spread it on the mattress.

It was a map of a large chunk of the state. At the bottom was Kuala Terengganu. At the top was Jerteh. There were lines drawn on it. One went along the main road between Permaisuri and Terengganu. At the state capital, it didn't loop around on Route Three like I had on my way up here. Instead, the line went west, past the largest lake in the country and then across the Highlands. I couldn't see where it ended up but knew Ipoh and the Kinta Valley were over in that direction. I figured this was the route Jenkins had taken tracking the killer: over the mountains to Terengganu and then north up Route Three. He'd gone too far and returned to this town.

Centred on Permaisuri was another line, a circle of about five miles radius. I wondered if this meant that Jenkins knew the killer was in the region but didn't know where. This was a search area. I'd have done the same.

Most of the area was jungle. Apart from Route Three there was a road that followed the river, left and right: south-west into the mountains and north-east to the sea. Further up, another road also went right until it joined the coast road that connected with the road that followed the river, forming a rough square.

I checked the clothes in case there was a clue in a pocket, but found nothing. The breast pocket of the hanging shirt was also empty.

I lifted a sheet that was strewn on the floor. There was nothing under it except for a mat. I looked under the mat at bare floorboards. The cracks between the wood revealed nothing. I also found no floorboards loose, so nothing secreted underneath.

Then I turned my attention to the bed. The thin green mattress was probably stuffed with horsehair. I felt around the mattress and found nothing unusual or any seam that had been unpicked.

There was nothing under the bed.

I carried on my search, checking in case the metal frame had a hollow section with something inserted. It didn't. The wardrobe had nothing but dust on top and underneath. It hadn't been moved in a long time.

The only other furniture in the room was a wooden chair and bedside table with a drawer. Neither revealed anything hidden or otherwise.

The last thing to check was the window. Thin curtains hid nothing, and looking out of the window to the ground below showed nothing hanging there or fallen to the ground.

I looked around again. Someone had been in here and turned it over. They expected to find something. Maybe they had. Maybe they hadn't.

In my SIB role, I always kept a notebook. I'm sure Jenkins did too. Either he had it with him—wherever he was—or the searcher had found it.

It would have been useful. The map helped but it wasn't as good as an investigator's notes.

Nothing.

Then the curtain pole caught my eye. There was a finial on each end. The one on the right was at a slight angle. I went over and twisted it and it came away in my hand. The pole was hollow. I poked my finger in and touched something that moved, but I couldn't grasp it.

Dismantling the pole, I raised the other end and shook it. A coin fell out. That's what I first thought, but it wasn't metal. It was a wooden disk like a poker chip. The face had the number one painted on it.

I turned the chip over. Something had been written—or, rather, scratched—on the other side.

One word: BlackJack.

TWENTY-SIX

BlackJack.

Three possibilities sprang to mind: The first was that since I'd mentioned the name, Jenkins had scratched it onto the first thing he could lay his hands on. I thought that was unlikely. Why stick it in the pole? Why hide it? Much better to hide his whole notebook. The second possibility was that he had found it. Again, why put it in the curtain pole?

The most likely explanation was that it had been deliberately left here. Which meant by the killer. BlackJack had been the one who'd turned over the room. And he was playing games. He'd planted the clue so that an investigator would find it.

Had he left it for Jenkins? I thought not. Jenkins hadn't returned. This was a message for me.

BlackJack wanted me to know that he'd been here.

This led to a more disturbing thought: he wanted me to know that he'd dealt with Jenkins.

After staring at it for a second, I stuck the chip in my pocket, collected the map, and went downstairs.

The landlord was in the café and tracked me with his eyes as I walked from the bottom of the stairs.

"What car was he driving?" I asked him.

"A dark green Land Rover. Not new, but not beaten-up like yours." He was right, my jeep was pretty dented. There were also bullet holes in the back courtesy of a Chinese terrorist a few months back. I'd left it like that. Apart from avoiding the outlay, I felt the holes added a touch of credibility to my job. Although I briefly wondered whether this attracted the desperate housewives like Mrs Slone.

I said, "And you've not seen it since he went out yesterday?"

"No."

"What time did you last see him?"

"About four in the afternoon. I don't know for certain. I wasn't checking on him."

I nodded. "Did you see anyone else go up there?" This guy ran a café. He would be distracted for the evening and I was sure anyone could slip up there without him noticing.

"No," he said again.

"Does the name BlackJack mean anything to you?"

He looked at me like I was being funny. "The card game?"

"A name. Like the card game."

"No. Do you gamble?"

"I found the name in the room."

"Did your friend gamble?"

I shook my head, ordered lunch from him and sat outside in the shade with the map open.

"What's out there?" I asked when he returned with a bowl of noodles for me. I ran my finger around the circle on the map.

If I'd hoped that buying lunch from him would make him less laconic, I would be disappointed. He replied, "Not much."

"Anything you can tell me about this area?"

142

"Permaisuri? It was once booming. There was a gold rush in these parts but it turned out the gold is way off to the west. Mostly fishing and farming now. And of course, the capital moved to Kuala Terengganu. People just pass through here now."

"And disappear."

"Maybe he's coming back."

I shook my head and focused on lunch. Jenkins wasn't coming back.

I drove north-east out of the town, following the river as it twisted and finally settled on an easterly course. I passed small kampongs and subsistence farmers and kept going towards the sea. There I expected beaches and palm trees like I'd seen further south that morning, but instead I met with wetlands.

I'd driven beyond Jenkins's search perimeter and turned around. Trekking back to the road I'd seen on the map, I turned right and went roughly parallel with the coast. There were more arable farms here, and all struggling to survive in pretty harsh terrain. Over on the west coast, the land was flat and fertile and ideal for rice and tapioca. The rubber plantations and the wealth were on the western side too.

The British hadn't bothered with these parts of Malaya.

I came to a junction and recognized the left turn. This was the second road leading back to Route Three. I took it, and a mile later I crossed a river and came upon a large village. Even here, the people appeared to be scratching an existence from the land. They came out, excited to see someone driving on their road. However, if they wanted to sell me anything, they were too late by the time they got their acts together.

I kept going west and was back in the jungle, which went all the way to the main road.

North would take me to Jerteh. Kelantan was the next large town, maybe forty miles away. I didn't know it, apart from being on the border with Thailand.

That was to my right. Ahead, I could see a track disappearing into the trees. It wasn't on the map and it was overgrown. Oxen and carts left deep ruts in most of the tracks, many of which I figured had never seen a motor vehicle. This one hadn't seen a car or oxen for years, I thought. No point in going that way.

Left was Permaisuri, the centre of the search area. Not right to Kelantan. Jenkins had ended it about here. He must have known that the killer was somewhere close. But where?

I turned left and drove back to the town with trees either side and hills on my right.

At Permaisuri I drove straight through and explored the road to the south. However, the next town was much more than five miles and I saw nothing significant.

Back at the town, I followed the road that went southwest, although it quickly petered out into a rough track. Progress became slow and I eventually stopped at the top of a rise. There was another kampong up here and I recognized vast swathes of pepper trees with their bright green leaves and masses of red berries.

The whole time I was out, I didn't see another white person, nor did I spot a green Land Rover.

Disappointed, I returned to the town and did a circuit, checking for any partially hidden vehicle. Jenkins's jeep must be somewhere, but I didn't find it.

Just before six I parked outside the little post office and went in to use the phone.

When the operator connected me to my office I told Madam Chau that I was checking in. I was touched that

I could hear the relief in her voice but disappointed that she had no news for me about Lieutenant Jenkins.

I'd held out a vain hope that I'd been wrong about the SIB man, that he'd moved on and would check in from another town.

He hadn't.

I'd also hoped Styles at BVD 221 might have come up with something, or maybe Captain Robshaw. But the information she had for me wasn't about the case.

She said, "Inspector Singh called. It's about the fire."

"He questioned Mr Wu?"

"You were right. He confessed to setting fire to the door. He did wear his old shop overalls."

"Did he say why?"

"He wants his shop back. He confessed that he wanted you to get the new manager arrested. After what you did for the man. It's disgusting! I actually felt sorry for him."

"He lost his son and his business," I said, trying to understand.

"Well, he hurt the only person who helped." She carried on grumbling and it made me smile. She really cared.

When I put the phone down, the post office lady was looking at me.

"I'm sorry," she said.

"Why?"

"I could have told you something yesterday, but I didn't know you."

"What changed your mind?"

"You asked the operator for the same address as that other man."

"It's my office," I said. "I'm worried about him."

"Yes, I can see that now."

"You said you could have told me something."

145

"I saw where he ate. I know who he spoke to. Maybe it will help. Maybe he went there after he called you."

I could see something else in her eyes, like she was holding back.

"What is it?" I asked.

I saw her teeth clench before she finally let the words out. "It was me who sent him there."

TWENTY-SEVEN

The eating place was on the west of town where the river went in a complete circle. I figured it would become an oxbow lake at some point, but not yet, not for a long time.

The sun was low and reflecting off the water. It was a pleasant spot, the town rising behind and a marshy island nearby with burgeoning plant and birdlife. I'm no expert on birds but I recognized grebes because of their bright orange eyes. They were in the water and all over the island's riverbank.

Directly opposite me was a row of small boats, and I judged the men in the café to be fishermen. They had hard faces and suspicious eyes.

"They're wary of you," the waitress said.

"Why?"

"Because you are white."

"You don't get many white people here," I said, as a statement rather than a question. I'd still seen none during the whole day. Even driving around. Not one white person.

"Do you want to eat?"

When I nodded she told me what was on offer. No choice, just one thing on the menu, so I ordered it. She left me and I resumed my observation of the fishermen.

The lady in the post office hadn't told me anything, but I suspected one or all of these men knew something.

I took out the photograph of Lieutenant Jenkins and held it up. Every single one of the fishermen turned their heads. It wasn't an awkward glance and look away. Not like being caught out staring at someone. These guys saw the photograph and deliberately showed me they weren't interested.

I started to get up.

"Sit down," a young woman said. She wasn't the waitress who had taken my order, but this one placed my bowl of noodles on the table. "No one will talk to you."

"Why not?"

"Because you are white."

I shook my head, not comprehending.

"We don't trust white people."

I held up the photograph of Jenkins. "He came here, didn't he?"

"Yes."

"Did one of these men cause trouble?" I nodded towards the locals watching me intently.

She snorted at my foolishness then sat down at my table.

A man immediately came out of the kitchen and I guessed he owned the place when he barked at her in Malay. She waved him away, looked at me earnestly and with her hands clenched together. Then she unclenched them and bit her thumbnail, maybe making a decision.

"Are you his friend?"

"Yes, I'm looking for him."

"I think he's in danger," she said.

"When did he speak to you?"

"Saturday and Sunday. The first time I wasn't sure I could trust him." She glanced at the fishermen. "We can't trust white people."

"But you changed your mind?"

"Yes. He was different and I am desperate."

I studied her for the first time. She was of Indian descent and her light golden skin suggested the north of the country. Her long sleek hair was the colour of a raven's wing. Large, deep brown eyes either side of a straight-edged nose added up to a very attractive young girl. I figured she was only sixteen or seventeen.

"How was my friend different?" I asked.

"He listened. He wanted to help."

"Tell me why you're desperate."

"They have my sister."

"Who has your sister?"

"The white men. I told your friend and he said he would get her out."

My head was spinning with the fragmented information this girl was giving me. "Start at the beginning," I said. "Tell me about the white men."

She took a breath and tried to stop the nervousness I could hear in her voice. "There is a town. People call it Bandar Putih."

"White town," I said.

"Right. We call it that because it is run by white men. One in particular. He's called Jeremiah. But they are all bad."

If this girl hadn't been so earnest I would have suspected she was simple. However, I think it was partly the language and partly fear that made her speech so staccato. I waited for her to say more.

"They take people and don't let them leave their town."

"Like your sister?" I asked.

"Yes. It is hard living here, and my sister said she was going to Terengganu to find work. That was five years ago. I was too young then. Now I've been looking for

149

her. She's there, but the white men have fences and guns."

Now I was interested.

The man who I'd guessed was the owner bustled over and spoke sharply to the girl.

"It's all right," I said, not understanding his words. "It's all right."

"I don't want her bothering you," he said. "She's a bit crazy."

"Please, just two more minutes."

He bowed, uncertain, and then backed away.

To the girl, I said, "You were saying that my friend wanted to help?"

"Yes."

"Did he say why he was in this town?"

"He'd followed two men."

I nodded encouragement.

She continued: "He told me they had disappeared off the main road. I know where. It's the same place. It's Bandar Putih. It's where my sister is being held."

I saw the owner watching from inside the kitchen. His body language said that the two minutes were up but he didn't come back out.

I pulled out the map I'd found in Jenkins's room. "Show me where it is."

"It's not a town on any map—it's not marked," she said, but she looked closely as I opened it up.

"Here," she said, and touched the paper. Her finger was beyond Jenkins's circle but only just. It was west of the disused track I'd seen at the crossroads where I'd turned left back to Permaisuri. But she wasn't pointing to a road, she was touching a spot in the jungle between the hills.

"Out there?" I said.

"It's at the end of a road that's not on this map. Just past the crossroads." She pointed to the junction where I'd seen the track disappear into the jungle.

"And they've built a town there?"

"Yes. With a big fence around it. They won't let the women leave."

I wondered how she'd take my next question and watched for a reaction. "How do you know? How do you know they can't leave? How do you know your sister wants to leave?"

"I've been here for almost a year. I can't get too close because they'll catch me and I won't be able to get my sister out if I'm in there as well."

I nodded.

She said, "A long time ago, they used to let women come into town to buy provisions. I found some people who told me a little. They remembered seeing my sister because we look alike. I think someone escaped a few years ago and now they don't let the women out. And there's something worse."

She took a breath. "The woman said they kill the babies." She broke down then and couldn't speak.

I waited. The sun touched the distant tree-covered mountains and the clouds became orange and purple streaks.

"What do you mean *they kill the babies*?"

"When the babies are born, if they aren't white, then the men kill them. That's what I was told."

"What about the police?" I said. "Tell them."

She pulled herself together and shook her head. "They're in the pockets of Jeremiah. If I say something they are as likely to take me to the town and leave me there. I've heard of it happening. Everyone is afraid. No one dare say anything."

"Except for you."

"Will you help me? Will you help my sister?"

"What's your name?"

"Shalaa."

"And your sister?"

"Safiya."

"I'll do my best." I tapped the picture of Jenkins. "You said the same to my friend yesterday?"

"No, it was the day before. I told him about Bandar Putih and he went to have a look."

"And yesterday?"

"He came here and said he was going in. I told him what to say."

"What was that?"

"The white men were all soldiers, so say that you are ex-army. That you are looking for a new home—looking for paradise. That's what they call it." She shook her head. "How can it be paradise if you're a slave?"

"He drove there?"

She nodded. Of course.

"A Land Rover, like mine but dark green?"

"Yes."

I stood and thanked her, realized I hadn't touched the food but handed her a pile of notes.

As I left, she said, "Please bring back my sister. And beware of Jeremiah. You'll know him by his looks. He's an albino."

TWENTY-EIGHT

The light was fading fast when I found the track two hundred yards after the crossroads. It cut through dark forest, twisting around the hills one way and then the other. My jeep bounced and jolted and I figured this wasn't designed for cars.

The girl at the café had pointed to a spot a little over a mile from the road, but that was as the crow flies. I was no crow and judged the twisting would double the distance.

When I came to a bridge, I backed up and parked. Ideally, I'd have pulled off the track, but there was nowhere to go so I just left it there, blocking the way.

With my Beretta in one hand and a torch in the other, I continued on foot.

The bridge could have been fifty years old, maybe a hundred. It was wooden and creaky, wide enough for my jeep and would take the weight but only just. This bridge had been built for much lighter traffic, people, bicycles, maybe animals.

On the far side, the track went right and I came to a big metal gate with wire mesh, similar to the one at the BVD place. The only difference was that this had barbed wire looped along the top. That wasn't a hundred years old. I doubted it was even ten. In the moonlight, it looked fairly new.

Fencing of similar design ran left and right, disappearing into the dark jungle.

I could see a wooden guard hut designed for one man, although I saw no sign of anyone patrolling, or doing anything for that matter. I wondered if there were guard dogs but heard no sounds above the ambient jungle hum.

A heavy chain looped through two gaps in the mesh bound together by a hand-sized padlock. The gate and fence were eight feet high. In addition to the barbed wire, the uprights were each finished with a nasty-looking spike.

What is this, I asked myself, a military installation?

I might have believed it was something left over from the war but I touched the padlock and felt no rust. Recently used, I guessed from the spring's give.

Beyond the gate, the track continued and curved right, but I couldn't see much. I decided to follow the track from my side of the fence and went right. There was no path, but I found it easier despite an incline and must have walked two hundred yards. The fence kept on going and I had two thoughts: one, the area could be huge; and two, this fence could keep unwanted visitors out. It could also keep people inside.

They take people and don't let them leave.

Was Jenkins also in there now? Was he trapped too?

I waited and listened to the night insects, bird calls and occasional monkey chatter. And then I heard a bell ring. It was like the sort of bell that churches use to call people to prayer, but shorter. Five rings and a diminishing echo.

I kept climbing for about another hundred yards before the fence began to drop down the other side of the hill.

Using a reasonable climbing tree, I got above the top of the fence. Now I could see buildings on the far side. They were scattered around, dark blocky shapes in the pale moonlight, too far away to see any detail. My sense was of a Malay village.

Beyond them there seemed to be a wide, flat expanse with more substantial buildings in the distance. Thinking of the bell I'd heard, I figured one was a church.

Despite having a reasonable view of the place, I still saw no one. If it hadn't been for the bell, I might have considered this a ghost town.

There were no lights and no sound of people.

Where was everyone?

Clouds had been moving in from the east. Suddenly the moon was consumed by them and I could no longer see the buildings.

But the darkness also brought a moment of stillness, and I thought I heard something. A single human voice. A preacher perhaps? Or maybe that was my imagination based on the church bell. But before I could discern any words, it was lost in the background jungle noise.

I waited another few minutes and was about to climb down when I saw a pinprick of light.

Another ten minutes later, I saw shapes as people moved around the village. The murmur of voices carried on the air and then was gone.

I expected fires or lights as the people returned to their huts, but it got quieter and quieter. No lights appeared, and after another ten minutes, I realized they never would. That was it.

My watch said quarter to ten, and the town had seemingly shut down for the night.

I went back down the hill to the gate and followed the fence to the left. The stream was on my left and fireflies flickered through the night air. If it hadn't been for the circumstances I'd have appreciated the beauty of the scene.

When the moon came out, I could make good progress, but it also meant I was exposed. However, I saw no one and nothing on the far side of the fence for about half a mile. I almost stopped when I got to the first of two ditches but was glad I continued. Soon after, I came to the series of buildings I'd glimpsed before. Their squat shapes seemed out of place with the village, and behind them was the bigger building.

Although I now crept along, careful in case anyone should be in or around the buildings, I still saw no one.

The fence continued, looping right and then left towards distant hills. After the buildings, all I could see were trees inside.

I'd seen enough. The fence continued but I doubted there would be anything of interest, and I could be out here all night. I figured I'd covered a mile and learned little. My legs were scratched from the undergrowth, I'd been bitten by a thousand insects, and I was dead tired.

Time to go back to Jenkins's room.

* * *

Over two hundred hard-driving miles west, Slugger Stevenson was in the Batu Gajah police station. The police chief wiped his sweaty brow and stretched his neck.

"You said the jeep was army property. They claimed the faceless man's body but the jeep's still here."

Slugger nodded like he knew. The PPF had a good relationship with the police but the chief could be tricky.

He knew or had something, Slugger was certain of it. That's why he was looking uncomfortable.

Slugger said, "There's a secret investigation. I can't tell you about it."

The chief's eyes narrowed. He was interested.

"I'm involved," Slugger said. "I'm helping the Special Investigation Branch."

The chief nodded.

"Anything you've got you should let me have. You've found something, right?"

With palpable relief, the chief dropped a hand into a desk drawer and pulled out a thin black notebook.

"We found this in the jeep. Jammed under the driver's seat. It got a bit wet in the hole, but... well, you can see it's intact."

Slugger held out his hand and took the book. It was still damp but not too wet that the pages wouldn't separate.

"Good job," he said.

"You'll sign for it?"

"Of course."

Twenty minutes, later, Slugger was at home looking at the pages when Cindy came in from a late shift helping at the medical clinic.

She kissed him. "What've you got there?"

"Just a book."

Cindy shook her head. "I know you, Scott Stevenson..."

"It was in the army jeep they found in the disused mine."

"This is about Ash, isn't it?" She didn't hold a high opinion of his friend ever since he'd left the town six months ago. He'd been dating Doctor Heidi Allan—Cindy's boss—and she'd said she was happy for him to

157

go. But she wasn't. Not really. And Cindy couldn't forgive Carter for abandoning her.

"Not really," Stevenson said, but he knew his tone was anything but convincing.

"Whatever you've got there, hand it over to him. It's Ash's problem not yours." She sat on his lap and kissed him.

He set the book down. The writing looked like it was in code or some strange shorthand. It didn't make any sense to him.

"You're right," he said. "I'll give him a call tomorrow and hand it over."

TWENTY-NINE

In the morning, I went down for breakfast.

"What's your name?" I said to the landlord of the lodging house as he served me.

"Tuah," he said after looking me up and down. I was wearing the same clothes as last night and looked grubby. Probably worse. I'd brought clean clothes but they weren't suitable for what I had planned.

"Can you drive, Tuah?" I asked.

"Of course!"

"How would you like to double your money?"

"You've decided to stay longer?"

"Not really."

"I'd like you to drop me about five miles away and then look after my Land Rover."

He studied me, processing the strange request.

"For up to five days but maybe only one."

"And you'll pay the same price, whether it's one or five days?"

"I will."

"Three times the money."

I shook my head. "Looking after a jeep isn't the same as renting a room."

"Pay in advance?"

"You'll have the jeep as collateral."

He shrugged, like it was a hard decision, then reached out and I shook his hand.

"When do you want to go?" he asked.

I took the rucksack with some of Jenkins's clothes in and asked Tuah to drive me to the post office. I let him drive and realized I should have given him a test before agreeing the deal. Each time he changed gear he fought with the gearstick and created a sickening grinding of metal on metal.

I demonstrated the double-declutch technique and left him practising while I entered the post office.

Inside, the husband eyed me suspiciously.

"I just want to use the phone," I said, and he nodded, relieved. After picking up the receiver I spoke to the operator and asked for my office.

"Why are you calling me at this time?" Madam Chau asked. "Is everything all right?"

"It's fine, I just want to warn you that I won't call tonight. I might not call for a couple of nights. Just wanted to let you know, so you aren't worried."

"Of course I'll be worried. How will I know you're all right?"

"I'll be fine," I said. "Give me three days. If you don't hear from me by 7 pm on Friday, call Colonel Ambrose." I then described the location of the place the girl called Bandar Putih, before saying, "And if that happens, tell him to send in the whole bloody army like he promised."

Ten minutes later we passed the crossroads and I told him to stop at the track, with jungle all around and the mysterious town to the left. Tuah pulled over and I jumped out.

"You should have told me," he said, looking uncomfortable as I stood by the road.

"Why?"

"I might not have agreed."

"You didn't ask," I said.

"And I keep the Land Rover if you don't return in three days."

"Already agreed."

"Just checking, because you won't be coming back."

I laughed but realized it sounded faked and patted the holstered service revolver. He just shrugged, jolted the jeep into first, U-turned and drove back towards town.

I slung the rucksack over my shoulder and started the trek into the jungle.

When I got to the bridge, I saw that it was in even worse condition than I'd thought last night. I doubted it would have taken the weight of the jeep after all. Good job I'd stopped where I had.

Back at the lodgings, I'd stuffed my Beretta inside Jenkins's bag. On the far side of the bridge, I spotted a good hiding place under a tree root. Now I took out my gun and holster, wrapped them in one of Jenkins's shirts and hid it. Then I kept on going and walked right up to the gates.

The guard hut was still empty, but this time I noticed a bell to the side of the gate.

I pulled on its cord and then again, as I wondered whether anyone would hear the ringing. However, only a few minutes later a white man appeared, walking towards me up the track on the far side.

As he got closer I saw that he had a rifle over his shoulder. A decent-looking weapon. He wore a wide brimmed hat. That, in combination with his clothing, made me think of a cowboy.

He stopped smartly by the gates and held the gun at port arms. His grey-bearded face showed caution although his eyes looked pinched together, so I wasn't sure if it was his normal expression.

"I can't believe it," I said. "I'm finally here."

"Who are you?" He looked me up and down and had mistrust in his voice.

"A nobody, looking for somewhere to hang my hat," I said.

"Ex-army?"

"Sergeant," I said, and I gave him the name of a unit I'd worked with in the Middle East.

A flicker of a smile appeared before a frown fixed on his face. "Not heard of them in Malaya."

"No, sir," I said. "Palestine."

I could see him thinking, but he still didn't move to open the gate.

I said, "I've travelled a long way. I heard you'd created some kind of white paradise out here."

"We have. It's called Shangri-La."

"I'm hoping you'll let me join you."

"That'll be up to Jeremiah," he said, and finally he reached forward and opened the gate.

He pulled the gate inwards and I stepped over the threshold. As I did so, his gun swung up.

"Stop," he commanded when I was two paces away. "Arms out. Legs astride."

I complied and he immediately stepped forward and took my service revolver. He threw the rifle back over his shoulder and proceeded to pat me down. Then he checked the contents of my rucksack.

"Sorry for this but we have rules. No guns."

Despite the obvious contradiction since he had a weapon, I said, "Not a problem." In fact, I'd expected as

162

much. Having a gun made sense for my assumed role. Giving it up was a rite of passage.

"Right," he said. "Let's go and see what the boss has to say."

THIRTY

The cowboy said nothing else for a few paces.

"My name's Ash," I said, having decided my real name would be fine. No one would know me out here.

"Uh huh," he grunted.

"You called this Shangri-La."

"Yeah."

"Shangri-La was in the Himalayas."

"Uh huh."

Not much of a conversationalist then. I tried another approach. "What's your name, soldier?"

"Solomon. Solomon now, although I used to be called something else. You'll give up your old name too if you're allowed to stay."

I wondered if that meant this guy had chosen the name Solomon or if it had been chosen for him. Was his real name so bad?

The guy looked about fifty, I guessed. I couldn't place his accent, but he spoke slowly, and my first impression was that he wasn't very bright.

We had been walking towards the huts I'd spotted last night from my elevated position. They were attap huts, like I'd seen in a thousand traditional Malay villages. The hills dropped down behind them and rose again. I wondered where the perimeter of this little commune was.

We took a left fork and were now heading west, in the direction of the mountains. Initially green, they turned first grey and then blue in the far distance.

There were trees on my right and I caught a glimpse of the fence. So the perimeter probably looped around behind the Malay village rather than went on through the valley.

On my left were agricultural fields: a vast block, maybe more than three acres, or the same number of football pitches.

I saw people toiling there and then more around another building. This one had an attap roof but with a brick chimney at one end. There was also a wide undercover area with benches.

"Cookhouse," Solomon said.

Shortly after this, I had the big building on my left. It was twice the height of others and had a giant roof. In front was a broad area of baked earth around a water pump.

"I'm parched. Is it OK to drink?" I asked, steering towards the pump.

"Course!"

I grabbed hold of the handle and pumped water into my cupped hand then drank. It tasted clean and fresh and had spring water coolness.

I took my time studying the main building. Last night, because of the bell, I'd assumed it was a church. It had light grey shiplapped panels and no windows. The doors reinforced the impression of a church entrance, although I could see no evidence of a bell.

"What religion?" I asked, nodding towards the unattractive building.

"What?"

"The church…"

"Town hall," the guy said. "Come on. This way."

We didn't approach the town hall but kept right and passed a long chicken coop with maybe twenty birds inside. I could see the other buildings behind the big one and it confirmed what I thought last night. These were more modern blocks and reminded me of the prefabricated units used for army barracks and airfields.

I asked what they all were but Solomon picked up his pace and said nothing.

The path cut through the trees and the big building must have been more than two hundred yards behind before we came to another building: a long log cabin on stilts. Wooden steps led up to a door.

We climbed the steps and Solomon knocked. I waited patiently, like I had a thousand times outside a superior's office waiting for him to grant me an audience.

I saw movement through the windows before the door opened. I'd wondered whether it would be the albino guy, but it wasn't. The man staring at me had dark hair turning grey. He had a hard to read expression on his face, which sat on wide shoulders with no neck. He was about my height but seemed smaller because his body was about three feet across: boxy and heavy and a little intimidating.

"Who's this?"

Solomon handed him my service revolver, but before he could speak I responded.

"My name's Ash Carter. And I'd like to join you."

"Take him back to the gate, Solly."

"I'd heard you'd created a paradise here for men just like me," I said, and then I used the same phrase I'd used before. "I've travelled a long way."

The door closed on us.

166

"What now?" I looked at Solomon, but he had a thousand-yard stare and didn't respond.

I heard laughter and then the door opened.

"Do you vouch for him, Solomon?" the boxy man said.

The man beside me took a breath. "I suppose so."

"Fine. Take him to hut one and get him settled in."

"Hut one?"

"That's what I said."

The door closed again.

Solomon took a couple of paces down the steps before speaking again. "We give up our past lives when we join Shangri-La," he said. "You'll give up your old name too."

"You said that earlier. What will I be called?"

"Jeremiah will pick one for you."

"Was that Jeremiah?"

"No, that was Michael."

"Ah," I said. "So will I get a name from the Bible?"

He shook his head like I didn't get it. I suspected he was the one who didn't get it. Maybe he'd never read the Good Book.

I said, "Solomon was the wise king from the Bible."

He laughed uncertainly and I wondered whether the name had been a joke because it meant the opposite.

We started walking back towards the main building but then veered right, through trees, and came to three small huts. They looked like garden sheds. Maybe they had been garden sheds once upon a time.

"Hut one," he said approaching the first.

He opened the door and went inside, through tassels that would keep out flies. I saw a bed and hooks for clothes. I noticed that the uprights and wood in the eaves were bound by coiled rope, presumably to preserve it.

"Luxury," I said, dropping Jenkins's rucksack onto the bed.

"Uh huh."

"Why the laughter?"

"We don't normally use the huts for…"

"What?"

"It'll just be for starters. Once the others are happy with you, you'll move into the bunkhouse. You'll be one of us."

"The bunkhouse? Where's that?"

He raised his chin in the direction of the long building where I'd seen the other man. "Up in the woods."

"And how many of you are in this bunkhouse?"

"There are six of us…" he said, but his voice trailed off like he'd regretted telling me. Or for another reason. I decided not to continue with that line of questioning for now. I wanted to know about Jenkins but changed the conversation.

"You were telling me about religion," I prompted.

"Was I? Well, we don't follow one religion. All faiths are welcome here. Jeremiah's main rule is that everyone respects everyone else."

"It's a good rule," I said and sat on the bed. The mattress had no give in it. "Looks like this is where I hang my hat then."

"It's just the start," Solomon said. "You work hard, you fit in and you'll move up."

"What's Jeremiah like?"

The question seemed to throw him, like he'd never considered it before. "Er… he founded the place and sets the rules."

"Right."

Solomon went back outside and I followed him. "Come on, I'll show you around."

I'd hoped we'd go in the direction of the bunkhouse but we didn't. Solomon went east, back towards the big building.

"What do you mean, *move up*?"

"It's a small community," he said. "Do the right things and get rewarded. It's how all society works, isn't it? That's what Jeremiah says. Only here, we're more obvious about it. Have to be. It's much more straightforward here than out in the crazy world."

I nodded. "You said you'd vouch for me. What does that mean exactly?"

"I'm responsible for you," he said. "By that, I mean, if you do something wrong, then I'm equally responsible."

"What if I don't fit in?"

He stopped and looked at me hard.

"It's a fair question," I said, shrugging. "What if this isn't what I expected?"

"You can leave at any time." He shook his head but then smiled. "However, you won't want to."

"Oh, why's that?"

"Because it really is a paradise."

"Then why such a high fence?" I asked.

"Safety," he said. "When Jeremiah first established Shangri-La, he saw a tiger. That's why the houses are on stilts too."

"In case a tiger jumps the fence?" I said incredulously.

"No, I mean because of wild animals."

"What about the barbed wire?"

"Monkeys," he said. "They were the biggest problem, so the wire is a recent thing. But some still get over, and of course, the stilts don't stop them. Never have any food in your room and they won't be any trouble."

We walked around the first prefabricated building to the beaten earth beside the town hall.

"Can we go inside?" I said, nodding at the main building.

"Not until later."

"Why?"

He looked at me like it was a stupid question. "Because the doors don't open until later. That's when Jeremiah will talk to everyone."

He wouldn't explain further so I settled down to be shown around the grounds.

When we came out he nodded north. "For now, everything north and west of here, except for your hut, is out of bounds."

"But the first place you took me—where I saw Michael—that's just up there. So the bunkhouse is that way too. What else?"

"Don't cause me trouble," he said, with concern all over his face. "Remember, I vouched for you. It'll be worth it."

He nodded like he was convincing me and then started walking south, going along a curving line of buildings. He called the first one "the workshop". Then there was a storage room, a washhouse followed by a shower block and finally latrines. Behind them, through a thin line of trees, I could see the sweep of the river on the far side of the fence.

Solomon circled behind the town hall and I caught the smell of food coming from the cookhouse ahead.

I'd seen lots of people working although none was white, and as far as I could tell, they were all women. Some were pregnant but I saw no children.

They kill the babies. That's what Shalaa, the girl from the café, had said.

"You've already seen the cookhouse and dining area," Solomon said.

"How many people are here?" I asked, looking at the long table and benches.

"Between fifty and sixty," he said. "I forget the exact number."

"And how many men?"

Now Solomon smiled for only the second time.

"What?" I asked.

"There are plenty of girls to go round," he said. "If that's what you're worried about. It's one of the founding principles along with no practised religion. You can have as many women as you want here. The only restriction is that you can't take another man's woman unless he agrees."

"So how many men are there?"

"Eight plus you."

OK, that meant two others didn't share the bunkhouse. I wanted to ask where they lived, but more desperately, I wanted to ask about recent recruits. Had Jenkins joined a couple of days ago? Was he here? But instead, I said, "Ah, now I understand the attraction."

"And you'll want for nothing—providing you don't have material wants that is. Jeremiah says that materiality is a corr..."—he struggled—"...a corruption of the soul."

"I've not seen any children," I said, trying to sound casual. "I've seen pregnant women, so I'd expect some children too."

"Course there are children."

"Where?" Again I tried to sound curious rather than challenging.

"Oh, I didn't think you'd be interested. I suppose I can show you the nursery."

171

We went up past the chickens again and kept going. The office was in the trees to the left, when we came to another building, and he appeared solemn as he pulled back the door. But then he chuckled. Inside was a room with a few toddlers. Two Chinese women were trying to corral them. In other rooms, I could see cots and crawling babies.

"Are you all right?" Solomon was looking at me with concern.

He must have noticed my relief. I'd believed the girl in the café. I thought they killed the babies because they weren't white. Looking at these children, I saw mixed races and no pure white faces.

"I'm fine," I said. "Looks like a nice set-up you have here."

We went back outside.

"Oh, I forgot," he said. "We should get you some clothes. Back to the workshop."

This was the first prefabricated building, and when we entered I saw women making pottery and weaving palm leaves.

"They make everything," Solomon said proudly. "Furniture, rugs, even the ropes. And in this"—we walked into a small separate room—"they make all the clothes."

Michael had also looked a little cowboy-like. Everyone else I'd seen wore the same olive-green colour.

"You'll wear the same clothes as everyone else for now. It's so that no one is superior to anyone else," he said. "It's another of Jeremiah's rules. Pick some that fit you."

Equality was clearly nonsense, since he and Michael weren't wearing green. I nodded, but I wasn't thinking about the clothes.

There were two young ladies in the sewing room and I was staring at one.

She looked back at me with soft brown eyes and an eager smile.

I'd just found Safiya.

THIRTY-ONE

I knew it was Shalaa's sister because they had the same features, like twins, although I figured this girl was a couple of years older. And unlike Shalaa, this girl had severely cropped hair.

"As a new recruit you'll start in the fields," Solomon told me. I had changed into a khaki shirt and trousers. Although unstylish and loose, they fit just fine. We were in the beaten earth area that Solomon called the town square.

"What if I don't want to?"

He looked at me like I had two heads. "Everyone does the job they're told to." He started walking but stopped, confused because I hadn't taken another step.

"What's your job?"

He patted the rifle on his shoulder. "Patrol and supervision," he said. "Today anyway."

"And are you good at it?"

"Doesn't matter if I am good at it—"

"But it should," I said, interrupting. "Let's say you're a carpenter by trade."

He looked at me in a way I couldn't fathom—narrowed eyes and creased forehead. Then he relaxed, shook his head like he was dispelling bad thoughts, and said, "We have a carpenter."

"OK, a plumber or mechanic or a doctor or whatever. Let's say you have a skill. You'd be wasted doing patrol duty, just like I'd be wasted in the fields. And you said that I should work hard so I could *move up*. I can work hard at what I'm good at."

He was intrigued now. "So what are *you* good at?"

Investigating crimes, I thought, but said, "Not much that's useful if you discount boxing. However, I can sew." I shrugged as though embarrassed. "I know, it's not what you'd expect, but I noticed how much work the young ladies have in the sewing room and I can help."

His face contorted with thought.

"You said you were supervising today. A good supervisor deploys his staff where they're needed. And I noticed the girls in the sewing room looked under pressure. Make an executive decision."

"We do go through a lot of clothes," he said with a sigh, accepting my argument. "I suppose that would be all right."

"A wise decision."

He walked me back to the craft building and introduced me to the second lady rather than Safiya. She sat me at a table with a pile of pre-cut material and a needle and thread.

Solomon wished me a good day and said he'd see me at the town meeting.

The room's windows were high up and the air didn't circulate well, but the two young ladies didn't seem bothered. I wasn't next to Safiya and tried to catch her eye, but once I was settled in, both the women had their heads down.

After about thirty minutes of very poor sewing, I asked for a water break. A ladle and bucket of water were by a wall and this gave me a chance to pass the girl.

I whispered her name and she turned around and stared at me, her eyes full of questions.

After having a ladle of water, I hovered by the girl and loudly said, "Could you help me?"

Safiya looked at the one in charge and received a nod in return. Back at my table, I showed her where I was joining two pieces of material to make trousers. I'd misread her expression when I first set eyes upon her. What I thought had been an eager smile turned out to be a fairly fixed expression. Her warm eyes were more unfocused than I'd appreciated.

"Like this," she said, demonstrating.

"Your sister sent me," I whispered. "Can we talk?"

"At the lunch break." There was no intrigue or excitement, just acceptance that we could talk.

She left me to my incompetent stitching and I lasted until a bell sounded and we went outside. People came out of other buildings and I followed them to a spot under the trees where benches were set up like we were on a park picnic.

Safiya and I sat together at the end of a bench and we were served with chicken broth and noodles. Some of the other ladies glanced at me but no one really paid us any attention.

I made small talk before mentioning her sister again.

"How do you know my sister?" she asked with suspicion.

"I met her in Permaisuri yesterday."

"She's there?"

"In a café."

"What's her name?"

"Shalaa."

The girl took a breath and suddenly seemed more focused. "How is she?"

176

"Fine, but worried about you. She said you can't escape."

After a hesitation, she said, "We can't get out, but it's not too bad here."

"She said they kill the babies."

Safiya looked horrified. "No. They separate us from our children, but Jeremiah looks after them, educates them. We are safe and well."

"You have a child here?"

"Three."

I was surprised. She looked about eighteen. Twenty at the most.

"In the nursery?"

"No they're older. After the nursery they go to the school on other side of the hill. That's where Jeremiah teaches them."

"How long have you been here?" I asked her.

"Almost five years."

"Voluntarily?"

"In a way." She shrugged ruefully. "I didn't know what to expect. I thought I was coming to a better life. It's all right—and we're safe."

"Safe?"

"The fence protects us. The men protect us."

"From what?"

"From the terrorists... and the evil outside. We're safe here."

I got the sense she'd been indoctrinated to believe she was better off living in these conditions rather than in the free world.

"Your sister is safe. She asked me to get you out."

"It's impossible," she said. "Thank you, but please don't talk to me again." And with that, she got up and left me to eat the broth and noodles alone.

"You're not good at making clothes," Solomon said, confronting me as we returned to the workshop.

"I'm doing my best."

"It's not good enough. You're to work in the fields like I said before. Executive decision."

I didn't argue. I'd promised to save Safiya, but she didn't want my help. So I trailed after Solomon into the fields, where I was given a hoe and spent a sweltering afternoon turning over soil.

I used the shower block and got a bundle of fresh clothes. My dirty ones went in a huge pile and I guessed they'd be washed by the laundry team in the morning.

Dinner was in the covered area beside the cookhouse. We had rice and vegetables and noodle soup. Solomon met me and we found a table. We were the only whites in a room full of women and girls aged somewhere between fifteen and thirty I guessed.

"Who's that?" I asked when another white man arrived. Like me, he was wearing the green fatigues. We exchanged nods but he didn't join us. I judged him to be about sixty, with cropped grey hair and tight skin on hard muscles. His bare arms were covered in tattoos and I noticed one of them looked like a dagger.

"That's Doug. He's the carpenter."

Safiya sat on the table behind him, and despite me looking that way, she made no eye contact with me.

"How long has Shangri-La been here?" I asked Solomon.

"Seven years. There was a village here before but I think it was deserted when Jeremiah broke ground and declared this to be the sacred site." Which would have been shortly after the end of the war.

"Were you here then?"

"No, I've been here over four years."

"But you can't leave."

He looked at me like my words were sacrilegious.

"Why would I want to leave?"

I shrugged. "Free will."

He shook his head, not getting it. Then: "People do leave. Jeremiah doesn't like it. Coming and going disrupts the peace, disrupts the purity."

It sounded like nonsense to me. From what I'd interpreted, they didn't kill the babies, but keeping them separate from their mothers was like holding them to ransom. I couldn't imagine any woman leaving without her child.

I said, "All right, when was the last time someone left?"

"Recently. That's why we're uncomfortable about you."

"Why?"

"Because he came and then two days later he disappeared."

THIRTY-TWO

The man had taken the name Peter and been an ex-soldier from Singapore.

"He claimed to be AWOL," Solomon said, "but he was hiding something."

"Men on the run usually are," I said, thinking that Peter was Jenkins. I'd found evidence that the SIB man had been here. "Where did he go?"

"Like I said, he disappeared. We have no idea, but it's got us twitchy, Daniel especially."

"Daniel?"

"Jeremiah's the leader, and Daniel... well, he's sort of the sergeant major."

"Not Michael?" I asked, remembering that Solomon had called him the boss.

"No. Michael's... well, let's say he's number three."

"How did this Peter chap leave?" I asked, thinking of the fences.

"Just walked out."

"Where did he go?"

Solomon looked at me hard. "Peter asked a lot of questions. You ask a lot of questions."

"I'm not claiming to be AWOL," I said. "I'm just looking for somewhere to hang my hat, remember? Questions are normal."

"Peter asked lots of questions about the men. He poked around, if you know what I mean."

I ate my soup and acted casual. "Assume I don't."

"He wanted to know the men's backgrounds and said he was looking for a friend. Although I got the impression the person wasn't really a friend. And if the person was a friend then why didn't Peter know what he looked like?"

Jenkins looking for BlackJack.

"Daniel was going to ask him questions, but like I said, he disappeared," he told me a second time, then added: "I mean, Daniel was going to interrogate him. Asking questions sounds too friendly. I think Peter ran because he didn't want that cross-examination. He had something to hide—that's what everyone else thinks anyway."

"Did Peter make any friends here? Did you notice whether he talked to anyone—any girl—more than any other?" I was looking for evidence that he'd also spoken to Safiya.

"I think we should stop there."

"I'm just interested."

"No," Solomon said. "You're definitely asking too many questions."

At 8 pm the bell rang, calling everyone to the town hall. It was the same bell I'd heard last night. I went through the doors expecting yet another austere environment, but I was wrong. The walls were painted with images that I guessed were what someone imagined paradise looked like. Trees, mountains, butterflies and exotic birds. There was no sun. Instead, a central dark circle on a long stem radiated light.

There were electric lights inside like fake candles along the walls. The village huts and my little shed didn't

181

have electricity, but there were dim lights in other buildings around the square.

Like in a church, the seating was in rows, but chairs rather than pews. At the front was a raised stage with seven chairs on it: a row of six followed by a white sheet dangling from the ceiling and then another chair.

On the rear wall, the painting was of the dark sun-like object radiating light.

In the middle of the room, like a central support, was a giant pillar of rock from the floor to the ceiling. It made the space feel much smaller than it looked from outside. At about twenty feet high, even the ceiling felt lower than I had expected. When I looked up I saw swirls of green paint—not something that Michelangelo would have been proud of. This was no Sistine Chapel.

I took a seat near the back. The man who I'd seen at dinner, the carpenter, sat next to me. His breathing was heavy, a bit wheezy like a heavy smoker's. We were the only men in the audience. Safiya came in after I'd sat down but made no eye contact.

The carpenter held out a calloused hand and I shook it.

"Ash."

"Doug."

"Not biblical?"

He raised a finger. "Talk later," he whispered. "Don't really drink it."

I frowned at him, not understanding his last words, but he turned away as Michael led Solomon and three other white men down the left aisle. After climbing onto the stage, Solomon took the chair on the far end, then there were three other guys followed by an empty chair. The last chair before the sheet was taken by Michael. He flicked his eyes in my direction and then looked away.

Two empty chairs. One next to Michael over on the left and the solitary one to the right of the sheet.

The men all reminded me of cowboys, although none wore hats.

"Ex-soldiers?" I whispered, and Doug grunted his agreement.

Once everyone was in, the doors were shut with a heavy *thunk*, and I heard a lock turn. We were being locked in, which I didn't like.

The man who must have locked the doors walked between the aisles. I'd not seen him before and he had an air of authority. He mounted the stage and stood on the other side of the sheet, by the solitary chair.

Was he Jeremiah? Had Safiya's sister been wrong about him? This guy had a pale face but his hair was grey. Not remotely like an albino.

Doug must have read my mind. In an almost indiscernible whisper, he said, "That's Daniel."

I nodded. The second in command. The sergeant major.

"All rise," Daniel said, his voice harsh and too loud for the confined space.

The ex-soldiers also stood and the sheet wafted with the movement. I saw that it had four sides, about three feet square around and more than eight feet high.

I was looking at the remaining empty chair, thinking about it. Then I focused on the faces of the men and noticed they appeared expectant.

The lights flickered and I wondered if they would fail, but at the same time, the white sheet jerked upwards and there was a man standing where it had been. He was a giant. White haired, white robed. He raised his arms as though accepting our adoration.

No doubt about it, this was Jeremiah.

More than a head taller than the others, I judged him to be almost seven-foot tall. The white hair hung loosely to his shoulders. A long beard covered the bottom of his face and his skin looked as white as his gown. But he was no albino. Even though I was about twenty yards away, I could see he had striking blue eyes rather than red.

He lowered his hands and the congregation sat. Then the ex-soldiers sat and Jeremiah stepped forward.

I don't know how, but I could feel his presence. He wasn't just huge, this guy had charisma.

At that moment I wouldn't have been surprised if electricity had shot out of his palms. And when he spoke it wasn't like the man who had told us to stand. Jeremiah's voice was soft and full of warmth. He welcomed everyone and then he asked me to stand and then welcomed me.

He said this was a paradise for the righteous, a safe haven in an insane world, and then went on to make a speech about freedom and spirituality. His sermon appeared to be a jumble of religious teachings and philosophy.

Like a preacher, he did a reading—although he called it a story. And it was indeed a story, because he read an extract of *Lost Horizons*, the book about the mythical Shangri-La.

Then he told us about a nineteenth-century German philosopher, Arthur Schopenhauer, who had said there were three stages of truth. "First it is ridiculed. Second it is violently opposed. Third it is accepted as self-evident." He paused, perhaps to let the concept sink in before continuing. "When I created Shangri-La, people laughed. They said I was crazy. When you joined us, they said you were crazy, living behind a fence. They said you wanted to escape and you were trapped. They criticized and ridiculed what they didn't understand.

"That, according to Schopenhauer, is the first phase. And before the world comes to accept the truth we must pass through that second phase: the violence. The war is coming. The fence is not there to keep you in, it is there to protect us. The men"—he waved a gentle hand towards the ex-soldiers—"aren't armed to keep you in line. They are here to protect you. I will protect you." Again he opened his welcoming arms and the women rose up as one. Doug and I stood up as well, and I watched the front row queue in front of Jeremiah.

Daniel filled a jug from a barrel that I now saw at the back of the stage, where it had originally been hidden by the sheet. He returned and poured liquid into a chalice. The first woman mounted steps towards Jeremiah and he presented the chalice to her lips.

Unlike in any communion I had witnessed, the recipient was expected to drink the whole amount. After each drink, Daniel refilled the cup before Jeremiah presented it to the next person.

Soon my row filed out and Doug nudged me forward. We moved slowly down the centre, round the column of rock, towards Jeremiah.

Finally, it was my turn. Jeremiah smiled at me and said, "Welcome, Thomas," speaking to the congregation before holding out the cup. Without hesitation, I took the liquid in my mouth. But I didn't swallow. I held it there and lowered my head like I'd seen everyone else do. Then I walked back to my chair.

I glanced around, wondering where I could spit the liquid without being noticed. Nowhere. Just as I decided to spit it down my sleeve and then try and hide the wet patch, Doug pushed a piece of cloth into my hand.

I coughed into it and quickly stuck the soaked rag into a pocket.

As we sat down, I whispered, "Thanks," but Doug shook his head and looked away.

Once everyone was sitting, Jeremiah made a concluding speech, which again came out as a mishmash of religious teachings and philosophy, before stepping backward. The white sheet fell, the lights flickered, and then he was gone.

The doors behind us were unlocked and we filed out. No one spoke. Just like I'd seen last night, watching from a distance. There was none of the chat you get when people leave a church. They just walked away in the direction of the village huts. I looked for Doug, but he slipped away as soon as we were in the town square.

I glanced back and saw the ex-soldiers lined up by the door. Daniel had his eyes on me so I nodded and turned away. I went the opposite way to the women, past the workshop then through the trees and found my little hut.

I could still taste the liquid on my tongue. It had been sweet like watered-down honey, but I had no doubt it had been some kind of drug. I thought about the look I'd noticed in many of the people's eyes: a dull acceptance, I'd thought. Now I thought differently.

I opened out a mosquito net that hung from the roof, lay on the uncomfortable bed and stared upward. Outside I heard the hoots and cries of the jungle above the buzz of cicadas. There were no voices. People left the town hall and went to bed. There was hardly any talking. No entertainment. No fun.

I wanted to retrieve my gun but didn't dare. I was in, I was earning acceptance and I had learned that Jenkins had been here.

But I wasn't just going to lie there and sleep. I would wait at least two hours and slip out. I wanted to explore the out-of-bounds area. There was more to this place than a soporific paradise.

A twig snapped outside.
I jumped up and opened my door.
In the moonlight I saw a figure standing beside a tree.

THIRTY-THREE

"I'm taking a big risk," Doug whispered as I stepped over to him in the darkness.

"Why?"

He took a breath. "Because of Safiya. She's my girl, but I know it's wrong."

I didn't ask him to explain what he meant. Instead, I asked him about the communion.

"Some kind of opiate," he said. "It took me two years to get off it and then I persuaded Safiya. She thought everything was all right until she stopped taking it. Jeremiah uses it to open people's minds, he says, but it also makes everyone compliant."

"The soldiers don't take it."

"No, they don't. At least I've never seen them."

"Tell me about them," I said.

"Will you help us?"

"What do you want?"

He sighed. "We want to get out. I told Daniel and he went crazy. I thought he was going to kill me on the spot. I was punished for weeks after that conversation. I trusted the other chap who came here. He said he'd help but he just left."

"Tell me about him."

"Tall—not quite as tall as you—darkish hair. Maybe early thirties."

"Did he tell you his real name?"

"I just knew him as Peter. Maybe that was his real name. You know him?"

I shook my head.

"Don't be like him. Don't just leave us," he said, gripping my arm. "Help us get out first."

"Tell me more about Peter."

"He was looking for someone. He was very interested in the soldiers. There's Jeremiah, the ex-army chaps and then me. We're supposed to be equal but we aren't. They live in the houses while the rest of us live in huts. I built those bloody houses. Why can't I have one?"

I went back to an earlier question and said, "Tell me about them—the ex-soldiers."

"Daniel is in charge, day-to-day. He can be vicious and the girls are afraid of him. Safiya is afraid of him but I can't stop it."

"Stop what?"

"They take any woman they want. It's rape, plain and simple." His husky voice shook with emotion, and I waited until he composed himself.

Doug said, "Jeremiah is different but worse."

"In what way?"

"He has a shrine. He says the sacred stone is in there, says that it speaks to him."

"Have you seen it?"

"No, but I've heard the ceremonies he holds. And it's not just girls he takes in there. He takes the children too."

"And does what?"

"Use your imagination. He seems like a gentle religious man, but he has a warped sense of reality. I fell for his whole new world speech originally, then I kind of

189

got brainwashed and then the drugs..." Again he gripped my arm. "You've got to get us out."

"How?"

He handed me a vicious-looking knife. "You've got to kill Jeremiah."

THIRTY-FOUR

I handed the knife back to Doug and told him that I'd think about it. In reality, it wasn't something I would immediately consider. Doug had been all over the place. He'd been desperate and distressed and paranoid.

He'd spoken to Jenkins, who was looking for a killer. Had he pointed the finger at Jeremiah or someone else? Maybe Daniel.

As he walked away, I wondered about the knife and Doug's dagger tattoos. What did they tell me about the old man?

I waited another two hours before I ventured out of my hut again. With the intention of scoping the area beyond the office and nursery, I carried nothing with me except for one of Jenkins's shirts, which I wrapped around my waist.

The fence continued beside the river as I went through the trees. Eventually, I came to a long building on stilts. From what I could see in the dark, it was unlike the other buildings. This looked more like a British colonial house on a single floor with a long balcony. It wouldn't have looked out of place on a tea or rubber plantation.

I reckoned this was where the ex-soldiers lived. When I'd been at the office, Solomon had looked in this direction when he'd told me about the bunkhouse where they lived. Some kind of bunkhouse!

I kept going and within a few yards found a narrow-gauge railway line. Following it, I came to a tunnel. It was cut out of rock, and a gate covering the tunnel's mouth lay open.

The tunnel was the height of a man and the width of two. In absolute darkness, I ran my hand along a rough-hewn wall as a guide. Before entering, I had listened hard and heard nothing. Outside was the constant buzz of insects. Inside, I could only hear my breathing and the sound of my feet on stony ground.

The floor never rose or fell and I counted my paces. I reckoned I'd gone half a mile before I reached the end. There was no gate this time.

It was the other side of the hill, but what was here except for a valley with trees before more hills? The rail track kept going north and I followed it, although through the treeline rather than open ground.

As I wondered whether this rail line would go for miles, the light improved as clouds parted, and I saw something to my right. Not on the ground, but in the trees. I moved cautiously towards it and I realized I was looking at a huge treehouse.

It's stilts were twice my height with a structure on top that had a balcony and roof like a chalet. I figured it was about twenty feet long by eight feet. A ladder went up to the middle of the balcony.

I could hear the gentle groan of wood on wood but no human sound and there were no lights. The building puzzled me, and circling it, I found another rail line that ended right below the house. The undergrowth appeared to have been cleared, and as I went further north I walked beside the new line I'd found. This seemed to be a branch line that would join up with the first. However, before I could confirm this, I heard voices, quiet and relaxed.

I stepped further into the cover of trees and waited. Then I saw movement and two men came towards me from the north, thirty yards off. But they weren't heading my way.

I waited and they passed, their voices soon lost in the background hum. Rather than go back to the exposed track, I continued to explore but stayed deeper in the woods.

Making my way through undergrowth I could barely see, I stumbled. I took another couple of steps and stumbled again, only it wasn't roots that had tripped me, it was a mound of earth. And then I stepped over more mounds, some raised higher than others. The highest was about six inches off the ground, like a series of ridges meant to slow progress or make me divert. I counted eleven more before the ground flattened again and I could walk more easily.

After the mounds, I found a well-worn path that led me back to the rail line. Then it split left and right. Right along the line, left into the trees. Most people, given an unconscious choice, will turn left. It's natural for a right-handed person. I'm left-handed but I made a conscious choice. I went left.

At first, I thought I was looking at a snake. Unmoving and thick. Then I realized it was a cable running beside the path.

And then I came to a generator. I'd figured there must be one because of the lights. Villages out here weren't connected to a power station. Which meant fuel.

Which meant something else.

I smelled diesel and located a tank a few yards later. Diesel had to come from somewhere. It needed to be transported.

Although I wasn't a hundred per cent sure of my geographic location, I knew I was nowhere near the gate I'd originally come through and the track over the bridge had been unsuitable for a truck. So there had to be another way in. There had to be another road.

And then I saw a perimeter fence. So there was one after all. Like the other, it had barbed wire on top, but it was shorter at around six feet high. Following the fence, it took me five minutes to find a gate. It was a double gate, just wide enough for a vehicle, and locked with a big square-headed bolt. A padlock ran through a hole in the bolt so that it couldn't slide open.

The padlock felt new, whereas I could feel rust on the gate. I wondered then whether this fencing was much older than the eight-foot fence on the other side of the hill.

Pushing the two halves of the gate I found it had minimal movement. No way could I squeeze through the gap.

This is where Jenkins's shirt came in handy. I removed it from my waist, tore it in two and then scaled the gate. The barbed wire stopped and started again where the two gates met. Not an easy obstacle but one I was willing to attempt.

Balancing on the bolt and protecting my hands with the shirt, I pulled at one loose end of the wire. I locked it in place, creating a slightly wider gap. Then I set to work on the other side. By the time I'd finished, I'd created a space about eighteen inches wide. Still not comfortable, but with a shirt-covered hand on either side I managed to stand, straddling the gate, before I jumped down on the far side.

I landed with a thump as I misjudged the ground but then rolled to lessen the impact. I touched my calf where

I'd caught it on a barb then breathed a sigh of relief. It was just a scratch.

I looked back and wondered if I'd been foolish. What was I thinking? I had to climb back in and I'd bent the wire outwards. It would be harder getting back.

I shook the negative thoughts from my mind, stuffed the two pieces of shirt beside the road and walked away.

With moonlight cutting through the trees, I could see the road ahead and followed its curve until I came to a bridge over a river.

Unlike the rotten wooden bridge, this one could take weight. Not a tank, but certainly a heavy truck, one laden with people escaping. Alternatively, one filled with soldiers coming in.

Swatting away insects that I felt land on my skin, I continued. The scratch on my calf suddenly hurt and I flicked at something feeding there.

Then I saw a building ahead. It was mostly hidden by trees, and I soon recognized it as a garage of sorts, with sides and a roof and vehicles inside. Three of them. A Land Rover and two trucks. I didn't recognize their make. They were small and light with Chinese or Japanese writing on the back. It was hard to say in the semi-darkness but they seemed old and battered. Probably pre-war.

Both trucks had load beds, one covered, one open. Both empty.

I smelled lingering fumes, and the Land Rover's bonnet felt warm. The two men I'd seen had travelled by this vehicle, parked and walked into the compound.

It was an ex-army Land Rover with a hard roof. Army vehicles don't require a key. Too many potential drivers, too much opportunity to lose the key.

I got in and pushed the start button. The engine fired into life and I pulled out of the garage and turned right, away from the Jeremiah's strange fenced-in commune.

Again the road swept in a long arc moving from approximately north to east. I figured I'd eventually reach Route Three, although I had no sense of distance. Maybe another mile, I hoped.

Then I stopped abruptly.

Even though my lights were off, I saw a man walking towards me. He whipped out a gun.

My engine idled. I sat and waited. He had a weapon, I had the Land Rover. I didn't move. He didn't move. I figured he was deciding what to do.

He took two paces forward and stopped. His gun was still aimed at me. His right hand held something else. He raised it and flicked it on. A flashlight.

I made a decision, swung out of the Land Rover and raised my hands. Then I walked slowly towards him.

"Far enough," he said when I was seven or eight paces away. British, clear and crisp with the hint of an accent. My mind was processing, spinning, confused.

His torch blinded me and I shielded my eyes.

"Who the hell are you?" he said. I placed the accent as being from the English Midlands.

"Ash Carter," I said, trying to see the other man. "It can't be?"

"What can't?"

"You." I stepped closer. "Show yourself."

The torch flashed away from me and briefly showed his face. The shadows made him look like a monster. Maybe a ghoul would be a better description. But it was him all right.

The man standing before me was John Harwood.

THIRTY-FIVE

"You're dead," I said. We were in the Land Rover, although not moving.

He laughed. "I've been called worse things."

"No," I said. "I've seen your body. You were burned to death."

"Then you were obviously mistaken. I'm very much alive." He pinched himself. "At least I hope so."

I shook my head, still unable to comprehend what was going on. "Explain," I said.

"Let's get away from here first. But not in this. I've got a jeep hidden off the main road. You take this back and I'll pick you up. Then we'll talk. OK?"

He jumped out and jogged away.

The road was too narrow to turn on, and I didn't fancy trying to reverse in the dark. It took me a while, but I got the Land Rover back to the garage and then jogged back down the road.

Harwood picked me up after a short distance and then he too manoeuvred back and forth to turn around before we got going.

He put the lights on and moved fast, ignoring the jolts and thuds.

"You were going to explain," I said, after he wasn't forthcoming.

"You first. We've never met but I know of you. You're ex-SIB. What are you doing here, in the middle of the night in the Shangri-La Land Rover?"

"At the moment, I'm trying to make sense of everything. I was called in to investigate a helicopter crash, and we thought you were one of the victims. Then I was in contact with Jenkins and traced him here."

"He's here?"

"He was staying in Bandar Permaisuri. Last seen three nights ago. I thought he'd come to the commune."

Harwood shook his head. "Haven't seen him. I went in there for a couple of days. Jenkins wasn't there."

"That was you? I was told someone called Peter had been and gone. You were Peter. I just assumed it was Jenkins."

"It was me."

"Well, you certainly unsettled them." It was starting to make sense except I still didn't know where Jenkins had gone and why he hadn't reported in. And then there was the issue of the body and the helicopter crash.

We came to the main road and Harwood went straight over, still driving too fast for the poor quality surface in my opinion.

"What's going on, John? Why did we think you were dead? Why haven't you reported in?"

"Deep cover. I can't tell you why you thought I was dead, but I can tell you SIB Command didn't expect me to report."

After pulling off the track and switching off the engine and lights, he told me his story. He'd worked out that gold was being brought through unofficial channels. It started illegitimate and became legitimate and army personnel were at the end of it. When he referred to a pipeline, I interrupted.

"We think Major Chris Broom was involved?"

"He seemed to be at the end of the pipeline. He moved the gold to the end buyer. I followed him in Perak but he disappeared. You said *was* involved."

"Murdered brutally," I said. "His face was cut off. Do you know the name BlackJack?"

"No. Why?"

"We think it's the murderer's assumed name."

"Broom murdered." He took a long breath. "Doesn't surprise me. But Jenkins thought the murders were by more than one man. I think it has something to do with the gold. Soldiers or ex-soldiers are involved and they're getting taken out. It's possibly some kind of turf war."

That made me think of the Chinese Secret Societies. They were in Singapore and throughout Malaya.

"Chinese?" I asked.

He inclined his head. "Possibly. Where are the goldfields, Ash?"

"The Highlands?" I'd never seen any but knew they were in the middle of the country. The west had the tin, the centre had gold and the east had nothing.

"There are gold mines just a few miles north of here."

"Really?"

"In the jungle. Not big. Started before the war and abandoned. But the Chinese operate them now."

"By Chinese, you mean the terrorists?"

He nodded. "CTs. It's funding their activity."

"Then why hasn't—?"

"Why hasn't the army done something? Because the operations are small and scattered and well-defended. What the CTs don't have is a way of converting the gold into dollars."

"And that's where the pipeline comes in," I said.

"It's where this little unit comes in." He pointed into the jungle and I realized he meant the ex-soldiers from Jeremiah's commune. "They deal with the Chinese and pass the gold down the line. They take it over the mountains to Perak and bring the money back—taking a cut of course."

"OK," I said, "then you get the army in here."

He shook his head. "They're prepared for that. Have you met Jeremiah and Daniel?"

"Briefly."

"Jeremiah is a crank. I think he really believes he's creating some sort of paradise, although it's warped because it revolves around his needs." He took a breath as if something disturbed him. Then he said, "You can't trust anyone in there."

"No," I agreed, "you can't."

"But Jeremiah isn't the brains. He lives in his own fantasy world in a treehouse. Daniel has one too. They have an odd relationship. I don't think Jeremiah realizes that it's all funded by the CTs. Daniel sorts that out. He brings in the other things they need, like food and oil."

I nodded. "I'd figured their little farm wasn't producing enough food for them all. I've eaten chicken and they don't have enough to feed everyone."

"Daniel and his ex-soldiers get it all."

"You were telling me why you can't get the army in there to break it up."

"He'll kill them all. One of the men told me the town hall is wired with explosives. One sign of trouble and everyone is taken to the town hall. And *kaboom*. Fifty-odd innocent people dead."

"There must be a way."

"That's what I'm working on."

"Who told you about the explosives?"

"Noah. He's the one with the round glasses."

I pictured him sitting next to Solomon on the town hall stage.

"Can I trust him?"

"Don't trust anyone."

Rain suddenly started to pelt the windscreen, a rapid percussion that forced silence between us. We were still sitting beside the road and I was thinking of a comfortable bed. I could still taste the liquid in my mouth. A drug. My tongue would have absorbed some and it was probably making me drowsy.

"There's something you aren't telling me," I said above the noise.

"Like what?"

"Like why the deep cover?"

He waited a beat then said, "Because Major Broom wasn't the end of the pipeline. There's someone else, someone more senior involved."

"Someone in the British Army?"

"That's what I think."

"So you don't know who in the army you can trust?"

He treated it as rhetorical because he said nothing for a while. Maybe he was wondering if he could trust me.

"OK," he said, restarting the engine. "I'll drop you somewhere. Where can I take you? Bandar Permaisuri?"

Queen's town. I could return to the room where Jenkins had stayed. A good night's sleep and a big breakfast certainly appealed.

I breathed the night air deeply and let it out. "I'm going back in."

"This isn't your problem, Carter."

No, it wasn't. Harwood had matters in hand. This was his job and I was just butting in.

I said, "You can't go back because they're already twitchy. You need me inside. It's likely that one or more of them is BlackJack."

The rain pounded the windscreen and he said nothing.

I said, "Quitting isn't in my nature."

He reached over and shook my hand. "Good man. Earn their trust, find the explosives and disarm them."

THIRTY-SIX

Lights off, he drove me back down the road towards the commune. We stopped well before the garage.

He looked at me. "Did you leave the gate open?"

"I scaled it."

"Over the wire? They didn't trust you as part of the team?"

"Not yet. Like I said, they're twitchy after you came and went. How did you get out?"

"I came out with two of the guys. One had a key. I slipped away."

"That'll be why they don't trust me. You scared them. They're suspicious of me."

"You need to earn their trust, be part of the team."

I nodded. I'd already figured that out and had a plan. Since I was going back, I didn't want to carry on being the outsider.

He said, "So you'll climb over again."

"I bent the wire. It'll be harder going back in."

"Let's meet again tomorrow night, at 3 am. They work most nights but tomorrow they'll be later. You must have just missed them tonight."

"I saw two. They didn't see me."

"You were lucky," he said, then told me where to meet tomorrow.

I nodded.

"Did you see the generator?"

"Yes."

"I'll cut the wire near there. That'll get you through in case you haven't got a key."

"They won't give me a key," I said.

"Right."

He thought for a moment.

"What?" I asked.

"You came through the tunnel. That'll be locked now." He thought a moment longer and then fished a key out of his pocket and handed it to me.

"Unfortunately it's the only one I got."

"Thanks," I said, realizing this was a big moment for him. He was trusting *me*. "Let's be clear, I'll disarm the explosives, but I want you to do something."

He waited.

"I want you to call Lieutenant Colonel Ambrose at 200 Provost. You might not trust the army in general but you can trust him. We need men here."

He said nothing and the rain seemed more intense.

I said, "You can keep them back. Don't let them come in until everyone's safe, but having them here will mean they can react as soon as we need them. Otherwise, they'll get here a day too late."

Still no comment.

"John, we can't do this alone!"

"Fine," he said. "I'll call Ambrose."

He started the engine and rolled over the bridge and went towards the gates. All the way, so that the bumper nudged the fence. I saw what he was doing.

"Good luck."

"See you tomorrow night," I said, and I got out into the rain. "One last thing. We need a signal. If you hear the bells going crazy or see something unusual, like a fire, then I'm in trouble."

I retrieved my strips of shirt to protect my hands and climbed onto the jeep's bonnet. From there I clambered onto and over the fence.

It was still dark when I woke up in my hut. My watch said 5:30 am. A noise outside had disturbed me. Boots thumped on the earth and then one of the ex-soldiers pushed through my doorway.

This guy had been third in the line after Solomon and Noah.

"You're here," he said, almost surprised.

"Uh?" I said. Normally I wake up instantly, but my brain felt like syrup. I blinked hard, trying to shake the grogginess. Finally focusing, I noted the revolver held tightly in his right hand. There was another man behind him.

"You're wanted. Get down to the CR."

CR meant common room. I figured that was the long building—the office.

I got up. "Who wants me?"

"Just get moving."

THIRTY-SEVEN

"Oh, too easy," BlackJack thought as the ex-soldier called Noah walked past in the dark. He was alone and careless.

BlackJack slipped in behind him and walked four paces before Noah realized he was there.

The ex-soldier spun around and was met with an iron bar between the eyes, cattle prod style. His eyes were as wide as a cow's as well as he went backwards, open with shock despite his brain shutting down.

BlackJack checked the man's pulse to confirm he wasn't dead before dragging him through the trees. He moved through wet undergrowth to the fence and located the section he'd cut just fifteen minutes earlier.

Getting Noah through the hole required a twist and pull. The man's shirt snagged and BlackJack let it tear on the cut wire.

On the other side, he dragged the body for a few yards before lifting him and carrying Noah fireman-style.

This was one reason why he hadn't killed the man first. Blood would have made BlackJack messy, and one thing he prided himself on was being able to perform his tasks without mess—at least without getting blood on himself.

With Noah on his shoulder, BlackJack went up the slope he knew would lead to a boulder. In the dark and with the weight of a man on his shoulder, he found it harder than he'd anticipated. But BlackJack was fit and he refused to let himself feel any weakness. In fact, the exertion made his heartbeat even faster than the anticipation of the kill.

And a good kill it would be.

THIRTY-EIGHT

"You were wandering about last night, poking your nose in where it wasn't wanted."

I was in the common room, sitting on a hard-backed chair, my hands cuffed around the back. By my shoulders were two of the men: Sam and another man. I'd managed to get Sam's name out of him as we'd walked, but that was all I got.

Both men behind me had handguns out and ready.

There were plenty of comfortable chairs around, but not for me. The ceiling fans weren't rotating and the air was thick with the smell of stale cigarettes. I saw a locked metal cabinet, the sort for storing guns. By the door were three wooden pegs. One was just a peg, but the other two had wooden signs hanging from them. They were numbered "2" and "3". I figured that, whatever it represented, "1" was in use.

I saw a dartboard and round tables and posters of young film stars in bikinis stuck to all the walls. A typical men's common room.

Michael was the man challenging me. His face was hard, his eyes harder. I'd encountered worse, but I sensed this guy would take no nonsense. If he thought I was lying he'd probably get his men to pistol whip me until I told the truth.

I smiled disarmingly and shook my head. I needed to be part of the team, not the enemy.

"I took a walk," I said. "I don't deny it. My head felt funny after the communion. And anyway, I'm not stupid. I have a brain. I'm inquisitive."

"What d'you mean by that?"

"I knew there must be stuff coming in."

"You saw stuff coming in?"

"No, I found a narrow-gauge track. That went through a tunnel."

"You went through—into Cham?"

"Cham?"

"The northern compound."

"Of course I did. Why not? The gate was open. I'd already guessed you were bringing other goods in. There are electric lights so I figured there'd be a generator, and a generator meant diesel. Diesel isn't exactly a natural resource here, is it?"

One of the guys behind me stifled a chuckle, which was a good sign. They were relaxed. More than Michael appeared.

"What else?" he said.

"You're bringing in food too. The vegetable field you have here doesn't produce everything you're eating, plus a few chickens aren't providing enough meat."

"What else?"

"What else are you bringing in to Shangri-La?" I said, using the name to sound like I bought into Jeremiah's vision. "Anything, I guess. Anything you need. You must have transport somewhere. I can't imagine you allow deliveries here. I heard men walking around last night. I guessed they'd been out and got whatever you need."

"How did you cut your leg?"

I looked down, having forgotten that I'd caught it on the barbed wire. There was a line of blood, two inches long on my trousers.

I frowned. "I don't know. Must have fallen over, I guess. The drug maybe."

"Drug?"

"Come on. The communion drink had something in it. My brain still isn't functioning."

"Tell me about the fence."

I'd sat on both sides of a table like this. Interrogation was all about intimidation and disorientation, a fear of violence, a fear of torture. Questioning for a confession could be different. That tended to be more of a monologue to earn the other's trust. Make them think it was OK to confess.

I didn't know about Michael's history but I was sure he'd never had interrogation training of either sort. Which probably meant he hadn't been an officer. In fact, I doubted any of the men had been officer class except maybe Jeremiah.

"What about the fence?" I asked, relaxed.

"Why did you go out?"

"I didn't," I said, gambling that Michael didn't know the truth.

"You snipped the wire. That's how you cut your leg."

"Snipped the wire, with wire cutters?" I asked.

"Yes."

"*Wire cutters?*"

"Where did you get them from?" Frustration edged his voice.

Now I smiled. "Precisely. Where the heck would I get wire cutters? I don't know anything about anyone cutting a hole in any fence."

"I didn't say there was a hole."

"Well, what else would it be?" I shook my head. If there's genuinely a hole in your fence—if it's been cut—then I'd do a headcount."

This was another gamble. They'd lost Harwood recently. Yes, they were nervous about me, but I figured Michael was also concerned about losing men. Maybe.

"The women won't go through the tunnel."

I shook my head. "What about your men?"

He said nothing and tried to intimidate me with his eyes. I stared right back. After a good half-minute, he looked at the guys behind me and raised his chin. They filed out.

Michael said, "I don't trust you."

"Why not?"

He stood, leaned forward on the table so that his face was near. A dumb move, because we were alone and I could have jerked upwards and head-butted his ugly mug. Not a smart move with my hands cuffed behind me, but then again desperate prisoners do things that aren't smart.

"Think things over," he said. "I'll be back later."

Then they left me alone in the common room. It was still before sunrise, although the sky was lightening. The windows were all closed and I had no water.

The sun came up and shone through a window onto me. The room got warmer. After three hours, my clothes were soaked due to the humidity. The sun was still on me and I was without water.

Maybe this guy wasn't such a bad interrogator after all.

The three of them plus another man came back in after midday. The fourth guy had been the one just to the left of Jeremiah on stage. Daniel, second in command.

My eyes had been closed and I'd slept a little despite the heat and the uncomfortable position. And when I hadn't been asleep, I'd breathed slowly and imagined cool things rather than think about the heat.

When I opened my eyes, my focus returned to the room, the here and now. I breathed in air that burned my throat and lungs.

Daniel sat in the chair opposite me. Michael leaned on the wall behind him with menace in his eyes. I decided that his head looked too small for his bulk.

The other two men took up their positions slightly behind me as before.

"I don't trust you," Daniel said.

"Tell me who's missing," I said. "Who did you lose?"

He scrutinized me.

I said, "It wasn't one of the girls. It was one of your men, wasn't it?"

He said, "Why are you here?"

"Just looking for somewhere to hang my hat. I came here because I'd heard about... the benefits."

He blinked surprise.

"I want in."

He shook his head. "What are you talking about?"

"Gold."

Daniel laughed uncomfortably, looked at the men behind me and then back.

"Who did you hear that nonsense from?"

"A clerk at BVD 221," I said. "He works for Major Chris Broom." I used the present tense. If I knew too much they'd be suspicious and probably guess I was connected to the military police in some way. Maybe they didn't even know he was dead.

Daniel leaned on his elbows, his lips resting on clenched hands, thinking.

"I don't trust you," he said eventually.

"So you already said." I shrugged. "If you're a man down, I can be of help."

"But I don't use men I don't trust. That would be dumb, wouldn't it?"

"It would."

"So tell me the truth about yourself. No way were you just a sergeant. I know an officer when I smell one."

"You're right," I said. "I was a captain and I had to leave quickly because I did something I shouldn't have. I killed a bunch of guys."

"Who?"

"An Arab gang. Nasty pieces of work who did some terrible things. You can't trust the MPs or the police to do anything about it so I took matters into my own hands." The thing about a good lie is that it's based on the truth. I didn't mention that I was the MP or that the terrible things involved my snitch, but I did say: "They raped and murdered my girl. No one gets away with that and lives."

I said it with a flat, honest voice and could see the mutilated, desecrated bodies that the evil guys had left after their fun. I think Daniel read the pain in my eyes.

He removed his hands from his mouth. "Tell me something that'll make me trust you."

This was what he'd been building up to. I could see that he was waiting for the right time. I could see that he wanted me to be telling the truth.

I nodded. "You need to watch the carpenter. He asked me to kill Jeremiah."

Daniel's eyes flicked from my right and left, back and forth, assessing. And then he smiled. This is what he'd wanted to hear.

What he didn't know is that I'd already decided to confess about Doug's request. One, because Jeremiah

213

was not my objective, and two, because Doug wasn't who he purported to be.

Doug had told me that Safiya was his girlfriend and yet I'd not seen them together. Maybe she was, maybe she wasn't, but I was suspicious. Of course, he'd seen me sit with her at lunch, so he knew I was interested in her.

He'd gained my trust by warning me about the drug given at communion. But they'd made a foolish error. There had been a spare chair at the front. One of them wasn't where he should be, where he usually sat. That's because he was sitting next to me. Doug hadn't known it was safe to tell me to kill anyone. If he'd been genuine, he wouldn't have risked telling a stranger. He didn't know who I was or who I'd tell.

"Good," Daniel said. "I'd like you to meet Zach."

THIRTY-NINE

Zach was the carpenter. I feigned surprise when Doug came into the common room with Solomon. By then they had opened the windows, switched on fans and given me water. My hands were also untied.

Zach was a good actor. As the timid, paranoid Doug, he lacked the presence that I now saw in him.

"I should deck you for betraying me," he said.

I shrugged and felt like encouraging him to try, but I didn't. Everyone was there bar Jeremiah and Noah, the man with the round glasses. They all shook my hand except for Zach. I sensed some bad feeling, like he really had wanted me to kill Jeremiah or was really offended that I'd betrayed him.

I'd already met Solomon, Sam and, of course, Michael and Daniel. The other man—who I later learned was the one who'd choked back the laugh while I was being interrogated—was called Gabe, short for Gabriel.

When Daniel left the common room I sensed that Michael was now in charge. He looked at me with narrowed eyes and I knew he trusted me the least.

"How did you know one of our men was missing?" he asked.

"The cut fence," I said. "Plus the level of concern."

"Level of concern?" Zach asked.

"He was an officer," Michael said.

Zach spat, and I figured he had a thing against officers.

"Where would one of the women get wire cutters? They don't get out, do they?" I paused, then: "You're missing the one with the glasses."

Gabe sniggered. "That's Noah."

"Why would Noah leave?" Michael said.

"I don't know," I said. "Lots of reasons I suppose. Most of which will involve a level of happiness. Maybe you should be asking yourselves rather than me why Noah was unhappy."

Michael shook his head. "No reason he was unhappy."

"Maybe you just didn't know," Solomon opined.

Michael glared at the other man. "Trying to say something?"

"No."

"Good." Michael swivelled his attention back to me. "Daniel says you're to be trusted, but we made that mistake with Peter."

"Who was he?" I asked, despite knowing.

"Came and went," Sam said. "I thought he was all right."

Zach said, "But he asked a lot of questions and Noah vouched for him. Maybe they got too close. Maybe Peter planted silly thoughts in his mind and persuaded Noah to leave."

I thought, why cut the fence? But didn't speak up. Peter was Harwood, and he'd just walked through an open gate. Why would someone even more trusted not go the same way? It didn't make sense.

Not then anyway.

FORTY

I was taken to my new accommodation—the British colonial house to the left of the common room and closer to the river. Solomon had told me six of them lived here, but there were eight rooms. I was sharing with Solomon, Sam, Gabe, Zach, Michael, and Noah. Although no one knew where Noah had gone. I was told that Daniel had a home on the other side of the hill—the northern compound they called Cham—near Jeremiah's treehouse.

Inside, there were electric fans in all the rooms and white sheets that wafted in the created breeze. They made it look pretty but the real purpose was to keep the insects out. The furniture looked comfortable and it smelled clean and fresh. I had a decent sprung bed with crisp white sheets and a feather pillow. I had a window with mesh instead of glass, keeping the insects out and the air fresh.

"Better than a hotel," I said to Solomon, who showed me around.

"With hot and cold girls laid on," he said. "Everything a man could want."

I didn't like the lecherous expression on his face but ignored his comment.

Instead, I said, "You know about *my* history. You must have been in the war. Were you based here?"

He sat on the solitary chair in my room and I sat on the bed.

"I fought in North Africa. A tank gunner, me." He chuckled, although I didn't understand the joke. "Never came to Malaya. Had no idea what it was like, but I knew Michael—we come from the same village back home. And Michael knew Daniel, who had been out here—he'd been with Jeremiah. They were in Force 136, you know?"

Of course, I didn't know Daniel's or Jeremiah's backgrounds—didn't even know their real names—but I knew about Force 136. They were a clandestine unit that liaised with the Malayan Communist Party during the war. So that was how they had contacts with the Chinese communists. They'd worked with them, taught them guerrilla tactics. Ironic how things change. During the Second World War, the Chinese were not only our friends, but we armed and trained the bandits.

Jeremiah and Daniel hadn't stopped working with them.

"I'm impressed," I said. "They must know their weapons and explosives."

"And killing techniques," Solomon said conspiratorially. "You'd think Jeremiah was a saint the way he floats around—a modern Jesus—but he can snap a man's neck like that." He clicked his fingers and raised his eyebrows.

I'd hoped to get Solomon to tell me about the explosives in the town hall, but he seemed more interested in talking about death, because he went on to tell me about how Daniel and Michael were expert killers too.

"No one will mess with them," he said.

"Has anyone?"

"In the past you mean? 'Course."

I was thinking about the murders that Jenkins was focused on. Harwood thought they were possibly Chinese gang-related. A turf war removing the pipeline. I wasn't so convinced. To me, it made more sense that it was one or more from this team.

"I heard that Major Broom chap was dead," I said, fishing.

"Did you? I wouldn't know about that. I don't help on that side."

"Who does help with the pipeline?" I was taking a risk asking questions like this, but Solomon wasn't the sharpest tool in the bag and he seemed happy to talk.

"Everyone except me and Gabe."

"Was Noah involved with the gold?"

Maybe I'd gone too far because he looked at me askance, possibly starting to think I was asking a lot of questions.

I laughed. "I'm just hoping that he's gone and I can take his place, that's all. I've had nothing to my name for so long, I've almost forgotten what money looks like."

"How'd you know about the gold?"

"I suspected from someone I met. They told me about Broom."

"We shouldn't talk about it,"

"Daniel confirmed it."

"Oh, OK." Solomon relaxed. "They won't let you near it, I'm afraid. They'll use you for general supplies."

"In what way?"

"Daniel will tell you where to go and you'll meet someone and pick up whatever you're there for."

"At night?"

"Yeah, always at night because it's all black market. You know, there's people out there who we trade with. They even get the girls."

"What do you mean?"

He grinned. "They don't come of their own free will now, do they. The men talk about getting fresh blood."

I forced a smile while my stomach turned over. I wanted to do something there and then: grab Solomon's gun and shoot the whole sick bunch of them. Could I do it? Could I hunt them down one at a time? But before I could formulate a plan I saw Solomon's face change and I realized he was acting.

"You're not one of them, are you?" I said. A statement, not a question.

He swallowed. "I have to go along with it. They get all whipped up with excitement. They get crazy." He swallowed again. "So, yeah, I pretend I like it, but I don't."

"Then do something."

He shrugged and then shook his face, like a dog with his jowls flapping. When he focused on me again he was smiling as though our conversation had never happened. As though he'd never confessed his doubts. "So, you'll get waited on hand and foot now you're one of us. You get to choose a maid whose sole responsibility is making sure you're happy."

"I get to choose?"

"Yeah. Most of the men go for the pretty ones, but I'm smarter." He tapped his nose. "Get an older one who knows what they're doing. My room is the cleanest and my bedding the crispest. I need a bath or a massage, I get one. I need tea or a snack, I get one. It's like she reads my mind. Most of the girls do their job because they have to. My girl, Jasmine, looks after me because she wants to." He tapped his nose again. "There's a difference see?"

"I see."

"I can help you pick one."

"The girl in the sewing room, Safiya."

Solomon looked disappointed. I'd chosen a pretty girl despite his advice.

But then he surprised me. "I'm not sure that's wise."

"Why?"

"She was someone's special girl."

I thought of what Zach had told me while he was pretending to be my friend. "She really was Zach's?"

"No."

"Then whose?"

"No one's. Not for a long time."

"Good. Then she's the one I'll have as my maid." I stood up and opened the door. "Let's go for a walk. Yesterday, you showed me around. Now I'm one of the team, you can show me more."

I headed for the tunnel and asked him to open the gate. Of course, I had a key, but it was better that he didn't know. In the daylight, I saw the electricity cable running along the bottom right-hand edge in places before it went underground.

On the far side, we followed the rail track and he took me all the way down to the gates that I'd climbed last night.

"These are the upper gates. The one you came in through is the lower gate." He pointed down the road on the far side. "We've got a garage down there. Three vehicles."

I tested the lock as though for the first time. "Can I have the key to this."

"Not yet. Not until they trust you." He pointed along the fence. The generator's down that way. Want to see it?"

"No," I said, and set off back, although I veered off into the trees beyond the branch line.

"Where are you going?" he said as we were tramping through undergrowth.

"Just a bit further," I said, and I kept going until I saw what I'd stumbled over last night: mounds of earth. Many of them were covered by vegetation but I could see lots. Last night I figured around thirteen or fourteen. Now I saw a large plot with more than fifty mounds. Not some tactical formation to discourage access. These were graves. I could see them clearly now and my stomach churned.

I could hear Solomon breathing raggedly through his nose, and I looked at him.

He said nothing.

"Who are they?"

He swallowed.

"Solomon, it's OK, you can tell me."

"People die. That's life, right?"

"There's a lot of graves for seven or so years," I said, shaking my head. "And most of the people here are young."

He waited a beat then said, "That's what I thought. Daniel explained that it's because we don't have proper medicine. Children get ill and die—and some of the girls too."

We stood in silence looking at the mounds that looked so innocent beneath the trees, and I couldn't help wonder what terrible story each one of them held beneath the soil.

Finally, he said, "Jeremiah has a treehouse just up here—although we aren't allowed within twenty feet.

222

Invitation only, and the likes of you and me won't get invited."

"Who does?"

"Daniel."

"Anyone else?"

"I don't know, just that it'll never be me. Nor in Daniel's place, which is further over that way in the trees."

We went back across the branch line and then across the main rail line.

As we walked I said, "Zach told me that Jeremiah has a shrine. Is that true?"

"It's in the town hall. You must have seen it."

"The huge column?"

"Yes. He had the town hall built around it."

"And so he calls it a shrine?"

He shrugged. "In the early days, he held ceremonies there after the meetings."

"Did you ever go along?"

"No." He shook his head vigorously.

"Anyone else go?"

"Everyone except me and Noah. And it was before Zach and Gabe joined us."

"Why not you two?"

"We didn't want to." He swallowed and took a slow breath, then spoke quietly. "I've heard the sounds."

"Sounds?"

He was walking away now, and I scooted up next to him. "Solomon, what sounds?"

"Screams," he whispered, and he took another long juddering breath.

"Why don't you do something about it?"

He turned and looked at me like I was insane. I thought he was about to say something, like he didn't stand a chance against the others, Michael and Daniel in particular.

But he didn't.

"This is Shangri-La," he said, like it explained everything. Then he smiled. "I've got everything I could possibly want. And anyway, it all changed shortly after I got here. He stopped the ceremonies."

We carried on walking south-west through the trees. He started to whistle a happy tune, as though he'd forgotten the graves and the shrine conversation.

"Happy?" I asked.

"Why wouldn't I be? You? Hey, how do you feel about your new name? Thomas is a good name, right?"

"I prefer Tom," I said, although I thought Moses would have been more appropriate. I'd come here looking for Jenkins but now I had a more important, more desperate objective. I needed to get the innocent women and children out of this place.

"Tom it is then," he said with a nod.

"Where's the school—where they take the children after the nursery? I was told it was on this side of the hill."

"Over there," he said, pointing almost north. Between west and where the generator is."

"Let's go that way," I said, turning.

"Out of bounds. Only Jeremiah goes there."

I wanted to see it, but that would have to wait. So I said, "Show me where the fence was cut."

"Just up here."

We turned towards the hills, blue mountains looming in the far distance, and walked through the trees. Eventually, I could see the perimeter fence before the ground rose.

"There," he said, taking me closer. I could see a gash in the chain links, about six feet high and pulled apart like tent flaps.

The ground was now dry despite the heavy rain in the night. Before the gap in the fence, the ground was churned up with footprints. I could also see marks just the other side and into the undergrowth.

I knew then that I wasn't looking at where someone had escaped.

Two people had been through here, but only one of them walking. The other had been dragged into the woods.

FORTY-ONE

We were still standing at the hole in the fence when Michael and Gabe approached us.

"What are you doing?" Michael asked.

"Just looking," I said. "Solomon was giving me a tour."

Michael scowled at the other man before speaking to me.

"Don't get any silly ideas, Thomas."

"Like what?"

He shrugged. "Anyway, we're here to fix it."

Gabe held up a roll of wire in one hand and a pair of pliers in the other.

"We should investigate," I said, "before you close it up."

"Investigate?"

"Find out what happened to Noah."

They all looked at me, concern in their eyes.

Gabe said, "What do you mean?"

I pointed to the marks on the ground. "Whoever went through here didn't go voluntarily. Are you sure none of the women are missing."

"They're all still here," Michael said.

"You're certain?"

"Yes!"

I nodded. "Then my conclusion is that it was Noah. Someone dragged Noah through the hole."

While they made various comments about the situation, I also thought something else: whoever pulled Noah through must have known the ground was wet. They must have known there would be the tell-tale drag marks.

I ducked through the gap in the fence and started looking at the ground. The others scrabbled after me and clustered on the far side.

"This way," I said, and headed into the trees. I could see footprints and judged it was a man carrying a heavy weight.

"What are you expecting?" Michael asked me.

"Nothing good."

"Why?"

"If Noah was leaving of his own free will, why pick here? Why not go through a gate? What's over the hill?"

"Nothing but more hills."

"No road?"

"Hills and trees, that's all," Michael said.

I nodded and kept going up a slope. Where the path rose steeply, I could see evidence that my heavy man had found an easier route.

We went up and up.

Gabe complained about the effort but stayed with us.

I stopped. On the ground was a pair of glasses. The same round ones I'd seen Noah wearing. Michael picked them up and stuffed them in his pocket without commenting.

We continued up the slope and the path turned as it avoided a massive rock. We went around and found the other side was flat and wide.

And it was covered with flies feasting. The rock was streaked with blood. Lots of it.

227

Someone behind me threw up.

I walked on and then tasted my own bile. Hidden from sight by a bush, I found blue-grey strips and black stuff. Guts, I realized.

I tore my eyes away from the horror and stepped back. All three men looked at me, their faces pale with shock.

"Was this Noah?" Gabe asked.

I nodded. "I'm afraid that won't be the worst of it."

"What?" Solomon managed to say.

"He was killed here. Now we have to find his body."

The ground was well trampled by the killer, but it didn't take me long to work out where he'd gone. The intestines were the clue. I realized they weren't complete, and after a few yards in the same direction, I found more, then a chunk of fly-infested liver, I think. Every few yards I found another piece of internal organ.

Michael saw the body before I did. It was hanging from a tree, naked and buzzing with flies. It dangled with arms outstretched, bound to tree branches like a man crucified.

I was expecting him to be disembowelled. What I hadn't expected was the stick in each eye. They were like insect antennae with black streaks that ran down his cheeks.

I breathed out long and hard.

"Jesus!" Solomon cursed.

Gabe chuckled and then apologized. "The pose," he said guiltily. I knew this was gallows humour and his way of coping, but Michael wasn't impressed.

"You're sick!"

Gabe hung his head.

Solomon said, "What do we do?"

"We get the police," I said.

"No," Michael said. "We get Daniel."

"If we aren't going to report it, we should cut him down," I said. "Does anyone have a knife?"

Michael pulled a flick knife from his pocket, spun it between his fingers then handed it to Gabe. "Cut him down."

"Why me? Why not Solly?"

"Because I said you," Michael said firmly. "Cut him down!"

It took a lot of sawing back and forth to cut the ropes, and after the first one, the body dangled grotesquely from one arm before Gabe got the second one cut.

I picked up a piece of the rope and felt its coarseness between my finger and thumb.

"What are you doing?" Michael asked, his voice tense.

"This is the same rope the women make, isn't it?"

Michael looked at it as I held the sample out. "I suppose."

I nodded.

With hard eyes locked on mine, he said, "Carry the body back."

I said nothing for a moment, thinking about rebellion. The idea of lugging a stinking dead body down the hill back to the commune wasn't the most appealing thing I could imagine.

Michael took the knife off Gabe and weighed it in his hand, looking at me, waiting. My eyes met his challenge but neither of us spoke. Then, to my surprise, he walked away, avoiding a confrontation.

"I'll expect to see the body at the bunker in half an hour."

I found two sturdy branches and stripped them, then removed my shirt. The other two copied me once they saw what I was doing. We threaded the arms along the branches and made a stretcher.

I took Noah's legs and they took an arm each. Rigor mortis hadn't set in yet and the body flopped onto the shirts.

When we lifted it up, the stretcher bent under Noah's weight, but it held, and together we carried him through the woods, down the hill back to the hole in the fence.

As we man-handled it to the other side, it struck me again that the killer had known he'd leave a trail. He'd deliberately left the scuffs, the glasses, blood on the rock, and then the crucified body for us to find.

And that made me think of one man: BlackJack.

FORTY-TWO

Scott "Slugger" Stevenson called Ash Carter's office and a woman answered.

"Is Ash Carter available?" he asked.

"No."

"Do you know when he'll be back?"

"No."

Slugger laughed. "You must be Madam Chau. He told me about your charm."

"How can I help you, Mr…?"

"Slugger. Tell him Slugger called."

"And what shall I tell Mr Carter you called regarding?"

"The body he came to see in Ipoh."

There was a pause on the line and he heard a sound like she was sucking air through her teeth—thinking probably. "Ah," she said finally, "Mr Stevenson. Of the PPF?"

"Correct."

"With the glass eye."

"I'd rather be thought of as a friend rather than by a physical attribute."

"So what can I tell your friend, Mr Stevenson?"

"When did you say he'll be back?"

"I didn't." She paused. "I don't know when he'll return. He's gone upcountry. The last time he called it was from a small town called Bandar Permaisuri, north of Terengganu."

Slugger scanned across the map, used his finger and found Terengganu on the east coast, almost the same latitude from where he was in Batu Gajah. A road cut across the mountains in the middle of the country. It explained a lot.

"Mr Stevenson, are you still there?"

Slugger realized he was just nodding to himself. "When Ash calls, tell him I found a Land Rover. I found information about the pipeline."

"The pipeline?"

"He'll understand. I think he's at one end and I'm at the other."

"Shall I ask him to call you?"

"No. When he calls you, find out how I can get hold of him. I'll call you again tomorrow."

Slugger ended the call and stared out of the window for a second. Did he dare go through with this? He'd intended to ask Carter what he thought, but this was the same damned case. Carter had followed leads to the east coast and Slugger had traced the connection in the west.

He'd promised Cindy that he'd call Carter the following day but he'd become fascinated by the code in the notebook and worked on it for two days. Now he understood. Major Chris Broom was part of the pipeline. He'd drive into the Highlands directly east towards Terengganu.

There he would meet the man who would hand him the latest shipment of gold. Broom would then pass it on in Kuala Lumpur, and two days later the money would make the reverse journey.

Broom didn't provide the contact's name but he did provide dates, times and locations. Once Slugger had figured out the code it had been simple.

The next one was tonight, and Slugger didn't need Carter's approval. No, he had every intention of making that rendezvous and finding out what was going on.

FORTY-THREE

The bunker turned out to be more of a pillbox. It was over by the tunnel and hidden by trees. I hadn't spotted it before but noted how well-trodden the earth was around it.

"What's it for?" I asked as we waited. We were still shirtless; none of us wanted to remove our clothes from the stretcher.

"Don't know," Solomon said. "It was from the war."

"Before the war," Gabe corrected. I thought he was going to say something else, but he swallowed any words and looked east.

Michael and Daniel appeared through the trees. I wondered if they'd come from Daniel's or Jeremiah's place.

"Thank you, men," Daniel said. "That'll be all."

I started to walk then hesitated. I wanted to say something. They knew Noah had been murdered but did they know about BlackJack?

Any one of these guys could be the killer. He probably didn't kill Noah straight off. The victim might have been lured outside, but he was most likely rendered unconscious first before being dragged and carried to the rock where he'd been killed and gutted.

Should I confess to knowing about BlackJack? If one of these men was the killer, I'd be making a mistake. I decided to say nothing. Michael glared at me, probably wondering why I was still standing there. Maybe for another reason. I gave him a thin smile and walked away.

Our shoes sounded particularly loud as we walked through the tunnel, no one speaking until we reached the other side.

I said, "You were all out last night. Who was with who?"

"I wasn't out," Solomon said.

Gabe said, "I was with Sam. Daniel, Michael and Noah were together at some point."

"What about Zach?"

I don't think Solomon got the implication, but Gabe did. He pursed his lips and shook his head.

"What?" Solomon said, stopping.

"He thinks one of us killed Noah." Gabe looked at me. "That's right isn't it?"

"It's a possibility."

"Why? Why would one of us do it?"

I shrugged. "You tell me, or at least think about it."

We started walking again and I could tell they were thinking, but neither said anything more.

I ate a good meal in the common room with all of the men except Daniel and Michael. I'd somehow got the impression that Shangri-La was alcohol-free. I was wrong. All of the men had bottles of beer with their cigarettes.

I declined both, which I could tell didn't impress my new colleagues.

Sam and Zach wanted the detail about Noah and what we'd found. I let Gabe talk while I watched everyone's faces.

They were sombre and tense but no one speculated, although Zach glanced at me a few times and I sensed malice.

Of the four of them, only Zach was lean. The others were out of condition with paunches and soft flesh. I couldn't imagine any of them were capable of hoisting a body up a tree, let alone carry it to the flat rock. Except for Zach. He may be sixty, but I figured years of hard work had left his muscles defined and taut.

Of the others, Daniel looked in reasonable condition. Neither he nor Michael had let themselves go, and despite, or maybe because of his shape, I suspected Michael was strong.

And then there was the giant, Jeremiah.

If there was one killer then I figured it was either Zach, Michael, Daniel or Jeremiah.

Sam disappeared early and took the label numbered "2" off its peg. I noticed that there was now a number "1" on the previously empty peg.

Safiya was waiting outside my room when I arrived after dinner. She bowed low, her hands clasped together as I approached.

"Master."

I raised her chin and looked into dead eyes. "You don't call me that. I'm going to get you out."

She blinked and stared up at me.

I opened my door and asked her to sit on the chair. I sat on the bed like I had when Solomon had chatted to me in here.

"I really am going to get you out. Get everyone out."

"How?"

"I'm working on it."

For the first time, her eyes softened and I could see even more of her sister in her. A beautiful girl, but with anguish behind those big brown eyes.

"Are you all right?"

She shook her head. "If you call being raped almost every day for a year being all right then I guess I am. You can never recover from that."

"It stopped after a year?"

"I was pregnant. There are plenty of girls, so the pregnant ones aren't so in demand."

"Your children—who's the father?"

"I don't know. It's not just one man. Daniel most likely, but it could have been any of them that were here then. So not Zachary or Noah. I had three children and then put a stop to it. Some of the women take that option. We also try to make ourselves look as unattractive as possible." She stroked her roughly cropped hair as an illustration. "They talk about fresh blood. They prefer the new girls they find, and it's bad for them—but not as bad as it used to be."

"Why?"

"It was before my time, but there are some who were here then. The men used to have parties. They'd abuse the girls, cut them, that sort of thing."

I shook the image from my head. These guys were depraved.

"I'm sorry," I said.

"It's not your fault."

"When I first met you, you told me the children were safe and being educated. You said you were fine with being separated from them."

"No mother is happy without her children."

"So you were lying."

"Of course. I didn't know you. It could have been a trick."

237

"It's not a trick. I really met your sister and promised I'd help."

"I haven't seen her for so long. She was just a kid when I left. What is she like? How is she?"

"Pretty, like you. She has a job in a café in Bandar Permaisuri." I didn't know what else to say. I didn't know the girl except that she worried about her sister and was desperate to get her out.

"That close?" Her eyes widened.

"She's been looking for you. But the locals won't help."

She nodded. "They have an arrangement. I've heard them talk about it. None of the girls they bring in here are locals. You know, I didn't choose to come here. I was picked up, held for a day and then bundled into a truck one night. There were fifteen of us and they brought us here. We were some of the first, and the drugs were stronger in the beginning. We know they make us compliant, but once you accept your situation, it gets easier—and we are safe here. Safe from the war."

"Your sister's safe too," I said. "Yes, there's a guerrilla war, but it's really between the communists and the British establishment. The bandits target enterprises like tin mines and plantations. The general public is safe."

She nodded and smiled.

I said, "I need to know where the explosives are."

"Explosives?"

"I've been told the town hall is set to explode if Shangri-La is attacked."

"But you said—"

"Jeremiah fears the army." I didn't bother explaining Jeremiah's link with the terrorists and the gold, and she just accepted what I told her.

She said, "He'll be hard to defeat. He has magical powers."

"No, he doesn't," I said.

"The town hall…" she started to say.

"Tell me, Safiya."

She shook her head and looked away.

I waited.

If she was going to tell me, she didn't get the chance. The bell calling us to the town hall interrupted our chat.

FORTY-FOUR

This time, I sat at the front with the other ex-soldiers. Seven chairs. Seven of us with me on the end sitting next to Solomon. He'd moved up in the hierarchy and Noah's place had gone. Zach was on the stage tonight, now that I'd been accepted. He sat next to Michael before the sheet. Daniel sat on the other side like before.

The same magic trick was performed. It had been hard to see from the back of the room. It was harder from the end of the line of ex-soldiers. The white sheet descended. One second there was nothing but a sheet hanging from the ceiling. Then it jerked up and Jeremiah stood there, looking like Jesus, his arms open as though accepting the adoration of the congregation.

I thought about Noah, tied up in the tree. I glanced along the line of men but couldn't see their faces. Were they thinking the same thing? In death, had Noah been deliberately posed like Jeremiah?

Jeremiah preached his mix of religion and philosophy but I only half-listened to his nonsense. I was looking for signs of explosives or perhaps wires.

I saw nothing obvious. The walls were plastered and painted on the inside.

Behind me was a rope that was attached to the bell. I'd glanced up as we'd trooped in, hoping to see into the bell tower. I couldn't. There was just a brass ring in the ceiling were the rope passed through.

Jeremiah did his reading from *Lost Horizons* again. I figured this was his Bible, although it was just the section following the one he'd read yesterday. Maybe it was just a story and he didn't intend any interpretation, because he certainly gave none.

Yesterday he'd talked about truth, concluding that the second phase may mean violence and war, which came before acceptance.

This time he talked about a Greek philosopher called Parmenides, who had written a poem called *The way of truth*.

"Reality is singular," Jeremiah said. "Existence is timeless and uniform. Being is being. There is nothing else, no other truth. What we sense is just interpretation: our eyes deceive us, our ears deceive us. Our minds create a duality that doesn't exist."

I looked at the faces of the girls and women before me. Most of them appeared mesmerized by Jeremiah. Did his words make sense to them or was it the drugs— or maybe the desire for their fix?

Jeremiah continued: "Good and evil, truth and untruth are mere human concepts. We must transcend this duality, create order out of chaos. And we will live forever."

Once again, people rose on command and filed forward to receive communion. We were first, and I had a rag in my pocket, prepared to spit the liquid out. It had struck me that the ex-soldiers couldn't do their jobs if they were hooked on an opiate, and I noticed that Daniel filled their cups from a different jug.

When I accepted the liquid from Jeremiah, I tasted normal wine.

I returned to my seat and watched the queue. As Safiya came forward I tried to catch her eye, but she didn't look at me and accepted communion like everyone else.

When the congregation settled once more, Jeremiah concluded with a chant that I think came from Hinduism:

"What one god set sacrifice in man here?
"Who set in him truth? Who untruth?
"Whence death? Whence the immortal?"

It made no sense to me except that the reference to immortality fit with his earlier statement about living forever and of course *Lost Horizons* and its theme of eternal youth.

The ex-soldiers were the last out of the town hall doors, leaving Jeremiah behind. He ended with a trance-like pose, face raised to the ceiling, arms out wide.

I had hoped to see where he went, how he got out, but he hadn't moved by the time the doors closed and then locked behind us.

I followed the men to the common room and this time we didn't have Zach but Michael joined us. He declined the beer and announced that there'd be no talk of Noah.

"Jeremiah always said it wasn't safe beyond the fence. Now we know it's true." He looked from man to man and elicited a nod from each. I shrugged.

"Good," he said. "Now, who's in for a game of cards?"

I didn't move, and while the others clustered around a table, Gabe approached me with a handful of darts.

"Do you play?" He nodded to the dartboard at the far end of the room.

"Sure," I said, and joined him.

We played two games of 501 and he beat me comfortably. During the third game, I said, "Where's Zach?"

"He'll be with a girl."

"Which one?" I threw a dart, and for a horrible second, I wondered whether Zach would deliberately choose Safiya.

"You look worried."

I threw another dart.

Gabe said, "He may not like you, but he wouldn't take your girl. It's one of the rules. Zach may be different, but he wouldn't go against that rule."

I was about to ask what he meant when Michael called out.

"Enough with the darts. I want you playing cards. Now!"

Gabe shrugged with a wry smile and we joined the card game. I was given a pile of poker chips. They were made of wood and looked identical to the one I'd found in Jenkins's room.

I'm a good poker player with an excellent memory for cards, but not this evening. And these guys weren't playing poker or one if its derivatives. The game was Newmarket, where the men bet on which card could be played during the round: jack of spades, queen of clubs, king of diamonds or ace of hearts. My mind was elsewhere, not helped by the cards.

Jack of spades. BlackJack.

What had happened to the missing ex-soldier, Noah? Was there really a killer around and was he one of these guys? Was this thing connected or had separate cases overlapped, like I'd overlapped and flipped from Jenkins to Harwood.

I thought about the way Noah had been displayed. Who was I kidding? This was the same case.

Michael was watching me closely with open hostility.

"I'm no good at cards," I lied. "Good job we're playing for chips."

"They're like an IOU," he said with a smirk. "Once we get some real money we can settle up. Ten bob a chip."

I smiled, not sure whether he was serious or not.

Gabe laughed, presumably at the look on my face. "Doubting Thomas!"

Michael nodded. "Good choice of name for you."

"I prefer Tom."

"Not a problem. We don't call Gabe, Gabriel."

"Thank goodness," Gabe said.

I said, "So, the chips... I don't have that sort of money."

"That's the point," Solomon said. "Now you're one of the team you'll be wealthy."

"Pro rata," Michael said. "Based on time served. That's only fair."

"How much?" I asked.

"A lot," Sam said.

We continued playing cards and I continued to lose. It was my deal and I hesitated. "So when? How long before I become rich?"

The other three looked at Michael, who gave me a thin smile. "Soon enough, but it's not something you should be worried about."

I was about to ask him what I *should* be worried about when Zach came in, got a beer and pulled up a chair.

"Good one?" Gabe asked him.

"Always!" He blew smoke in my direction. "She's a pretty one, that Safiya."

Gabe looked at me, his eyes wide.

244

I shook my head. Zach was trying to wind me up. I doubted he'd dare go against one of Jeremiah's rules.

"Let's change the game," I said, smiling back at Zach. "Let's play twenty-one."

FORTY-FIVE

Before I could gauge a reaction, the door opened and Daniel came in.

"We're about to play twenty-one," I said cheerfully, watching his face. However, he just strode in, ignoring me.

He raised his chin towards Michael, like a signal. "We're going earlier tonight."

"Who'd you want?"

Daniel scanned the men around the table. "You, Gabriel and Solomon."

The three men stood, and I thought Sam and Zach looked disappointed.

Michael said, "Tally up the chips, Sam," and strode over to the metal cabinet. He used a key, opened it up and took out three revolvers and two rifles. Gabe and Solomon took a revolver and rifle each. Then the four men went out, leaving a strange silence behind after their heavy footsteps.

Sam lit up a cigarette. "Bastard!"

"What's the matter?" I asked.

He shook his head like he didn't understand. "Why them? They don't deserve it. Chuckles and Charley"—I figured he was referring to Gabe and Solomon, in that order—"What have they done? What have we done?"

"An important job?" I asked.

Sam delayed his response as he sucked on the cigarette, and I thought he was about to say "Yes", but Zach spoke first.

"All jobs are important," he said. "Anyway, I'm pretty sure Daniel wanted us here to keep an eye on you. I think he couldn't trust you with the Two Stooges, so he left us here."

"Oh, right," Sam said, sounding convinced.

I said, "You don't need to keep an eye on me."

Zach leaned forward. "I don't like you, Carter!"

"I'm called Thomas or Tom now, remember?"

"If you're really one of us."

Sam said, "Daniel's accepted him."

"Well, I haven't. It's all too convenient." He scrutinized me. "So tell us again how you stumbled across our little village?"

I thought of ignoring his question but relented and repeated the story I'd told Michael when I first arrived. I said I'd heard they'd created a paradise and travelled through Malaya looking for it.

"How did you travel around?"

"Hitchhiked."

"For how long?"

"A month, give or take."

"You didn't look like you'd been on the road for a month. Your clothes looked too clean and you've no beard."

I'd worried about that. I knew I didn't look like a hobo and had thought I'd got away with it. Apparently not.

"I look after myself," I said. "It's called self-respect. It's something that sailor boys find hard to understand."

Zach jerked upright, his chair falling over.

247

Sam laughed. "How did you know he was navy?"

"The tattoos," I said. I stayed seated and relaxed. Zach would have to get across the table to reach me, which would give me plenty of time to react. Plus, my upward momentum would add to my uppercut.

Zach didn't move. He just glared at me, willing me to make a move, I guess.

"What did you serve on?" I asked him, as though genuinely interested.

"I was merchant navy in the last war," he said. "North Atlantic. Too old for the Royal Navy by then."

"You served in the Great War too?" I asked.

"I was a young lad on a destroyer. HMS *Shark*."

"One of the boats that went down," Sam said. "He was involved in the Battle of Jutland. Only six of them survived, rescued by a Danish steamer. Isn't that right, Zach?"

Zach was walking over to a cabinet where the beer was kept. He got a bottle and opened it.

"I'm impressed," I said.

"Doesn't change anything," he said, looking at me hard. "I still don't like you. You're an officer and your story stinks." Then he walked out of the door.

"Just you and me then," I said to Sam. "Shall we play blackjack?"

No reaction.

"Whist or darts?" he said. "You choose."

I dealt the cards for whist.

"So why is the northern compound called Cham?" I asked as we played.

"Easier to say than *Xiamian*," he said.

I nodded. "Funny name."

"Old Chinese name," he said. "I think it means below, although it's north. Most people would say a northern place was above, wouldn't they?"

I dealt some cards. "Who do you think killed Noah?"

He shook his head.

"You must have a theory."

"A local?" he opined. "I'm sure there are people out there who don't like us."

"Enough to kill one of you like that?"

He shrugged.

"I've got to ask," I said. "I don't know everyone like you do. Isn't it possible that it's one of the men here did it?"

He was about to play a card and stopped. "Who?"

"I'm asking you."

"You're just trying to distract me. You must have noticed Gabe does that when we're playing cards."

"It's a serious question, Sam. Someone not only murdered Noah, but he gutted him and strung him up. He was displayed for us to find."

"To scare us, you mean?"

"Possibly. Could it be one of the other men?"

"It could be you."

"Yes, it could," I said. "But it's not. And it isn't you."

"Definitely not."

"What about Daniel? Could he do it?"

"Why?"

"I don't know. What's going on tonight? Everyone was expecting the job but it was brought forward."

Now Sam said, "I don't know. Daniel doesn't talk to me. I just do what I'm told."

"Is it the pipeline job tonight?"

"I heard you knew about that. Yes, twice a week we do the trip over the mountains."

"And trade the gold."

"Yes, but we shouldn't be talking about it."

"Why not?"

249

"Because Michael said not to tell you too much. Not yet. When they trust you, then you'll get a set of keys and your gun back."

We played some more cards and he got tipsy on the beer.

I broached another subject: "Solly told me about Jeremiah's shrine and the ceremonies."

He looked uncomfortable. "That was a long time ago."

"And?"

He put his cards down, mid-game, and got up. "And I don't think it's a conversation we're having."

Walking over to the pegs, he took number "3" and left me alone in the common room.

I found Safiya waiting outside my room. She opened my door and I walked in.

"Was Zach here earlier?"

"Yes."

"Did he bother you?"

She shook her head and looked surprised at my question, which was a relief.

She said, "Is there anything I can get for you?"

"Nothing. Thanks," I said, removing my shirt. "Except for clean clothes."

"Of course. You'll get clean clothes twice a day, master."

I shook my head. "I'm not your master. Call me Ash."

My shorts came off and I handed them to her.

"Would you like me to remove my clothes?" she asked, her voice soft and quiet.

"No," I said, shocked. "No!"

She nodded, and I think I saw a slight smile of relief.

★ ★ ★

Cindy held Slugger's hand. "Don't go," she said.

He'd confessed that he'd worked out the code in Broom's notebook and that Ash Carter hadn't been in his office.

"I need to," he said.

"No, you don't, Scott. It's not your job."

"For me. I need to do this for me. I love being here with you, but the protection force stuff isn't exactly challenging—"

"We don't need challenging."

He pulled her in close. "Your job is satisfying. You're helping... saving people every day. My job is about driving around and making sure the bandits don't attack. And quite honestly that's boring."

"But a vital role," she said desperately.

"Is it? There haven't been any incidents for three months."

"That's because of you and your team."

"It doesn't change matters," he said. "If you sat in the surgery all day every day and no one was sick, would you feel any job satisfaction?"

"That's not the same."

He said, "All I'm saying is that I need a bit of spice."

"And I'm not enough?"

"I love you."

"Then marry me," she said, and he spluttered. "What, you don't want to marry me?"

"Of course I do!" he said, swallowing his surprise. "I was just waiting for the right moment to ask."

She held him at arm's length and looked expectant. "Now I'm asking you."

He laughed. "Then I accept."

251

"Mrs Cindy Stevenson," she said. "It has a nice ring to it."

He laughed again. "Of course. We'll go to KL and pick out a ring at the weekend."

"Then we should talk about the future. If you don't want to stay with the PPF, that's fine. I'll even leave Malaya if that's what you want. Which suits me because this is no place to bring up our four children."

"Four?"

"I've already picked out their names."

"Of course you have!"

They hugged and kissed but then he pulled away.

"Tell me you're not still going!"

"I have to."

"Where is it?"

"A place called Gua Musang. It's in the Highlands."

She shook her head and tears ran down her pretty cheeks.

"I won't be long, darling. When I come back you can tell me all about our four kids."

FORTY-SIX

The others hadn't returned, and I slipped out of the bunkhouse after checking that Sam and Zach were asleep.

When I emerged on the far side of the tunnel, I darted left into the trees and listened hard. I believed Michael, Solomon, and Gabe were out working, but I had no idea whether Daniel and Jeremiah had left or stayed.

I also had no weapon except for a hefty torch, and I had every reason to believe that there was a killer about.

After a few minutes, I risked moving north and first came to the bunker where we'd left Noah's body. In the pale moonlight, the squat concrete structure gave me the shivers. It would make an ideal place for someone to lie in wait. I had an urge to shine my torch inside and check, but I resisted. Better to continue with doubts than broadcast my position to the killer.

I gave it a wide berth, keeping my noise to a minimum, and continued north. Halfway to the upper gate, I spotted another building through the trees. I'd expected it. This was the school I'd been told about.

I moved in close and circled the single-storey, flat-roofed building. The concrete looked old, like the bunker's, and I found only one window and a solitary door.

Glancing in through the window I glimpsed a row of beds. They looked empty but I couldn't be sure. Again I wanted to use my torch but resisted. Instead, I tested the door and found it locked.

Why lock a school door? I wondered.

There was nothing more I could do there so I continued until I came to the generator. Now I risked flicking the torchlight over the fence behind it.

As promised, Harwood had cut the wire and used short strips to hold it back together. That's what I would have done and it's what Noah's killer should have done. But he'd wanted us to find the body.

Unclipping the wires, I squeezed through and made my way towards the track.

As I passed the garage, I checked and noted that both a truck and the jeep were out. Then I crossed the bridge and walked towards the main road. Once there, I turned right and jogged to the crossroads.

We'd prearranged a signal and he flashed his headlights in response to my torch. A minute later I was in the passenger seat of Harwood's jeep.

"They've not gone out tonight," he said. "What's going on?"

"They went early."

"Damn, I missed them! Why leave earlier than usual?"

"I don't know, but they've been unnerved. You said Noah had talked to you. Well, he's dead."

Even in the darkness, I read surprise on Harwood's face. "What? How?"

I gave him the details and ended with: "It bears all the hallmarks of our killer. BlackJack."

Harwood blew out air. "Christ! Maybe it is one of them and they're cleaning house."

"It could be."

"Then watch out, you could be next."

I nodded.

He said, "Have you found the explosives?"

"Not yet. Have you called Ambrose?"

"Yes."

"And he's on his way?"

"I didn't speak directly to him. I left a message last night—early hours—after we spoke."

"He'll be on his way," I said. "He'll be here soon. Listen and watch out for my signal, because this is happening sometime tomorrow."

* * *

BlackJack tracked Carter as he moved through the trees. He made sure the ex-SIB officer disappeared into the tunnel before he turned back.

The bunker was his target. He'd been hiding there when Carter went past the first time. Now he was sure the coast was clear, he returned.

Once inside, he located the hatch and lifted it. A second later he was descending a ladder into the darkness.

FORTY-SEVEN

Slugger checked his watch: twenty minutes before one in the morning. He was early. Thirty-five minutes early. Would they be on time? It was a long drive through the mountains. The timing could vary a lot. Maybe they'd changed the schedule. Maybe this was a dumb idea after all. His second in command back at the PPF had said as much.

"You need backup—me, a couple of the men..." Cranfield had said.

"For what?"

"In case it goes tits up."

Slugger had shaken his head. He didn't need to explain but he did anyway. "The plan is to become accepted," he'd said. "They spot anyone else, they'll know I'm not kosher. If I'm to get any intel this needs to seem legit."

"Intel? You're talking like a bloody MP!"

"That's because I'm helping one." He could have added that he liked the excitement. Working with Carter provided an adrenaline rush he didn't get from his protection force job.

Cranfield raised his eyebrows and pulled some kind of quirky smile.

"And I can take care of myself," Slugger added.

"You're nuts."

Now that Slugger sat in Broom's Land Rover on the crest of a hill in total darkness except for the wash of stars across the heavens, he wondered if he was a little nuts. He could be home, cuddled up with his gorgeous wife-to-be instead of sitting out in the middle of nowhere expecting God-knows-what.

A distant light drew his attention like a homing beacon. It swung and bobbed and disappeared and then reappeared. A vehicle's headlights. It was about a mile off, on the road that snaked down from the hill cutting through the trees. But it couldn't be them.

This vehicle was approaching from the west—the way he'd come.

Slugger watched anyway, mesmerized by the way the lights appeared and disappeared in the dark.

Closer and closer.

Slugger ducked down. The last thing he wanted was someone else stopping. It might scare off the men with the gold.

The vehicle crested a rise. Two hundred yards away. One hundred. Fifty. It slowed suddenly then stopped.

A minute passed and then the vehicle rolled forward slowly and halved the distance before stopping again.

Headlights flashed. Off on. Off on. Off on.

Slugger waited a beat. This was it. They were here. He'd just assumed they'd come from the east. But they'd come the same way as him.

Now or never.

He fired up the engine, turned on the lights and swung the jeep around. Now facing the other way, his headlights showed the front of the other vehicle: a covered Land Rover.

Jesus! A thought suddenly struck him. What if these were Chinese? What if Broom had been dealing with the damned bandits? He breathed in and blew out slowly.

Why were they just sitting there? Were they discussing the situation? Were they expecting him to get out?

Just as Slugger started to open his door, the other Land Rover moved forward again.

Maybe it's part of the routine, he thought.

It stopped ahead, across the road from him, and he saw two people inside. They both got out, one held a rifle, the other a revolver. But they weren't Chinese. He could immediately see they were two white guys wearing identical dark clothes, almost military-style. Soldiers. It made sense. Broom was army; these guys were army.

Here we go! Slugger muttered to himself and opened his door.

He stood in the truck's beams and held out his arms. No weapon.

The two guys had separated. Not a single target. The guy with the revolver stepped forward. He had a soft round face with a grey beard. "Who are you?" he challenged.

"The new man."

"New man?"

"The replacement."

"Who are you replacing?"

"Broom," Slugger said, trying to sound slightly irritated by the questioning. "The boss said something had happened to him, said I had to meet you here tonight. I'm the new man."

"OK." He said it slowly, like it was more of a question.

Slugger noticed the second man moving slowly, positioning himself to Slugger's left, hard to see.

258

"Let's get on with it!" Slugger said with more irritation in his tone.

The man in front shook his head. "You'll understand we need to be cautious."

"Of course. It's gold after all."

"Solly, check the jeep."

Slugger glanced left and saw the second man move. Now he circled all the way behind and looked into the back.

"Empty," Solly finally said. Slugger thought he heard relief. The jeep was for collecting goods off these guys, not exchanging.

The man in front nodded. "All right. Let's get this gold loaded."

"You can put the gun down," Slugger said. "We're on the same side."

"Sure." The man lowered his gun and smiled. "Come round the back and help us with the load."

Slugger walked over to the other vehicle and followed the first guy around the back. The guy hesitated, glanced left and right and then unclipped the rear cover.

In the darkness, it took a second for Slugger to register that the rear was empty. It took another second to realize his problem—which was too long. He swivelled just as something big and hard slammed into the side of his head.

FORTY-EIGHT

"Who was that?" I asked as Safiya brought me a breakfast of fruit and tea. I'd heard someone in boots walk down the steps outside.

"Master Zach," she said.

"What time did the others get back?"

"I don't think they're back yet, which is unusual. Twice a week they go out for a long time but they're normally back by now."

And they left early, I thought. Something has definitely changed.

"I need to find out about the explosives. Did you ask the other women?"

"No one knows anything. Perhaps they are in the north—the other side of the tunnel."

"Have you been there?"

"We're not allowed through the tunnel. It's forbidden."

I nodded. Having the explosives there didn't make sense unless this was all about the children. Blow up the school rather than the town hall. Could that be Jeremiah's plan?

"I saw the school last night," I said. "How many children have there been?"

She looked up, thinking. "Thirty-two. No, wait. Thirty-three."

"Not counting the young ones in the nursery?"

"Yes."

I nodded and said nothing.

"Your tea will go cold," she said.

"I'm getting you all out, tonight."

Her eyes went wide. "How?"

"My friends are coming. Don't say a word," I said. "Not yet. Just be prepared. When the time comes, I'll tell you what to do."

She nodded, and I couldn't read whether she was excited or afraid. Probably both, I decided.

When she spoke again, she said, "You know I told you about them getting new girls?"

"Fresh blood?"

"The new ones they kidnap and bring here. Every now and again they go out and come back with a girl or two." Her voice trembled. "Those poor kids."

I nodded. "They'll be rescued too. Don't worry."

Her eyes brimmed now. "Yes but it's already happened. Is already happening."

"What?"

"You don't know?" When I shook my head, she continued: "They hold them in the huts. There are three of them."

"Yes. They put me in hut one the first night."

"That'll have been their little joke. They didn't visit you there did they?"

I remembered hearing Gabe laugh before Michael had told Solomon to take me to hut one. And Solomon had been going to tell me but had stopped himself.

The numbered pegs in the Common Room!

"Where's Zach gone?" I asked, heading for the door.

"He'll be in hut three."

I was barefoot and slipped on the wet ground as I ran to the huts. Even before I got there, I could hear the cries.

The door flew open as I kicked it and I was inside before it bounced off the side wall. Zach was there. Naked and on top of a girl. She was shaking beneath him and howling like a wounded animal.

I didn't stop. I lunged, wrapped my arm around his neck and pulled. I kept on pulling him, out of the hut onto the earth. Once there, I thrust him forwards so that his face thudded into the ground.

For an old man, he was surprisingly agile. One second he was prostrate on the floor, the next he'd sprung up and was swinging at me, screaming like a banshee.

A fist flailed past as I stepped out of his reach. Then I stepped back in with a straight left. He yelped and came at me again. This time I hit him harder, and when his nose exploded with blood, he dropped to his knees.

"You busted my nose!" he spluttered.

I walked past him and into the hut. The girl cowered in the corner of the room, hugging her knees. She looked about fifteen or sixteen, and I couldn't speak. Instead, I removed my shirt, handed it to her and stepped back outside.

Safiya was there, staring at Zach and staring at me.

I nodded to the hut and noticed the wooden label pegged beside the door. Notification that one of the men was inside. They selected them from the common room and took their turns with the fresh blood.

"Take care of her," I said. "And the girl in hut two."

Zach had blood all over his face, in a line down over his lips and beard.

"You'll regret that," he snarled nasally.

"I don't think so," I said, watching Safiya lead the poor girl away. "You started it."

262

"I didn't!"

"Your word against mine."

Zach pulled himself up and spat blood on my feet. He took a step towards the hut, presumably aiming to retrieve his clothes.

"No," I said, barring his way. "No one goes in the huts anymore. Go and get cleaned up and get some new clothes."

He snorted and walked in the direction of the town square, looking naked and pathetic. I hoped he felt uncomfortable, although I doubted he'd feel the shame I wished for him.

I picked up Zach's shirt from hut three and, after breaking hut two's locked door, gave it to the frightened girl inside.

Ideally, I'd have set fire to the three huts, but then Harwood might think that was the signal and I wasn't ready. Not yet. So I broke the hut doors off their hinges instead. At least now nobody could lock a girl inside.

Satisfied, I returned to the bunkhouse, where I found Solomon looking agitated.

"You're back," I said without a better greeting. "Have you seen Zach?"

"No," he said. "Have you seen Michael or Daniel?"

"Weren't they with you?"

"No, it was just me and Gabe. They went off in the jeep. We took the truck and something happened."

"What?"

I followed him and Gabe to the tunnel and through to Cham, then beside the track through the upper gates to the garage. The Land Rover was parked inside on its own.

"I made an executive decision," Solomon said, trying to smile.

"A mistake more like it," Gabe snapped.

"What?" I said, starting to feel uncomfortable.

Gabe had his hand on the rear flap. He unclipped and lifted it up.

On the floor, a large man had been squeezed in.

I recognized Slugger immediately.

"He's dead," Solomon said. "He's bloody dead."

FORTY-NINE

For a good minute I couldn't speak. My hand shaking, I reached in and checked for a pulse, desperately hoping Solomon was mistaken.

Slugger, my friend, was definitely dead.

Eventually, I forced myself to say, "What happened?"

"You know about the pipeline, right?" Gabe said. "Well we were doing the run, only the plan had changed. Daniel said we'd be meeting a new man in a new place."

"That's why we had to leave early," Solomon said. "It was further than we normally go."

"Anyway, on the way back, we're coming up to the old meeting place and there's this car there."

"A Land Rover," Solomon added.

"Whatever. We should have just driven on, but Solly decided to find out who it was."

"And it was this big chap. He claimed he was Broom's replacement—Broom was the one we used to meet. But he wasn't."

"We panicked a bit," Gabe said.

"No, we didn't. You hit him too hard!"

"I thought if I knocked him out, Daniel and Michael would be pleased. We could question him. Find out what he was doing there."

"But he's not answering any questions now, is he?"

"You should never have stopped in the first place!"

I listened to them argue, too concerned for themselves to notice my shock. I had no idea how Slugger had worked out their plan—their old plan—but he had, and he'd taken it upon himself to take Broom's place.

I felt like screaming at him. *Why didn't you tell me? Why didn't you have backup?*

Instead, I composed myself and said, "We've got a problem. I recognize him."

"Who is he?"

"He's military police," I lied. "He's trouble."

"Oh God!" Solomon moaned.

"There'll be more, and Daniel will be furious that you brought him here. You'll be for it. Both of you. You've put the whole operation in jeopardy."

Solomon put his head in his hands, and Gabe asked, "What can we do?"

"Get rid of the body before anyone finds out."

I could see Gabe thinking.

"Bury him quickly," I said.

"There's a couple of shovels in the garage," Gabe said. He was already moving and swung up into the cab. Solomon ran round the other side and I got in the back with Slugger.

I had two aims: I didn't want the commune going into lockdown right before I tried to get the women and children out. My other objective was to preserve Slugger's body so that I could retrieve it later.

We buried him behind the garage and agreed that we'd tell no one about the stop or the dead cop. On the way back through the tunnel, Gabe suddenly asked, "Why?"

"Why what?"

"Why did you help us back there, Tom?"

"Because I have a secret of my own. I know what you did and I want you to back me up."

"What did you do?"

"I had a fight with Zach. If anyone asks, I want you to say he started it. Remember he threatened to deck me yesterday?"

"Yeah, he did," Gabe agreed.

"So you came back, parked, walked back and saw him attack me over by the three huts. We had a squabble about one of the girls and he went berserk."

"He can do that," Solomon said.

"Why?" Gabe asked.

"I didn't know the system and we went for the same girl. Like I said, he went crazy and smashed the doors open then he went for me."

"Serves him right!" Solomon said. "He's never really been one of us."

I said, "He'll claim it was me, but I need you to back me up. I was just defending myself."

"Deal!" Gabe said, and shook my hand. "We stick to our stories."

After showering and a change of clothes, we hit the common room and played darts. Zach didn't appear. The clouds opened and rain pounded the windows and roof.

"Who's doing the patrol today?" I asked eventually.

They both looked unsure, before Gabe said, "Michael didn't say." Then they looked relieved as I volunteered.

"How do I get a rifle?" I asked, looking at the gun locker.

"Get it from Michael or Daniel," Gabe said.

"You don't have a key?"

"Not to the locker. You beat Zach, I'm sure you can take care of yourself."

I raised my fists like a pugilist and they grinned.

267

"I'll just do a circuit," I said. "Won't stay out there too long."

I dashed into the rain as though running for cover, although the rain was all the cover I needed. I figured that the other men—wherever they were—wouldn't be out in this deluge. And quite right too. Within seconds, I was soaked through with my hair plastered to my skull.

I kept to the trees for as much protection as possible and headed for the town square.

I could see women in the workshop and in the blocks further down. I could also see them ahead under the cover of the cookhouse. But I wasn't going that way.

My target was the town hall.

First I tried the big wooden doors on the off chance they weren't locked, but they were. Then I went around the building, checking the ground and the walls for anything buried. I was looking for signs of the explosives, and circumnavigated the building twice, but found nothing.

If there were explosives, they would be inside, probably under the floor. But I couldn't get inside. The doors looked sturdy and I didn't want to attract too much attention. I'd find it hard to explain why I'd broken the doors open.

I stopped for lunch and ate on my own by the cookhouse. The whole time I sat and stared at the town hall and thought. I remembered what Mr Wu had done, setting fire to my office, and a plan quickly formed. I might not be able to find the explosives but I could use them to my advantage. Providing I did it before Jeremiah got everyone inside, I could set fire to the place. It would destroy his weapon and serve as another signal to the army, which was surely here by now.

The cookhouse had a giant oven. That would be my source. I could get diesel from the generator. If I couldn't find a barrel, I would soak something in the fuel and set fire to that.

I collected a bundle of towels from the shower block and made my way to the bunkhouse. There I collected Jenkins's rucksack and stuffed the towels inside.

The tunnel was locked when I got there. I went to take the key from my pocket then hesitated. Gabe and Solomon hadn't locked it. Which meant someone else had.

"Thomas!"

I spun around. Sam ran towards me. "You're wanted."

"Who by?"

"Michael."

FIFTY

"What were you doing?" Michael snapped. We were face to face, and he reminded me of a pub brawler, not fast or effective, but with presence. He'd be in anyone's face no matter how big they were.

Everyone bar Daniel and Jeremiah were in the common room and all eyes were on me. Zach had a patch over his nose and his eyes were already starting to discolour.

"I was patrolling," I said innocently.

"In the pouring rain?"

"What difference does the weather make? You were a soldier. You know that."

His eyes acknowledged my argument, but then he said, "Give your bag to Sam."

I handed it over.

Sam pulled out three towels. He looked surprised. I guess he'd expected a getaway kit or at least a change of clothes.

"Towels!" he said unnecessarily.

Michael said, "What are they for?"

"Drying."

"Don't be a smart arse!"

I shrugged. "No, seriously, they were for drying me off as I patrolled. I thought it was a good idea."

Gabe and Solomon raised their eyebrows, as if they agreed with my logic.

Don't be on my side too soon, guys, I thought.

Michael clenched his teeth. "Can I trust you, Thomas?"

"Yes, sir."

"Why did you attack Zach?"

"Broke my bloody nose," Zach grumbled.

"Self-defence," I said, relaxed. "He attacked me."

"Lying sod!" Zach said.

"Just because you lost, doesn't mean you didn't throw the first punch!" I said.

He shook his head and snorted. "Why would I have done that?"

"Because you had a stupid issue with me. Because you wanted to prove you were better than me. It's a hierarchy thing. You're one down from Michael and I'm a threat to your position."

"You're not buying this are you, boss?" Zach asked Michael.

Now I looked at the Two Stooges as Zach had called them last night. Solomon swallowed but Gabe spoke.

"Solly and I saw it," he said.

"What?" Michael asked. "What did you see?"

"The fight," Solomon said, finding his voice.

Gabe continued: "We saw Zach going berserk, slamming the hut doors."

"The girls ran off," Solomon said, and I was impressed with his improvisation.

Zach started to speak but was cut off.

"Shut up!" Michael shouted at him. Then to Solomon: "Who threw the first punch?"

For a heartbeat, I thought he'd let me down. He swallowed, licked his lips and said, "I saw Zach attack him. Tom just... Like he said, it was self-defence."

"What?" Zach glared at Solomon, who looked away. "You bloody liar!"

Gabe said, "It's what we saw, that's all. Maybe we saw wrong."

Zach started to shake his head but stopped. I figured it made his broken nose hurt. "You—"

"Enough!" Michael stopped him again, and for a second time, I was impressed at his control over these men. "Fifty-fifty," he said. "Shake hands and forget about it. These things happen, and I'm not putting up with a pair of squabbling kids."

"But look at me!" Zach pleaded. "Look what he did to my nose."

"You got beaten," Michael said. "That's all. You had a fight, now lick your wounds and move on."

I held out my hand. Zach looked at it scornfully.

"Zach!" Michael bellowed.

He reached out and touched my hand rather than shook it, then grabbed a beer and sat alone looking out at the pouring rain.

"Right, lads, who's ready to lose some more money?" Michael swung into a chair and pulled out a pack of playing cards.

Everyone except Zach gathered around the table.

"Blackjack," I said, studying Michael's face in particular.

"Newmarket," he said without a flinch.

Damn. He was either a great actor or the killer was someone else.

We played game after game and the rain eased. Zach joined us briefly, but a few hands later he said his nose hurt so he was going for a lie-down.

I'd been wondering whether my plan could still work. Could I soak some towels in diesel and set fire to the town hall? But now Zach was abroad, I doubted I could risk being spotted again.

Minutes after he left, Safiya came into the common room with some other women and served us lunch. I exchanged glances with her and hoped she understood.

"Need a piss," I said once the men started eating.

I got up and found her waiting for me outside.

"Watch out for Zach. He might see you as a way of getting revenge."

She nodded.

"How are the two girls?" I asked.

"Distressed, but grateful you released them." She shrugged. "However, we expect they'll be put back. You can't stand up to the whole lot of them."

"I don't need to," I said. "We're getting everyone out of here."

"When?"

"Do you trust all of the other women?"

Her hesitation told me everything. Despite this, she said, "I think so."

"Which means you can't, so don't tell anyone. Not yet anyway."

She nodded. "So when?"

"Tonight," I said. "We go tonight at the latest."

The common room door opened and Michael took a pace towards me.

FIFTY-ONE

Michael looked at me hard, and for a second I wondered whether he'd overheard us.

Safiya bowed and walked away.

"There better be no trouble," Michael said. "If I hear of anything else between you and Zach, then I'm blaming you. Got it?"

"Yes, sir."

"You can drop the 'sir'," he said. "Michael will do. It's your respect and obedience we need. Not your salute."

I nodded.

"And if there's any more strange behaviour, like carrying towels in a rucksack, I won't hesitate to assume the worst. Get my meaning."

"Yes, and there won't be," I said meekly.

"Right. I'm off for a kip," he said. "Long night last night, and who knows about tonight."

I watched him go and then went back into the common room. Sam was quizzing the others about last night and they looked uncomfortable.

"So you met the new pipeline man?"

"Yes," Solomon said.

"Trust him?"

Gabe shrugged. "I don't worry about that. He just has to do his job."

"And he was there on time?"

"Yes."

"No problems?"

"No," Gabe said.

"Not this time," Solomon added.

I wondered whether he'd let something slip. If Sam worked out they'd met Slugger and killed him, he'd ask more questions and find my connection. Then he'd know they lied about the fight with Zach. I figured Sam wasn't unintelligent and he might start wondering what my true motive had been. He might even guess that I knew my old friend.

Sam shook his head. "Don't go thinking you two are the men now. Just because you did the new run doesn't mean you'll always do it from now on. And anyway, Zach and I were needed here."

"Oh?" Solomon said.

"Keeping an eye on officer boy here." Sam nodded in my direction.

I said nothing.

"What have you got to say about that?" Sam asked, looking at me. I guess he wondered if I'd challenge him. Maybe he wanted the challenge, like another pecking order thing.

"Just thinking about Zach," I said. "Do you think he'll try and get revenge?"

Sam nodded. "I would."

Gabe and Solomon took the opportunity to get up from the table and head for the door.

"Going for a lie-down," Gabe said.

This left me and Sam. If he was going to confront me, I didn't want it now. So I also got up.

"We could play cards again," Sam said.

I shook my head. "I think it's about time I got properly acquainted with my girl."

He laughed, and I wondered whether he'd been the worried one. Was he afraid of me challenging him?

"Enjoy yourself then, mate," he said.

When I reached my room, I told Safiya that I was going to sleep for a while. "Are the others all here?"

"Masters Michael, Gabriel, and Solomon are all in the house. No sign of Master Zachary or Master Samuel."

I told her I'd left Sam in the common room. "After you've got me some fresh clothes, I'd like you to watch the door."

"Watch the door?"

"While I sleep. Wake me if there's any trouble."

As soon as she'd gone, I lay on the bed and felt enveloped by the comfortable mattress. I shut my eyes and must have fallen asleep, because the next thing I knew, Safiya was shaking my arm.

"Master Sam is coming."

I looked at the time: 7 pm. The town hall service would happen in another hour and I'd have another chance to locate any explosives.

I heard his boots on the steps and then knocking on two doors before mine.

I was up and ready for him, but Sam was unarmed. He stood in my doorway and just looked at me.

"CR in ten minutes," he said. "Urgent."

I reminded Safiya to be prepared, and I hurried with the rest of the men to the common room.

Daniel and Zach were waiting for us, and for a fleeting moment I worried that my adversary had said something to Daniel.

"Roster for tonight," the second in command said. "Gabriel and the new boy, Thomas, are going to the

276

yard in Terengganu. Zach, you'll stay here. The rest of you will have orders after the service."

Michael opened the gun box.

"What, we're going now?" I asked.

"You have a problem with that?"

Of course I did. It meant I wouldn't get inside the town hall, but I just said, "No."

Michael handed Gabe a revolver then shut the cabinet.

"What about me?" I asked.

Zach grinned at me. "You're a fighter. Use your fists."

We went outside but then Daniel called Gabe back. I figured he was being given some instructions that they didn't want me privy to. They still didn't trust me.

Or was there a more sinister reason?

Had Gabe just been given instructions to get rid of me?

FIFTY-TWO

All three vehicles were in the garage and Gabe got into the covered truck. I slid alongside. It smelled of dirt and damp and oil.

He dropped the gun in the door well and the engine turned over a bunch of times before it fired up.

"Heap of Chinese junk," he said.

I could see both of his hands. While I knew he wasn't holding the gun, I could relax.

"Where are we going?"

"Terengganu. You were there when Daniel told us."

"Of course, but where exactly? It's a big place. And what are we picking up?"

"Nothing important," Gabe said.

He drove us out onto the main road and turned south. I glanced left at the crossroads, wondering if Harwood was down there in his jeep. Was he watching? Would he be following? And where was the army?

"What about the others? What did they tell you when you went back in?"

"Nothing important," Gabe said again.

He said nothing for a while so I prompted him.

"It must have been scary last night. Is that the first time you've done the run with the gold."

Gabe swivelled and scrutinized me briefly.

"I'm just putting two and two together. Solomon confirmed the trade in gold and you did the pipeline run last night."

He nodded but didn't answer my question.

We drove in silence through Bandar Permaisuri. I could see he was thinking. Maybe he was still wondering how much I knew.

"Michael mentioned us being wealthy. Will we get paid in gold?"

"We shouldn't talk about it," he said. It was the same expression Solomon had used.

But he started talking after we passed the mosque on the outskirts of town. "The gold needs to get processed. It's just in the rock before that, right? Jeremiah and Daniel set up a trade many years ago and we're just part of the pipeline. They arrange for it to come to us, then we take it over the mountains and hand it over."

"And you did that last night?"

"Not the gold," he said, as though I was being foolish. "That was why it was so odd when the cop took the usual man's place. He should have known we didn't have gold ore in a jeep—and how would he take it off us? No, last night we were picking up the money. That's why it was good to be trusted by Daniel.

"So we get paid in normal money, not gold?"

"Right!" Gabe looked at me. "We take the ore and hand it over. Two days later, the money comes back the other way. We take our cut and the rest goes to the er... miners."

I figured he knew the Chinese terrorists were involved but he couldn't admit it. probably one of the reasons they couldn't talk about it. That and the fear of ambush.

I said, "Just the two of you last night was a bit risky, wasn't it."

"Yeah."

"Why? Why not more of an armed guard?"

"There were other things to be done."

"Like what?"

He blew out air. "Look, I don't know everything and I suggest you don't go asking Michael or Daniel. Anyway, we have it made: money building up and fun doing it." He paused. "Jeremiah has created a paradise, but—"

"But he's mad."

"I wouldn't say that."

"Doesn't change the fact that he is."

Gabe laughed, suddenly more relaxed, maybe because I'd switched the subject away from the gold. "That damn book, *Lost Horizons*. He's obsessed by the bloody thing."

"And the mumbo jumbo he talks. He loves himself."

"Oh, God, he thinks he's Jesus or something. And we just have to go along with it." He paused and became more serious. "But Michael thinks we're getting close to the end."

I nodded. "What about Daniel?"

"I suppose he does. Jeremiah keeps talking about violence and war. He's expecting the army to attack."

"But he has a plan?"

"I'm sure he does, but he doesn't share it with me. Maybe Daniel knows it. They were in Force 136 together, you know?"

"Solomon told me. It must have been tough."

"They saw some terrible things, but Jeremiah's faith got them through it."

I listened to the rattle of old metal springs for a while.

"What do you think Jeremiah's plan is, Gabe?"

"I don't know."

"But if you were to guess?"

"Cause a diversion," he said. "That's what guerrillas do. Distract and disrupt, that's a phrase I've heard Daniel use."

"Which would be what?"

"Kill everyone."

I waited a beat. "Explosives in the town hall?"

He glanced at me with a curious look on his face.

"What?" I said.

"Why would he use explosives?"

"I just—"

He shook his head. "No. He'd do it with poison."

This was either good or bad news.

Good if I didn't have to worry about Jeremiah blowing everyone up in the town hall. Bad if he'd poisoned everyone this evening.

I knew things were moving at a pace, but I convinced myself that he wouldn't do it. Not yet anyway. Sending me and Gabe out on a mission didn't fit with that scenario.

Unless Jeremiah and Daniel had different agendas.

And that brought me back to the possibility of Gabe shooting me.

I remembered driving through Terengganu on the way up here; the industry on the estuary, warehouses, cargo lorries and the pervading smell of fish. It had only been four days ago but felt like an age.

Gabe drove us to an oil depot, through a yard, and into an alleyway with no lights. I could just see him in the darkness.

He reached for the gun.

FIFTY-THREE

"Gabe—" I started.

"Just sit tight," he said. "There shouldn't be any trouble. The gun is just a precaution."

I saw movement in the side mirror. Nothing distinct, just shapes in the darkness. The tailgate was unclipped and came down, then I heard stuff being loaded into the rear.

I looked at Gabe and he just nodded like he was saying it's OK.

The loading stopped and Gabe pulled an envelope from beneath his shirt. He still had the gun in the other hand and held the envelope out of his window. I saw a hand come up and take it and then we were alone.

Gabe reversed out of the yard, across the depot and into the street. I glanced back and saw someone closing gates behind us. I breathed out. Not only had this been a genuine collection, I could tell by the loading sounds that we hadn't picked up young women.

From what the men had said earlier, I'd worried that our mission had been to kidnap what they referred to as *fresh blood*. I'm not sure how I would have handled that. I'd told myself that I would go along with it and rescue them later, but I wondered if I could have waited that long. But that wasn't going to be a problem.

"What was it?" I asked as we got on the main road again.

"Just barrels."

"What's in the barrels?"

"Don't worry about it."

"Like I shouldn't worry about the poison?"

He said nothing.

"I presume it'll be in the communion drink."

"Jeremiah won't poison us. We're Daniel's team. He wouldn't allow it."

Really? I thought. If this madman—and he surely was insane—decided that his paradise was being invaded, he would end it all. For everyone. He spoke about immortality and the meaning of existence. My sense was that Jeremiah had a very different view of reality and interpretation of what it meant to be alive from most sane people.

I thought about what poison meant. Harwood was outside the commune waiting for me to defuse the explosives, but there weren't any. Could we move things forward? Harwood had called 200 Provost straight after we'd met. They should be waiting nearby, waiting for my signal.

What if the army hadn't arrived yet?

Did it matter? Did Harwood and I have to wait for them before rescuing people? The two of us could do it tonight. Cut the wire near the lower gate and get the women out. Although there was one problem: the children.

We were on the long road north. Mile after mile went by with the old truck grumbling and jarring whenever we hit a bump. I heard a barrel go over and roll until it thudded against the cab. I kept looking in the side mirror wondering if we'd be followed, hoping to see Harwood's jeep or maybe MPs. But I saw no evidence of a tail.

"After the nursery, where do the children go?" I asked.

"The school."

"It's not very big."

"It's big enough."

OK, I thought, then it wasn't just a matter of getting the women and babies out through the lower gate. We'd need to get the children from the other side of the tunnel. Maybe one of us could do one side and the other get the children. Would the women leave without knowing the children were safe? I hoped so.

"Why the interest?" he asked.

"No reason. Just making conversation."

He nodded, and we went another mile before he said, "You think one of the team killed Noah, don't you?"

"Why'd you say that?"

"The way you were looking at us in the CR."

"Two things I know," I said. "Someone has a taste for murder and your operation seems to be coming to an end."

He said nothing.

After letting him think about it, I said, "Was Zach on his own for long, last night?"

Gabe didn't comment.

"He's different, isn't he?"

"You mean because he's navy? Yes, he's different, but I don't think he'd kill Noah. They were friends."

"What about the others?"

"Solly's too stupid, and Sam—well, I just don't see it."

"What about Daniel and Michael?"

"I don't know Daniel well enough."

"OK. What about Michael?"

"Michael doesn't trust anyone."

284

I noted the lack of a ringing endorsement and said, "Tell me more."

"Sometimes he thinks he should be leader, not Daniel. He thinks we should take our cut of the money now."

I nodded. I'd sensed tension between the two men.

Gabe continued: "Because Jeremiah keeps talking about the end and violence. Michael told me we should get out before it all goes tits up."

"What do you think?"

He didn't answer, and I heard his breathing above the noise in the cab.

"What do the others think?"

"I don't know. Michael told me not to discuss it openly. He said he'd let me know when the time came."

We drove into Permaisuri. I thought about Shalaa, Safiya's sister, and then about Jenkins. Where was he? Could he have been killed by BlackJack as well? If so, where was his body?

We crossed the river out of the town. Not far now.

"Gabe?"

"Yes?"

"Where does Jeremiah get the opium from?"

He glanced at me, screwing up his face. "Opium?"

"The stuff at communion. The stuff he gives to the women."

"Ah!" He chuckled. "Jeremiah's old man was a chemist—worked with animals. He discovered something that calmed animals down, and it works on humans too. It's not opium."

"What is it then?"

I saw him shrug in the dim light. "Don't know. But it's not too bad. Jeremiah mixes it up in his lab. I've taken it a few times, and it made me feel super relaxed but a bit weird."

285

"Weird in what way?"

"Like the room spun. Like being drunk but with your senses... I don't know. Seeing colours and details I didn't see before. I don't do it much. Zach, on the other hand, does it all the time. He can be a bit crazy on it."

"You mentioned a lab. Where's that?"

He rubbed his chin. "Lots of dumb questions."

"What's wrong with telling me that?"

"All right, it's in the same building as the school as far as I know."

"Where do they hold the ceremonies?"

"What?"

"The ceremonies. They used to have them in the town hall."

"Who told you about that?"

"Solomon."

"That was a long time ago. Anyway, they didn't have ceremonies in the town hall. And they stopped them years ago."

In the dark, it looked like he was gripping the steering wheel harder than before. His knuckles seemed tense.

He said, "I think we should stop talking now."

Moments later, Gabe passed the crossroads. I looked for any sign of Harwood but didn't see him, and neither did I really expect to. He was smarter than that. If he was waiting, he'd be hidden. If he was following it would be subtle.

We turned into the jungle, crossed the bridge and drove to the garage. The other truck and Land Rover weren't there. The others had left and weren't back yet.

Before we entered, Gabe punched the gears into reverse and came out again. We were heading for the gate but now going backwards.

Gabe sounded the horn three times. A signal. Then he stopped with the tailgate close to the fence.

"What now?" I asked as we waited.

As if in answer, I heard the square bolt slide and a creak as the gates opened.

Gabe reversed another thirty yards—about as far as he could go on the track before the ground got too uneven. He switched off the engine and we both got out. I saw a couple of carts on the rail tracks right behind us.

Zach appeared, and I figured he'd been the one to open the gates.

"How did it go?"

Gabe responded. "No problems."

I was thinking: the gate's open. They're both armed but maybe this is my chance. Maybe I don't wait for Harwood. I just do this now.

The tailgate came down. "Shit!" Zach said. "One of the barrels is over. If the goods are damaged..."

Gabe said, "Don't blame me. I didn't pack them."

"Yeah, but you did the driving!"

I went around the back and could just see four barrels inside. One was on its side.

"Jump in, Tom," Zach grunted at me. "Pass the first one down."

I looked at him, about three fast paces away. I could get to him before he drew his revolver. I nodded, using the moment to glance towards Gabe. He wasn't close enough. The rail carts were in the way. He'd have plenty of time to draw and shoot.

I swung up onto the load bed, took hold of the nearest barrel and rolled it to the edge. It was the size of a small oil drum, but plastic, and I knew what liquid felt like in a rolling drum. Whatever was inside this wasn't liquid. The weight was at the bottom and uneven.

"Careful!" Zach said. He came to the tailgate and reached out for the barrel. Again I checked how far away Gabe was and decided against a move.

287

Zach took the barrel and lowered it onto the first trolley. Then Gabe moved in and took the second. Zach held back. It was like they knew to keep apart so that I couldn't get them both.

Zach took the third and I went to the last one, which was on its side.

Righting it, I rotated the barrel to the end of the truck where Gabe closed in, arms out, ready to take the load. Zach started to pull his trolley. He wasn't looking.

As Gabe took the barrel, I poleaxed him. A left-handed jab between his eyes. Lower would have been better but the barrel restricted my blow.

It felt good. That's for killing Slugger, I said to myself.

Gabe went backwards like a felled tree.

The barrel followed him and I leapt from the truck.

As it struck the ground, the lid of the barrel popped off.

Something spilled out. Pale and thin.

I staggered. My plan had been to sprint for Zach, get there before he drew his weapon. But instead, I hesitated. My brain screamed.

A child! There's a child in the barrel!

FIFTY-FOUR

Before I could run at Zach, I saw something out of the corner of my eye. Something moving fast.

"Hands up!"

I swivelled and looked into the muzzle of a revolver. On the other end of it was Michael, baring his teeth in a kind of grin.

"Children—children in the barrels," I said.

"Oh, and you're pretending that's why you hit Gabe?"

"What are you doing with children?"

"Hands up! Last fucking chance," Michael growled.

I raised my hands.

"I knew you were no good," he said.

I looked down at the barrel with the child hanging out of it. A boy, pretty malnourished and about three years old. I saw him move like he was dreaming in his sleep.

"Just tell me—what the hell's going on?" I said.

"None of your business, that's what. Now move!"

Gabe staggered to his feet and together he and Zach righted the barrel and jammed on the lid.

"Move!" Michael barked again, because I continued to stare at the barrel. "Or I'll just fucking shoot you!"

Four barrels, four children. This was all about-face. Safiya's sister had said they killed the babies. They

289

weren't killing babies here, they were bringing children in. Why the hell were they doing that?

Michael cocked his gun and told Gabe to get hold of me.

I shook off his grasp and started walking. Michael barked at Zach to take the barrels over to the school then Michael walked a pace behind us.

I followed the track towards the tunnel.

"I knew you would be trouble," Michael said. "It was suspicious you arriving just after another one. Peter was dodgy and you are too."

I said, "You're focused on the wrong issue. It's not me you should be worried about, it's whoever killed Noah."

Gabe said, "He thinks you might've done it."

Back in the truck, I thought I'd won Gabe over. I guess my punch had changed his mind.

Michael laughed. "Based on what?"

"Because of the situation and Jeremiah's plans."

"If I was the killer, I'd have shot you back there, wouldn't I?"

Not necessarily, I thought. There were witnesses, and BlackJack preferred a knife.

We left the side called Cham and went into the tunnel. They both had torches, and I felt a gun between my shoulder blades.

I said, "If it's not you, who is it, Michael?" My voice echoed in the darkness.

Michael said nothing.

"Is it Zach?"

"Right," he said. "I should worry that he's coming up behind me. I should turn and check and you'll escape."

Gabe laughed.

We walked on in silence except for the echo of our footfall.

On the other side, I tried again. "Jeremiah's mad, isn't he?"

No comment.

"He's planning to kill everyone. His preaching is all about the violent end. He thinks it's coming, and it is, Michael."

Michael said nothing.

"Maybe he's getting Daniel to kill the team off one at a time before he poisons everyone else."

"What's your plan?" he said, surprising me.

"We get out now. We get everyone out before the others get back."

"What about the money?" Michael asked, then: "Keep moving!"

I had slowed down as we'd passed the common room and I knew from his command that he was just playing along. He had no intention of running.

We kept going all the way to the town square.

"Where now?" I said, slowing again.

Michael jabbed me in the back. "Inside. The town hall."

I went around to the doors but stopped suddenly. I tensed, waiting for the jab of the gun, ready to rotate and snatch it.

No nudge from the gun this time. No chance for me to risk grabbing for it. I lurched forward as the sole of his boot made contact with my lower back.

"To the doors, if you'd be so kind."

I walked forward.

"Gabe, get the doors open," Michael barked. The other man jogged forward, pulled out a bunch of keys and got the door unlocked.

"Inside," Michael said to me, and he gave me another kick.

I staggered forward into the darkness and then turned to face them. The two of them stood there like a firing squad but I knew they weren't going to shoot. Not here. If there was going to be a firing squad it would have been earlier, by the truck maybe. They were keeping me alive. Which meant something.

Michael said, "Lock him in."

Gabe moved.

I said, "Wait. There's been a misunderstanding."

"If it was up to me, you'd be dead already," Michael said. He nodded at Gabe, who started to close the doors.

"But it's not up to you, is it?" I said. "You have to wait for Daniel. Because you can't make a decision on your own."

The doors shut and I heard the locking mechanism click in place.

"Michael," I shouted through the crack between the doors, "it's not just Noah."

There was no reply, but then I heard feet on the other side of the doors.

"Michael?"

No answer.

"I know about Major Broom. He was murdered too."

"How do you know what happened to Broom?"

He sounded closer now, and I figured he was right outside. It was a shame I couldn't burst the doors open into his face, but these were sturdy, made of solid wood with good hinges and a good lock. I'd just bounce off the door and ruin my initiative.

I said, "It's not just here. Someone is cleaning shop."

"What do you mean?"

"People connected to your business are dying all of a sudden. This little thing can't last forever. Someone knows the end is coming and is planning to clean up—remove the evidence."

He said nothing.

"They'll take all the money. You won't get anything."

"Who will?"

I tried to sound mysterious. "Someone who knows where it's kept."

"Daniel?"

I'd had no idea until he said that. So Daniel was in charge of the money. He worked the pipeline while Jeremiah lived his crazy dream, playing God.

"You can't trust him."

Michael said nothing for a few beats, then: "I can't trust you, you mean."

"He killed Peter too!" I lied. "Broom, Peter, Noah and many more."

Michael made a sound somewhere between a grunt and a laugh. "Tell that to Daniel when he gets back." Then he walked away, and I was left in the darkness of the hall.

FIFTY-FIVE

At first, the darkness seemed absolute, then my eyes got used to it—or at least partially. Because of the moonlight, I could see the outline of the doors. When I turned around I thought I could see something inside the hall.

Maybe my retinas picked out random photons, because I could see faint traces of light that appeared to dance before my eyes and then disappear. I couldn't focus on them, and when I tried to identify where the light came from, I couldn't. Phantom images, I decided; my brain compensating for the lack of visual input.

How to get out? I could break a chair and use a leg, wedge it somewhere around the door and try to lever it open. If the chairs had been made of metal, it might have worked, but the doors fit snugly and the gap around the frame was too small for a chair leg.

With my back to the doors, I visualized the room: rows of chairs with the central aisle; the rock that supported the ceiling; the stage at the back with the sheet that had revealed Jeremiah; the trapdoor he came through; and, the bell rope. The bell rope.

Feeling my way around the wall, I went left, got to the corner and continued all the way to the stage. Pulling myself up, I located the end chair where I'd been sitting only a few hours ago. Behind that was the rope.

I felt for it and took hold of the rope. Again I could see faint light, and I'd expected it. The rope went through the ceiling, which meant a hole, and I could just make it out. An option might be to climb the rope and test the ceiling there. Surely there was access to the bell? However, staring up, I could only see the point where the rope went through but no other light suggesting a hatch.

And there was the secondary issue: if I climbed the rope, I'd be ringing the bell like crazy. That would call Harwood, but what if the military police hadn't arrived yet? It would be Harwood against the men here, and I couldn't help.

There might still be a way out of here. Feeling my way, I went along the line of seven chairs until I reached the sheet. Then I knelt down and felt around the floor for the trapdoor I knew must be there. Jeremiah looked weird as hell, but I didn't believe in supernatural powers. His appearance was definitely a party trick.

My fingers located a line in the wood, a crack that I followed in the shape of a square. Two feet by two feet, I figured. It would be a squeeze, but large enough to fit Jeremiah's shoulders at an angle.

And then I found a switch.

I flicked the little lever and the trapdoor lowered with a subtle whoosh of air. Feeling for the edge, I lowered my legs over and rotated to squeeze down.

Jeremiah was a huge man, and I expected to drop seven feet, maybe more. But I didn't. My feet touched the bottom with my shoulders just through the hole.

The stage was about two and a half feet off the ground. This hole was about five feet deep.

I crouched, felt around and touched nothing. No sides, just a platform that didn't reach the ground. I saw nothing but blackness. My brain didn't even see phantom light down here.

Jeremiah could crouch here before he climbed onto the platform and appeared on stage. I'd already figured the method of propulsion: pneumatics. The whoosh I'd heard as the trapdoor descended was air in pipes. I could now feel the mechanism underneath: a metal frame and metal pipes and a thick rubber cable—a power line.

I followed it along hard earth and then stopped. I'd reached a wall, and the cable just went into the ground. From there I felt around the edges of the underground area and gained nothing except an appreciation that this was the size of the stage. So there was a space under the stage, with the pneumatic platform for Jeremiah, but not what I'd expected. There was no door. No escape route.

Which meant that the self-made messiah went into the town hall before the evening sermon, waited in this hot hole with little air and crouched on the platform before appearing as if from nowhere and impressing no one but himself.

How long did he wait down here? Ten minutes? Twenty? More? It seemed crazy, but then again he was crazy.

I shook my head with disappointment. He'd been locked in after we'd trooped out. I'd been sure he'd have another way in and out of the town hall. But he didn't. Which meant I didn't either.

There was another switch beside the platform, and standing on the raised section, I kicked the switch. The pneumatics worked in reverse, this time powering me upwards.

I felt the sheet waft and rise as I came up at speed, and as it stopped, the momentum made my feet leave the ground. Jeremiah had appeared suddenly and without a similar jerk. I figured he'd perfected the timing, bending his knees at the right moment to hide the jerk upwards.

So I was back above ground on the stage where Jeremiah preached his nonsense. I couldn't break through the doors and there was no secret passageway.

I'd found no evidence of explosives in the town hall. And if Jeremiah planned to kill everyone, he'd do it here.

While the women were on the outside they were relatively safe.

The men had found me out, locked me in here and I couldn't get away. Now I needed help.

No choice.

I rang the bell again and again knowing it was echoing off the hills and expecting the sound to travel maybe two miles. I'd told Harwood to listen for my signal. This was the call. I couldn't do any more.

FIFTY-SIX

It didn't take them long to get the doors unlocked. I stood to one side with a broken chair in my hands ready to strike, but they weren't stupid.

The door was kicked open and they shone torches inside.

I was behind the door on the right now, and they quickly located me without getting too close. Just Sam and Zach. So Sam was back. No Michael this time or Gabe. At least nowhere I could see them.

"You're an idiot!" Zach spat at me. "Drop your pathetic attempt at a weapon and get out."

After a second's delay, I discarded the chair piece and stepped from behind the door.

"Outside!" Zach commanded, waving the rifle at me.

I still took my time, evaluating, but they kept their distance and the guns pointed at me. Once beyond the town hall's double doors, they moved to my right and told me to keep walking, so I went left, walking slowly.

"Where are we going now?" I asked.

No reply.

I stopped and turned to face them. "If you're going to shoot me, do it here."

Zach grinned. "Don't tempt me."

I relaxed.

Sam said, "Daniel's still not back."

"We'll shoot you as soon as he gives the order," Zach said.

"That'll be too late," I said.

Sam looked confused and then worried.

Zach said, "Shut up and keep walking." He got closer and I thought about grabbing his rifle, but as I was about to move he drew back the bolt and snarled. "I will shoot you if I have to. Maybe we'll just say you went for us and we had no choice."

I took a step back. "The army is on its way."

Zach scoffed. "Shut up and walk."

I turned away from them and took a couple of paces. "They told me to ring the bell as a signal."

"Who did?" Sam asked.

"The army."

"Bollocks!" Zach said, but then I heard them whispering. Sam believed me, or at least half of his brain did.

"Right. In there!" Zach said after the short exchange between them.

"Where?" I was at the end of the workshop. There was the small outbuilding, that Solomon had called the storeroom, and then the washhouse.

Sam jogged ahead towards the storeroom.

"Follow!" Zach grunted behind me.

I went that way, and when we reached the little building, Sam fumbled with the door. The locking mechanism sounded old. I heard a click and clunk and then Sam swung the door inwards.

"In there!" Zach said, and he jabbed the barrel of his gun in my back. It was still locked and loaded. I'd known old rifles to go off with too much of jerk.

"Easy," I said, and walked into the storeroom.

The door slammed behind me and I was in darkness once more. Only this time I didn't even get the random images, just black. The door felt like steel, and when I kicked it, there was no give.

From the outside, I'd gauged the interior to be about ten by eight feet. The floor was wooden and the walls were rough brick. Feeling about, I soon located hessian sacks, wooden boxes, and barrels crammed in the small area, which made sense for a storeroom.

I stood on a box and felt the roof. It had the usual rope binding the frame followed by thatched palm leaves. There was no give when I prodded it.

I hefted a barrel as high as I could and dropped it. Coffee beans spilled out as the barrel broke open. Pulling apart the wooden staves, I levered off the top metal ring. Then I clambered back on the box and tried sawing at the thatch.

Five minutes later I sat down, sweating hard. I'd pushed and poked the ceiling with minimal effect. I was stuck in there and all I could do was wait.

Positioning myself by the door, I held a wooden stave in each hand. My plan was simple. When the men came back, I'd charge whoever opened the door. Not a great plan, but all I had.

I closed my eyes and breathed calmly like I'd taught myself as a child. My father had been a tough parent who lived by the motto "Spare the rod and spoil the child". He would lock me in the understairs cupboard for many hours as punishment, and I'd learned to use the time to good effect. Now I imagined I was in a comfortable chair with a cool drink, pondering this convoluted case.

For me, it had begun with the helicopter crash and the murder of the pilot and the other man. From the message at the airfield and the burnt warrant card we'd thought SIB officer John Harwood had been the dead man, but it hadn't been him. Harwood was deep

300

undercover following the thread of the pipeline, working out that Jeremiah and his motley crew were passing Chinese gold across the country, using men like Major Broom to legitimize it. In return, the bandits got their money and Jeremiah's squad received their cut.

The other SIB officer, Lieutenant Jenkins, had been tracking a killer or killers and had also ended up at Jeremiah's commune. Or had he? I rewound and remembered that Safiya's sister had directed him here but there had been no sign of him.

My assumption at this point was that Jenkins had stumbled across the killer and met an unfortunate end. The dog tag from the helicopter gave us the name BlackJack. I'd found evidence of BlackJack where Jenkins had stayed in the nearby town.

Did it make sense that BlackJack was one of the ex-soldiers in the commune? I thought Jeremiah was an unlikely candidate. If he wanted to destroy his business, he could just do it. He didn't need to kill people off first.

Daniel was a good candidate because of his history. Force 136 had been brutal. It had turned Jeremiah into a madman. Had it given Daniel a taste for blood?

Michael was a tough guy with a motive. He didn't have access to the gold money so he couldn't rely on Daniel and Jeremiah splitting the spoils. And I'd seen the way he handled a knife. When he pulled out his flick knife and handed it to Gabe, he'd spun it in his fingers, subconsciously, which told me he liked the feel of it in his hand.

BlackJack's signature was definitely the knife. He liked to cut his victims.

I was thinking about each one and whether they seemed the sort—not that I knew what "the sort" looked like. I'd met some nasty men but never such a prolific, brutal killer.

Solomon, Sam and Gabe were all too soft. They were foot soldiers without the hard edge of a killer, in my opinion. But Zach was a different matter. I hadn't seen him use a blade but he had the dagger tattoos on his arms. Plus he was ex-navy and therefore not quite one of the team.

How did the helicopter crash victims fit in? If it hadn't been for the dog tag, I would never have known about BlackJack's involvement. He'd shot the pilot and burned the other man to death. I'd thought that man was Harwood but it wasn't. So who was he? Why did BlackJack kill him?

For some reason, I flashed back to being at home. Maybe it was thinking about pilots and death. That reminded me of my father. But in my flashback I wasn't under the stairs. He'd thrust me into an attic space that was barely big enough for my ten-year-old body.

I'd been in the silence and darkness, like I was now, but after an hour I thought I'd try and get out. The door he'd forced me through was locked, but I found a gap between the beams and eaves. I remembered the wood scraping my back and worrying that I'd be stuck. Looking back, I could see how foolish I'd been, but I hadn't panicked. I just kept inching forward until I got to another attic space. Once out of the eaves I was into the spare bedroom and freedom.

If only this room had the equivalent crawl space.

In picturing the room, I realized the goods were stacked left and right with a corridor between. That made sense for ease of access, but why not use the back? The attic crawl space had been at the back. My subconscious had been trying to tell me that the layout felt wrong.

I hopped down from my box, crunching coffee beans as I landed, then searched the rear of the room. The far wall was solid brick. I'd already tested it when checking the first time. However, I stamped my foot and found a section by the wall that sounded different.

Scrabbling with the metal barrel ring, I found an edge. Seconds later, a trapdoor came up and back and I found the top of a metal ladder.

With nothing to lose, I climbed down and into a rough, walled tunnel that I could almost stand upright in.

Cool air smelled of old brick and earth. Ahead I saw a faint light, and as I moved forward, I knew I was heading for the town hall.

The tunnel ended abruptly and the space opened up. I was in a long, thin area, just wide enough to walk down. A faint ambient light came from above and I figured it was moonlight filtered through the roof. Apart from another door in the long wall, it was curiously empty.

I turned the handle and found another dark space beyond.

Even with a small amount of illumination, I could see I was back under the stage. Ahead was the hydraulic frame holding the trapdoor in place.

When I'd first entered the town hall, I'd sensed the room looked smaller on the inside. Now I knew why.

This was how Jeremiah got in. He didn't wait under the stage. He went into the storeroom, under the square, and through the narrow space.

What I couldn't figure is why the convoluted route? Why not just a tunnel straight under the square under the stage? Unless the tunnel was already built. From the smell of it, I figured that was likely. It smelled old. Maybe from way back, before the war.

I flicked the switch for the trapdoor, waited for it to descend, climbed onto it and then shot up to the stage.

My hope was that the guys hadn't locked the town hall doors after moving me to the storeroom.

But they had. I cursed my misfortune and wondered what to do now.

I could stay here or go back to the storeroom. I considered my original thought about climbing the bell rope to test the ceiling but discarded the idea. For now. Before that, I'd search the area I'd passed through.

There wasn't a handle on this side of the door and I realized that was why I hadn't found the exit before.

I stepped back into the long thin area and continued. Before the end, I found a ladder set into the wall.

So this was how they got to the bell.

Like the length of the town hall, the ceiling was lower than I'd guessed. Now I suspected there was a room up there.

The pillar went through the ceiling.

I put my hand on the ladder and froze.

Scuffling sounds came down the tunnel. Someone was coming.

FIFTY-SEVEN

Zach didn't like what was going on. Not one little bit. First the guy they'd called Peter and then Thomas. They'd had no one new at the commune for three years. He had arrived and then, two months later, Gabe. Zachary and Gabriel. Daft names, but they'd gone along with it, for the girls, the easy life and the promise of gold at the end of it.

But the new guy, Tom, had made him rethink the logic. How would it end? He'd asked Michael once but couldn't remember the answer now. It had seemed OK at the time but didn't make sense. You don't just walk away from a criminal operation like this—and Zach had no illusions about the illegitimate nature of the operation. They were dealing with the enemy. They took the gold from the Chinese and passed it across country so that it could be traded legally. Dirty gold came out and clean money came back.

That didn't trouble him. He'd served his country for most of his life, for what? A pittance! He'd lost more friends than he wanted to count. He'd had two wives leave him and his best pal had died in his arms while hoping to be picked up by the British, afraid the Germans would get them first. Instead, the remaining six had been saved by the neutral Danes. Not the British.

Just some random steamer. No. He'd served his country and owed them nothing.

But he did want his share of the gold money and he knew just where to look for it. No one ever saw where Daniel took their cut of the precious metal, but he certainly didn't keep it in the main commune because it never came through the tunnel. He wouldn't keep it in his or Jeremiah's house. Which left one place.

Zach was supposed to be manning the gate for when the others returned but decided that this was his opportunity.

He'd checked, and Jeremiah was asleep in his treehouse. Daniel still wasn't back. Michael was in the CR and Sam was on patrol. So he was alone out here in the woods and he'd go into the tunnel beneath the bunker.

"Zach?"

Zach jumped at the sudden voice, loud in the darkness.

"Who's there?" he said, unsure whether he recognized the voice. He looked hard but only saw a ghostly light between the trees. Or maybe a shadow.

But he was looking the wrong way.

A sound behind him made him swivel. He saw the other man's face, right up close, and felt a prick under his chin. At the same time, he felt his legs swept away.

Zach tried to open his mouth and scream, but he couldn't. The other man's hand was hard under his chin and the pain was immense.

It was all he could think of until the darkness enveloped him.

★ ★ ★

BlackJack gave the stiletto blade one last push into the other man's brain. He knew that Zach was dead despite his twitching body. It reminded him of the pigeon he'd killed all those years ago.

"Just putting you out of your misery, old man," he said, before pulling the blade from beneath Zach's chin.

FIFTY-EIGHT

A light shone down into the tunnel.

"Thomas?" Safiya called quietly.

I hurried from the space behind the town hall and through the tunnel and into the torchlight.

"Are you all right?" she asked, stepping back as I climbed the ladder into the storeroom.

I nodded. "How—?"

"Sam."

"What about him?"

I followed her through the open door and saw a body on the floor.

"I hit him with a big stone. Is he dead?" she asked as I checked him.

He was breathing but unresponsive.

I picked up his revolver, dragged Sam into the room and checked his pockets. All he had was a whistle and a pack of cigarettes, matches, and a hunting knife attached to his belt along with his holster. I pulled the knife from its sheath and tested the blade. Not razor sharp but not blunt either. I used it to cut lengths of the rope from the ceiling supports. Then I bound Sam's wrists and ankles with it.

I took the torch from Safiya and flicked it over the bindings, checking they were secure. The revolver had six bullets, and I stuck the gun in my waistband.

The final thing I took was a roll of the rope in case I needed to tie up anyone else.

The keys were still in the door, and I locked Sam inside before stuffing the bunch in my pocket.

"Go and get the women. Lead them to the lower gate. I'll unlock it."

I left her and ran to the lower gate. Once there, I pulled out Sam's bunch of keys. Solomon had opened the gate on the first day I'd arrived. He was bottom of the pecking order so I was pretty sure that one of the four on Sam's keyring would fit this padlock. The smallest key went in, turned, and... *click...* the pin released.

A couple of minutes later I was at the bridge. Using the torch, I found the tree roots and dug out my bundle. My Beretta was there. Fifteen bullets.

Six in Sam's revolver gave me a total of twenty-one. More than enough to handle six men.

I left the gate open and headed back. Safiya stepped out of the shadows as I approached the town square.

"Why are you here?" I asked. I'd wanted her out of the way before I confronted anyone. And it might all start very soon.

"I can't go yet. I told you, we won't leave without the children."

"Where did they used to hold ceremonies?" I asked.

"People never talked."

"Is there a room above the town hall? Is that where his shrine is?"

Her eyes showed distress. "Yes."

"Were you ever taken there?"

"No, I was lucky. I think it was because Daniel favoured me."

"Did some of the girls die?"

"Yes."

"When did the ceremonies—the parties—stop?"

"About a year after I was brought here."

"Three years after this place started."

"Yes."

"Stay here," I said, and I drew back the hammer on Sam's gun.

"But I can't shoot."

"Just aim dead centre and pull the trigger." I redirected the barrel away from me. "In the meantime, keep your hand on the stock, away from the trigger."

She nodded towards the storeroom, twenty yards away. "You're going back in?"

"Yes," I said, positioning her in among the trees with a good line of sight. "If you see any of the men, shoot them. No questions. No hesitation. Understood?"

She nodded and I left her there.

Inside the storeroom, I flicked the torchlight at Sam, checking whether he was still unconscious.

I stepped backwards in surprise. Sam had a wooden shard rammed through his throat and another in his right eye.

In the twenty minutes it had taken to go out of the lower gate and return, someone had been in here and murdered Sam.

FIFTY-NINE

Rather than use the torch, I let my eyes adjust and then edged my way down the tunnel, Beretta at the ready and listening hard. Could the killer be down here? Had he killed Sam and then gone to the town hall or room above?

The door to the under-stage area was shut. When I got to the ladder, I looked up and waited. Not a sound. Even the ever-present jungle hum couldn't be heard down here.

Climbing with my gun wasn't easy, and I kept stopping to listen. Still nothing.

At the top, I waited again and then came up quickly.

I saw the same phantom green lights that I thought I'd imagined down below. My torch came on and I flicked it around the room.

The space was vast—almost as large as the town hall below, but it looked bigger because there was just a rock in the middle, the bell, and four benches positioned around it.

I closed in on the rock, but now I saw that the pillar came up through the floor with the stone perched on top.

And I felt bile rise up from my stomach. There were marks on the ugly grey-brown stone. Unnatural marks. Streaks of blood, I was sure.

I touched them and realized they were old stains. Years old.

And then I saw something else in the room: bottles. Most were empty, but some had a clear liquid and three were red.

As soon as I picked up a bottle with red liquid I knew it was blood: the way it clung to the sides as I swirled it.

Smelling the clear liquid, I figured these were full of the drug Jeremiah administered in his communions.

I came out of the storeroom and breathed deeply as I scanned for movement. I'd been through the tunnel and up into a room above the hall. The killer hadn't been there. But he might have been in the town hall and he might still be there.

Safiya came out from her hiding place, her eyes wide and both hands clenching the gun.

"Did you see anyone?" I asked.

"No one."

* * *

Earlier, BlackJack had seen Carter and the young woman moving through the darkness away from the storeroom. Things were happening faster than he'd anticipated, but this was now the finale and he had to act fast. He had a lot of men to kill in a short time. Not that he minded, of course. This was what it had been building up to ever since he'd realized they were all guilty.

Deciding the order that the men should die would be interesting. Deciding how they would die—well, that was the fun part.

312

He had driven the stake into Sam's chest like he was killing a vampire. It hadn't given him the same pleasure as a knife, but it had been fun. The shards of wood into the dead man's eye was a little creative touch.

Then he'd hurried down into the tunnel towards the town hall. He didn't realize that Carter knew about the tunnel and was surprised to hear the man return.

BlackJack slipped into the area under the stage and fixed the door latch so that he could open it soundlessly from the inside. Then he waited, his knife ready. If Carter came through the door, BlackJack would kill him without hesitation. Carter would be dead before he even realized.

But Carter went past. He must have been heading for the ladder. Seconds later this was confirmed by the creak of floorboards from the room above the town hall.

Then the noise stopped and BlackJack figured Carter was coming down the ladder again. Would he go straight past, through the tunnel and out or would he look under the stage? Again BlackJack prepared himself but the man just hurried past.

BlackJack eased through into the corridor and then along the tunnel. Coming up into the storeroom was a risk, but he figured Carter had a plan. He wouldn't hang around here.

But then he stopped. In the trees ahead, he spotted movement. The girl was there, watching the storeroom door.

He was trapped! Was Carter coming back after all?

Just as BlackJack considered running, he saw the girl move. She wasn't looking his way, she was walking towards the workshop.

BlackJack slipped out and followed and saw what the girl was looking at. Across the square, Carter ran into the cookhouse.

What was he doing?

Carter had been into the room and seen the shrine. Surely he should head for the school now. Ash Carter was far too inquisitive. He'd need to fully understand what was going on.

But this worked well, BlackJack decided. Carter was distracted while he had things to do and men to kill.

* * *

I got material from the workshop and oil from the cookhouse. Then I went to the town hall doors and did what I'd previously planned.

The rags caught alight quickly and we waited until the wood began to burn.

This would not only destroy Jeremiah's shrine but act as another signal to Harwood and the army if they hadn't heard the bell.

If Sam's killer was in there then he'd be flushed out and Safiya would shoot him.

But she appeared at my side, attracted by the fire. "That feels good," she said. "What now?"

"Save the babies and get everyone out of here."

"No," she said quietly. "We're going to the school."

SIXTY

I told Safiya that the army were on their way but I didn't know when they'd arrive. Then I reminded her about the gun and told her to shoot first and ask questions later.

"Get everyone out."

She just stood there looking at me.

"I need to see the school." Her jaw twitched with tension.

"No."

"Why?"

"Have you ever been to the other side?"

"Of course not."

"They aren't in the school." I paused. "The school isn't big enough." *Also, there are lots of graves over there in the woods.*

She said, "I need to see for myself."

We were in some kind of staring match and I finally relented. "All right. Let's go." I'd fight the battle with her again later.

We hurried along the perimeter and got as far as the common room. Just beyond it I saw something ahead, stopped Safiya and pointed.

At first, it was just a movement in the darkness, and then it took form: one of the men patrolling. He had his rifle out in front like he'd seen the enemy and was about to fire. But then the rifle moved and aimed the other way. I'd seen rookie soldiers behave this way. This guy was nervous and jumping at shadows.

The ex-soldier turned our way and walked towards us.

We hugged a tree and I unnecessarily raised a finger to my lips. I was pretty sure he wouldn't spot us in the trees unless he got within five yards, maybe ten.

The Beretta was in my hand but by my side, ready should he get too close.

He stopped and listened and looked right at me, but then away again and continued. He was fifteen yards, then ten. I held my breath.

I could see his shape and then his face now. Solomon. Personally, I wouldn't have given him a gun, and how he survived the army, I'll never know. He went past and I slipped out from behind the tree.

Five quick paces and I hit him with the Beretta while jerking his rifle away.

He let out a grunt, but nothing worse.

I pulled him into the trees and knelt on his chest.

Solomon's eyes rolled and my hand went over his mouth.

He focused on me.

"Tom!" he mumbled through my fingers.

His surprise made me think. Solomon hadn't expected me, then who had he expected?

"What's going on?" I asked, lifting my fingers, but ready to clamp my hand down again.

"Everyone is spooked," he said.

"Why?"

"We found out that someone else in the pipeline was murdered and then this evening we found Zach with his head cut off." He took a breath and I could feel his fear under my weight. "We thought you might be the killer—

but you were in the store..." He stopped breathing as panic gripped him. "Hold on! You're not in the storeroom!"

"I *was* in the storeroom. I've only just broken out."

He nodded. "Thank God!"

"Right."

"And Michael has disappeared. You don't think it's Michael do you?"

"I don't know."

"What are you...?" he said, alarmed.

I raised the Beretta and struck him on the temple. Lights out. Tearing a length of material from his shirt, I tied a gag around his mouth. Then I used more of the rope from my pocket and bound his arms to a tree behind him.

I gave Safiya Solomon's rifle and we left him there. At the tunnel, we found the entrance gate locked.

I saw the rifle shake in her hands.

"What's wrong?"

"Going through the tunnel is forbidden," she said, although I didn't think that was the real reason.

I'd found Jeremiah's shrine and the stone covered with old bloodstains, but I didn't think he'd killed anyone up there. Not for a long time, at least.

I think she knew or at least suspected. The children went from the nursery at around two years old. The shrine ceremonies had stopped three years after Jeremiah had founded this virtual prison. The time the first children will have gone to the school.

"You should turn back."

"No, I'm coming with you," she said, and she pulled open the gate as I unlocked it. Seconds later we were in the tunnel and total darkness.

I touched damp walls and breathed cold air. Safiya kept close behind me, one hand on my shirt as a guide.

317

We went in about a hundred paces before I risked turning on the torch, and I heard Safiya sigh with relief. Now that I had a light, I could see chisel marks where the tunnel had been cut out of the rock. It must have taken a huge effort to create this. No way did the ex-soldiers do this. This was from the war, probably dug by Chinese labourers under the instruction of the Force 136 unit.

We hurried along and I turned off the torch as we approached the end. In case anyone was waiting on the other side, I dived out, rolled, and came up with my Beretta at the ready.

Nothing. No movement and no sound except for the buzz of cicadas and distant jungle noises.

Two minutes later we were near the school. I positioned Safiya slightly uphill and out of sight.

"You're going in alone?"

"Yes."

"Why?" Her voice quaked.

"Because I need to know the truth," I said. "If any of the men come out, shoot them. If one of them approaches, shoot them. Understood?"

She nodded and I left her there.

I kicked the school door open and found four young children sleeping peacefully in the beds I'd seen before. But this was no school. It was more like a hospital. Drips hung down feeding their arms and a belt ran over each chest, pinning them to their beds.

I checked other rooms and found beds but no more children. Twenty beds in total.

And then I came to the room at the end.

SIXTY-ONE

BlackJack went along the track and was almost upon Solomon before he saw the ex-soldier tied to a tree.

Solomon had his head down, and BlackJack didn't spot the gag until he was up close.

"Good evening," BlackJack said quietly.

Solomon jumped, startled. His eyes locked onto BlackJack.

"Can't speak?"

Solomon shook his head.

"Want to die?"

Panic took over. Solomon jerked back into the tree. Nowhere to go.

"So you don't want to die?"

Solomon shook his head, but his eyes were still wide with alarm.

BlackJack selected his hunting knife and saw Solomon's eyes fixate on it.

"Don't worry," BlackJack said, his voice calm and reassuring. "I'm just going to cut your bonds."

He reached forward and snicked Solomon's wrist. "Oops! Clumsy ol' me."

Solomon was squirming now, thrashing from side to side trying to escape. And making too much noise.

BlackJack gripped him by the neck, his strong fingers digging deep into sinew. He could feel the man's arteries pulsing, fighting back against the pressure.

"Hold still, old man," BlackJack said in the same calm tones. "If you struggle, I might make a mistake. You wouldn't want that now, would you?"

Solomon froze for a second, probably hoping it would help. Of course, it didn't. Not for him anyway.

And then BlackJack thrust the blade into Solomon's throat and watched the blood froth and foam.

A shame it's so dark, he thought. This would look better in daylight.

★ ★ ★

Safiya was standing in front of the door when I came out.

"There are only four children," she said.

"Yes. They were brought here last night."

"Brought here?"

I closed the door behind me but she didn't move.

"What did you find in there?" she asked me.

"Confirmation."

"My children aren't alive, are they?"

"No."

Safiya didn't say anything. I was happy to stand there, barring her way for as long as it took.

Eventually, she said, "I knew they were dead. In my heart, I knew. I just couldn't accept it. None of us could. We were happy with the pretence. After all, there was nothing we could do, right?"

"Nothing."

I had found his laboratory, only it was more like an operating theatre.

"Tell me one thing. Did they die in pain?"

"I don't think so."

"How do you know?"

"I don't—not for certain—but I mean to find out."

"I should take a look," she said without conviction.

"No, you shouldn't. You'll regret it. You'll see pictures of your children and you'll imagine the worst."

There were pictures all around the room. Most were of toddlers, but there were also photographs of young women. His first victims, I guessed.

Safiya said, "Why? What's the worst?"

I hadn't wanted to explain, but she wasn't going away.

"There's a dead child in there."

"How did he die?" She forced the words out, her voice quaking.

"Jeremiah took his blood. Slowly. Maybe over a period of weeks."

"Harvested?" she said quietly.

"In the end, the kid won't have known. He'd have gone peacefully." I hoped I was right. With my arms around her, I held her tightly, felt her body trembling.

"Try and imagine them happy," I said. "Watch children at play and think of your children that way."

She didn't say anything for a while and her face showed she was struggling—her mind competing with her heart.

She breathed in and then out and let me guide her to the entrance. We passed the four sleeping children. "I can't just do nothing," she said. "Not now."

"Then help these poor children," I said. "Save them too."

She nodded. "What are you going to do?"

"I'm going to find Jeremiah," I said. "And then I'm going to kill him."

SIXTY-TWO

Safiya said she'd get the women and babies out and then come back with help for the four children in the school. Before she left, I swapped Sam's gun for the rifle. I figured she'd look suspicious and threatening if anyone saw a rifle in her hands. The revolver she could stash under her clothes.

I made sure she went into the tunnel before I went the other way.

A few minutes later I was outside Jeremiah's treehouse. No light showed, and I circled the dwelling wondering if I was going into a trap.

I tossed a stone through a window and saw the chiffon curtains flap and sway with the impact. Nothing. I tossed another and it clattered against wood. Still no response.

Only one way to find out, I thought, and I mounted the wooden ladder, Beretta at the ready. I got on the veranda and then walked quickly through the building. I saw no sign of life. He wasn't in his bed, but then I hadn't expected him to be. Solomon had said they were spooked, and I figured this included Jeremiah.

He was either in hiding or, more likely, he was out searching for the killer. Unless, of course, Jeremiah was the killer. Gabe had suggested the poisoning thing.

Maybe he was wrong. Maybe the violent end Jeremiah preached about was actually caused by him. Maybe he was the one cleaning up before he left with his ill-gotten gains.

If that was true then what about Daniel? Daniel clearly admired Jeremiah. They'd been in Force 136 together, Jeremiah the officer and Daniel the sergeant. They'd been through a hell of an ordeal. They'd survived and now Daniel and his band were Jeremiah's protectors.

Would Jeremiah cut Daniel out? And if not then did that mean they were both in on this. There could be more than one killer, after all. Joe Jenkins could have been right.

I looked for Daniel's house and found it forty yards on. As I circled the treehouse, I wondered where Harwood was. Had he seen the flames yet? Maybe not, but if he'd been tailing the other guys, he was surely back. Solomon had gone with the others. So had Zach.

A sudden noise made me halt. I listened hard and waited. Then an animal—probably a monkey or squirrel—scampered up a tree. Could that have been the noise?

I repeated the trick I'd tried at Jeremiah's treehouse with a couple of stones. Again I got no response. A minute later, I made my way to the steps and into the property.

No one there.

I came back down and looped around to the upper gate. It was locked. I checked Sam's keys and one worked.

After swinging the gates open wide, I jogged down the road to the garage checking whether anyone had taken flight, but all three vehicles were there. So it looked like they were still in the commune. But where were they?

I'd neutralized Sam and Solomon. Zach had been murdered, which left four: Gabe, Daniel, Michael and Jeremiah—and I figured at least one of them was the killer.

What I didn't know was whether they were searching or lying in wait. The smart money said the latter. That's what I would do if I didn't know where the others were—and thought one was the killer.

Leaving the gate wide open felt like it encouraged an early arrival of the army. I could see the glow from the burning town hall. Surely they'd be here soon.

Moving swiftly but with caution, I followed the rail track back towards the tunnel.

I was about halfway there when I found Zach. He was in a rail cart, and like Solomon had said, his head had been cut off. It had happened here, because a flick of my torch showed his blood pooled on the track. Either the killer had placed his head back inside the cart or one of the men had. It struck me that they could have moved the body.

Back through the tunnel I could see the town hall burning nicely. The roof was alight and flames leapt half as high again into the night sky.

The town square, I decided. That's where I would go. Maybe find a way up onto the roof. A sniper could pick people off if they got too close.

With Solomon's rifle over my shoulder and Beretta in hand, I followed the route that Safiya and I had taken earlier. It would take me past the common room rather than the other way past the bunkhouse.

When I came to where I'd tied up Solomon, I stopped short. He wasn't there. Damn! Hadn't I tied him well enough? Had he escaped?

But then I saw something white in the nearby trees. Stepping over, I realized it was Solomon. Upside down, he looked like he was doing a naked headstand. His legs were bound and his arms reached out to the sides. Like an upside-down crucifixion. Like Peter, the disciple had been crucified.

I flicked the torchlight over him and saw Solomon's wrists had been slashed. His throat had a puncture wound in it: a hole big enough to fit two fingers.

All of the men here were evil by association, but I figured Solomon was the least bad. He didn't have the mental capacity and just went along—if that was any excuse. In different circumstances, I might have felt a twinge of sympathy for him. But not right now.

A sudden noise behind me made me realize I'd been a fool. Solomon's body could have been a lure, displayed like this to attract my attention.

I dodged behind the tree, my gun hand poised. Something caught my attention, something moving fast and away. And even though it was dark, I was sure I'd seen a man.

My instinct was to give chase, but again this could have been a trick, so I tracked the movement and figured the person was now in the vicinity of the bunkhouse.

I stayed to the north, scanning ahead and checking for movement on the far side in case the person showed themselves again.

As I came level with the common room I stopped. Easing forward, I was ready in case someone was waiting behind the common room wall. There wasn't, but as soon as I edged south a gunshot cracked loud in the night. And then another.

SIXTY-THREE

The gunshots echoed in the mountains, but I placed the origin in the direction of the town square. Who was shooting? Could it be Harwood? Had the army finally arrived? Then I thought not. Only two shots. If the cavalry was here surely there would be a whole barrage of shots.

I moved through the trees to the bunkhouse and quickly checked it. No sign of anyone.

I set off again, this time following the perimeter with the river not far beyond. And I heard Gabe before I located him in the long grass. He'd been shot twice in the chest and was losing blood fast. I could also see it bubbling around his lips.

His eyes bulged with fear as I approached.

"Who shot you?"

"Don't... know," he said, spluttering blood. "Michael and... Daniel..."

"Are they fighting?" I gripped his shoulder as his eyes closed. "Gabe. Stay with me, Gabe."

"Tony... My name's..." The guy was dying and I realized he no longer wanted to be known by the name Jeremiah had given him.

"Stay with me, Tony," I said, but I could see it was pointless. He gave a final cough of blood and was gone.

Another one dead, just three left.

I started for the edge of the town square and the latrines but stopped. What if the sniper wasn't on a roof?

He could be ahead. Maybe Gabe had been a lure. After all, he was the first man who hadn't been killed outright.

A sniper could be in the trees just ahead of me, but that would have been foolish. A sniper wants one of two things: a spotter or a safe vantage point. Since I figured this was one man protecting himself, it meant there was no spotter. The trees provided cover but he'd also be exposed. He'd be lying in the undergrowth looking down his barrel at the pool of light created by the fire.

More shots rang out.

I decided to stay with the sniper-on-the-roof theory. Of course, I was assuming he had either intelligence or training. Either he would be on the cookhouse or washroom's roof. Both had a line of sight across the square.

Which one? There were other buildings either side of the washroom: the storeroom with Sam's dead body on one side, and the shower block and latrines on the other. The cookhouse was on its own except for the eating area.

The former had the benefit of the river and fence close on one side. The cookhouse had trees on two sides and the fields on the other.

The washroom might seem like the better option, but a good sniper also considers his exit, and more trees also meant more cover for an escape.

I stuck my Beretta away and swung Solomon's rifle into my hands and cut across to the northern perimeter fence before I reached the three huts. As I passed behind the chicken coop, I heard another exchange of fire.

I found a good position, aimed at the cookhouse roof and waited, checking left and right every few beats.

Nothing happened for five minutes and then suddenly there was another volley of shots. Scratch that. It was the rat-a-tat-tat of a machine gun and returning single shots. Two people in a fire fight or two people shooting at a third.

I saw movement on the cookhouse roof. The sniper. He did a crouching run to change position. I saw his rifle before he dived down and began shooting across the square.

From his boxy shape and size I guessed this was Michael.

While he was focused on the opposite side, I ran across the open land to the back of the cookhouse.

The gunfire ended and echoed off into the distance. Pulling a bench over, I clambered on it and peeked over the edge of the roof.

Single sporadic shots started again and I saw the shooter lying there, focused away from me, firing towards the buildings on the far side.

I pushed up and moved lightly over the roof. I got the whole way before Michael heard me. He jerked around, but too late as I landed a knee into his prone body and followed with a downward punch to his swivelling head.

Machine-gun fire made me flatten beside Michael. I knocked his rifle away and stuck my Beretta behind his ear.

"Where's Jeremiah?" I hissed.

"What?" His voice was strange and I heard the panic in his voice.

"Jeremiah—where is he?"

"Fuck Jeremiah," he said. "Daniel's gone fucking crazy."

Machine-gun fire forced our heads down.

"Daniel?" I asked.

"He's gone crazy."

More machine-gun fire, but this time away from us. I figured Daniel was moving around the back of the workshop and was shooting something else.

I grabbed Michael's collar and pulled him up.

"Get off the roof," I said.

He went for his rifle and I punched him again. "Don't tempt me," I snarled. "You're coming with me and we're finding Jeremiah."

I crouch ran back across the roof, pulling Michael with me. We made it all the way to where I'd left the bench. I dropped the rifle on the ground.

"Right—"

Before I could provide instructions, the air became alive with bullets. Instinctively I jumped onto the bench and bounced off it, immediately jumping again, onto the ground.

I'd started with Michael's collar in my hand but lost hold as we fell through the air. From the corner of my eye, I saw him hit. His body shuddered and then spun.

I grabbed the rifle and ran for cover. When I reached the trees, I dived for cover with the Beretta in my hand, ready to shoot.

Michael wasn't moving, and I saw Daniel across the way. He'd faked the move behind the workshop and doubled back. He appeared to be scanning the trees trying to spot me. I switched from my gun to the rifle and aimed at him, but he ducked back into the shadows and I now struggled to get a fix on his location.

I moved, found a good spot, stopped and swept through the trees opposite, looking for him. I saw movement over by the storeroom. So he'd doubled back again.

With a machine gun, he had an advantage, yet despite this, he moved away when I expected him to close me down.

Could this be another trick? Would he switch back yet again after luring me towards him? Nothing happened for more than five long minutes. I wanted Jeremiah but had no idea where he'd be. I needed Daniel alive. I needed Daniel to tell me where I'd find his boss.

I couldn't wait for Daniel to come to me and I figured we had about two hours before the sky lightened. Daylight would definitely give him a further advantage.

Instead of circling the town hall towards the workshop, I went the other way. I'd approach Daniel from behind if I was lucky.

Before I left the treeline, I saw movement opposite, near the latrines. Then a moment later I saw Daniel.

I raised my rifle and aimed at him, but my back brain was screaming at me. The movement I'd seen couldn't have been Daniel. There were two men.

The ex-soldier suddenly swung around and started shooting wildly. Then I saw him run.

Was Daniel now fighting Jeremiah?

He seemed to be going back the way he must have come, back past the washhouse, the storeroom, maybe as far as the workshop.

I ran the other way, past the cookhouse to the chicken coop. I went to the end and looked over towards the workshop. Someone ran through the woods on the far side, beyond the buildings. I waited a moment and then gave chase.

I cut across the land in front of the common room and headed for the bunkhouse.

I stopped and paused, checked behind, checked ahead. Then suddenly someone burst through the trees.

Daniel was running towards me and he had a Sten gun ready to fire.

SIXTY-FOUR

Daniel hadn't seen me. I stepped out of the darkness and he ran right into my rifle. I swung it out so that it caught him in the throat and almost knocked his head off. His legs came forward and he landed flat on his back. The machine gun spun off into the darkness.

"Where's Jeremiah?" I growled into his face after my knee jammed into his chest.

"Go to hell!"

"I think we're already there," I said, and stuck the Beretta under his chin.

He snarled back up at me.

"Don't think I won't blow your brains out."

"Then fucking do it!"

I pushed harder, forcing his head back. "You don't deserve it," I said, resisting the urge. "A bullet to the brain would be the easy way out. You're going to sweat in a stinking jail for the rest of your days—you and your sick friend Jeremiah."

I pushed harder still but could see it wasn't working, so I flipped him over onto his front and knelt on his back. Then I pulled his right arm behind him, my left still holding the gun.

"And your other arm," I snapped.

When he didn't move, I pistol-whipped him. Not hard enough to knock him out, but he'd have a sore head for a few days.

He yelped.

"I'll keep doing it until you give me your other arm."

Daniel's arm came back.

"Wrists together," I instructed, and he did it.

I pulled the rope from my pocket and repositioned so that a knee was on his neck. Only then did I tuck my gun under my arm so that I could cut the rope and tie his wrists with two hands.

As I did it, I mentally cursed that this was the last piece of rope. I'd used too much on Solomon and now I could only tie Daniel's hands.

When I was done, I got off him and yanked at his hands so he had to get up awkwardly.

"Last chance: where's Jeremiah?"

Daniel said nothing.

"Is he the killer?"

He snorted. "Don't be ridiculous! Jeremiah couldn't do that."

"Really? I've seen his shrine and been in the so-called school. The man is sick."

His eyes widened.

"And I've seen his lab," I said.

Daniel blinked, then let out an uncontrolled laugh before he stifled it.

"He's gone. You'll never find him," he said, but I was no longer listening. I was thinking about his reaction. I'd been in the laboratory and not found him. Could there be another hidden place, like in the town hall?

And then it struck me.

"*Xiamian*," I said, and his eyes gave it away. I'd planned to drag Daniel around with me, looking for his leader, but now I didn't need to.

333

Daniel was in the process of shaking his head, and before the return motion had completed, I landed an uppercut to his chin. His feet left the ground for the second time in five minutes, only this time he landed like a deadweight.

I spent a few seconds vainly searching for the Sten gun that Daniel had been carrying, then gave up. It was too dark and the grass too long. I was wasting time I didn't have.

I ran up to and through the tunnel that connected the two parts of the commune. I kept going until I reached the school. The door was open. Had we left it open? I thought not.

The four children were still inside.

With my gun out, I burst into the lab and immediately saw I had been right.

Xiamian—below.

There was a hatch in the floor and it was open. Faint light came from down below and I heard a scuffling sound.

Without hesitating, I went down steps into a tunnel like the one from the storeroom. The dim light came from two rooms, the first twenty yards ahead, the second another ten yards beyond.

With the gun ahead of me I moved lightly on my feet, covering the space quickly to the first room. Nothing there. A small empty room with a weak orange light bulb.

Then I realized the sounds were coming from the end room. Someone was moving around, not trying to be quiet.

Now I ran and burst into the second room, gun ready to shoot Jeremiah.

But what I saw made me freeze. This was the laboratory. There were cupboards all around with a

334

myriad of jars and bottles. There was a table in the middle of the room and spread-eagled on it was a naked body: a giant white-skinned, white-haired man. Jeremiah.

Blood ran over his chest and down his arms that hung over the edges, but that's not what first drew my attention. His stomach was sliced open and intestines looped from one side of the bench to the floor on the other.

And standing over Jeremiah's mutilated body was Harwood with a knife in his hand.

SIXTY-FIVE

"What the hell?" I said, staring at the SIB officer.

His hands were covered in blood and Harwood appeared to be in shock.

I pointed my gun at him but he stared at me with incomprehension.

"I'm arresting you for—"

"What are you talking about?" he said, shaking his head. "This isn't what it looks like!"

"Explain."

He took a breath. "I found him like this. I just arrived and found him like this. I'd decided the killer must be Jeremiah but it can't be."

"And the knife?"

"I'd just picked it up."

"You had the murder weapon in your hands, for Christ's sake, John!"

"It looks familiar. I think…"—he shook his head—"It can't be. You've got to believe me. It was on the floor."

I kept the gun trained on him.

"Why did you do it, John? Why all those men?"

"No, Ash. Give me time to think!"

I said, "You told me you'd called Gillman Barracks, but you hadn't, had you? The army isn't here, so you didn't call them."

"I did!"

I shook my head. "You called Tebrau Airfield and asked for Flight Lieutenant Tony Billings. You didn't leave your name but the clerk remembered your accent."

"No," Harwood said. His hand moved towards his holstered revolver.

"Don't move!" I barked. "Billings picked you and a prisoner up in the copter from Kahang and you somehow caused a crash. You shot him with a Chinese pistol and then burned the helicopter. You planted your warrant card on the prisoner and set fire to him—made sure he burned just enough to be unrecognizable but similar enough to you to be convincing."

"Ash, seriously, you've got this wrong!"

"You're BlackJack," I said. "You've been killing criminals, haven't you, John. Righteous kills, is that how you justified it?"

"It's not me, I tell you!"

"The names Jack and John are interchangeable, aren't they?"

He took a step towards me.

"Don't make me shoot you, John!"

Harwood raised his bloodied hands. "Wait, no, I can prove you're wrong. You said my warrant card was burned, but I have it here in my pocket. Let me just—"

Before I realized what was happening, I saw something in the corner of my eye. Something was moving fast in the darkness.

I swivelled but kept my gun on Harwood. His hand moved to his pocket. He hadn't seen the new arrival, but I had.

Daniel.

"Nooo!" Harwood shouted, and leapt into the air. Only he wasn't jumping, not of his own volition anyway.

337

The air filled with the ratter-tat of a Sten gun and Harwood's body danced one last time before slumping to the ground.

SIXTY-SIX

I dived under the table, rolled and aimed my Beretta at where Daniel had been standing. But instead of pulling the trigger, I hesitated.

Through the dust, I could see the machine gun on the floor. Daniel must have dropped it. And above the ringing in my ears, I could hear him sobbing.

I stood, aiming the gun at him. "Don't move!" I said, but I don't think he heard me. He was making too much noise because the sob had turned into a howl.

He was hunched over Jeremiah's bloody body, his hands on the dead man's shoulders, his head on Jeremiah's chest.

I stood on the other side of the table and poked Daniel hard with the gun. He raised his face. Jeremiah's blood formed a strange swirl around Daniel's eye socket and cheek like he'd been cut. He looked at me with blind eyes.

"Back away!" I said.

His eyes focused. "I loved him."

"Back away, Daniel!"

Finally, he straightened, closed his eyes and took a long breath.

I said, "It's over."

"Are you going to shoot me now?"

I'd considered it, but somehow his pathetic howling had stopped me. To shoot him now would be in cold blood. God knows he deserved it. He'd helped this monster feed his ego and insanity. Working with the Chinese terrorists was bad enough, but Daniel had participated in the abuse of women and murder of children. Directly or indirectly, he was as guilty as Jeremiah.

And yet I couldn't pull the trigger.

He was watching me, probably guessing my dilemma. Then he surprised me.

"I'll show you where the money's hidden."

I moved around the table and kicked his machine gun away. I glanced down at Harwood and saw his eyes bulge. Blood burbled in his throat seconds before he stopped moving.

Bullets had sprayed across his body and taken his right arm off at the elbow. His mouth froze open and I saw the light go from his eyes.

"The money," Daniel said again. "I know how to get it... and only me."

I looked up at him. "You can't bribe me."

"Not a bribe," he said. "Maybe it'll be taken into consideration. We shouldn't have dealt with the Chinese, but we did. You know we always did. In fact, this place used to be our base. Jeremiah"—he swallowed hard— "Jeremiah designed the tunnels and had the Chinese build it. We lived underground for years while the Japs occupied the country. That's why they called it *Xiamian*. It was the place below ground."

"Lead the way," I said with my gun on him. "Any sudden move and I shoot you."

We went back along the tunnel and into the room above.

"You guessed this wasn't the lab," he said. "I gave it away, didn't I?"

I didn't answer.

We walked through the last room where the four children were strapped into beds.

"How could you?" I said, with no attempt to hide my disgust.

"I loved him and it was his dream." He was talking about Jeremiah and continued once we were outside. He pointed for us to head towards the main tunnel through the hill. "He didn't want them to die, he just wanted the blood. He believed he'd discovered the secret to eternal youth."

"Shangri-La," I said.

"At first it was young women, but then the children grew and he became obsessed with it. He didn't want them to die. He was getting better at letting them live for longer."

I could barely listen to Daniel's rambling.

"Where are we going?" I said, after breathing and banishing images from my mind.

"The bunker," he said. "Is everyone dead?"

"Just you and me left."

"Peter killed Jeremiah. He was the killer all along, wasn't he?"

He was referring to Harwood of course, and I said, "Yes."

"He killed a lot of people."

"Probably more than you know," I said, thinking of the other cases the SIB men had been investigating. Not just the men here, but Major Broom and others involved. He'd only killed guilty men, but he'd been judge, jury and executioner. And the way he'd killed them—I knew Harwood had enjoyed it.

Daniel took me to the bunker. "There's a tunnel down here too."

I let him go first, locating the hatch, lifting it and descending the ladder into the dark. Sweeping the torch as we walked, I saw a series of rooms.

"Old munitions from the war," he said as we passed some. "You know I was Force 136. We were heroes. That must count for something, right?"

"Try it as your defence," I suggested without conviction.

We came to a locked door and Daniel used a key. After this, there was another door. This one had a wheel lock like you find on board ships—or bank vaults. He spun the wheel left and right and left again and then pulled the door open.

I shone the torch inside and he gasped.

"It's gone!"

I could see banknotes and boxes on the floor. There were boxes on shelves too.

We stepped into the small room.

"There was loads in here!" he said. The shock in his voice told me he wasn't lying.

"How much?"

"Millions. We converted the gold to cash and kept our cut."

I looked in a box. It was packed with notes and there were four more like this.

"There's still a lot of money in here," I said.

"Yes, but most is missing. There was a suitcase…"

"Where is it?"

"Someone's been here and beaten us to it."

We backed out.

"Who?"

"Only Jeremiah and I knew where this room was."

"Someone could have found it. Michael perhaps?"

He said nothing for a few paces. Our footsteps echoed against the tunnel walls.

"The money—Peter could have found it." Another pace, then: "I killed Peter. I killed the murderer. That must count for something even if we don't have all of the money, right? That'll get taken into consideration along with my service record?"

"Not up to me," I said. "But the biggest help will be if you tell us where the bandits are—at least the gold mines."

"I can do that," he said.

My torch picked out the ladder ahead.

As Daniel climbed, I had the Beretta trained on him. "Take it slow," I instructed. "Wait where I can see you. Too fast and I won't hesitate to shoot you."

I saw him reach the top and start to move aside. Slowly. And then I heard it. A banshee. A wild animal scream that froze my blood.

Above me, I saw a flash of movement and Daniel jerked away from the hole. And then he screamed too.

SIXTY-SEVEN

I took a breath, prepared myself and began to climb the rest of the way out of the hole. The screaming had stopped. All I could hear was Daniel moaning in agony.

My Beretta was in my left hand ready, but I didn't need it. I saw that straight away.

I'd already figured it was no animal that had attacked Daniel. Wild animals don't scream, attack and then stop.

Safiya stood two paces from the hole, watching me as I climbed out. Her hands were by her side and she stared at the heap on the ground. Daniel.

I shone my torch on him and saw a desperate face. A machete was wedged in his neck, maybe just above the fifth vertebrae. No artery had been severed but he was leaking blood and it was pooling under his head.

In shock, he was shaking, his eyes wide and desperate.

Safiya didn't move. She'd just delivered a merciless blow to Daniel and yet her face showed nothing.

"What shall I do?" she asked me, her voice calm and flat.

"We could leave him like this. Looks like you've severed his spinal cord. He's paralysed and bleeding."

"He's going to die?"

"Yes."

"Good."

"It'll take at least an hour. He'll die in terrible pain and fear. Or you could finish him off and put him out of his misery. Not that he deserves it, but it would be the merciful thing."

Her breathing sounded loud in the bunker.

"What would you do?"

"I'd shoot him in the head and get satisfaction from it."

She looked at my gun and back at me.

"But you should do it," I said.

"Yes." She held out her hand and took the Beretta, weighed it in her hand then gripped it hard.

She took a long breath. "This is for the children," she said, and stepped closer to Daniel. He focused on her and stopped shaking as she raised the gun.

She held it away as though it wasn't part of her and for a second I thought she wasn't going to do it.

Then she whispered, "For Arjun, Vihaan, and Sai. For my children. For all the children," and fired. She kept firing until she was sure the gun was empty.

Then she stepped back and nodded to me.

I said, "You came back."

We'd walked away from the bunker towards the main commune.

"I never left," she said. "I couldn't persuade the others to go. They're all at the nursery. They were afraid, and anyway, where do we go?"

"Your sister is waiting for you in Permaisuri."

"But what will she think of me?"

"She knows you've been a victim—and you don't need to tell her anything. Not until you're ready to talk. She loves you and will just be happy to have you back."

I saw her nod in the darkness.

She didn't say anything for a few paces, probably lost in her thoughts. Then she said, "And what about the children?"

"What about them?"

"They need help. They need a hospital. They're not mine but I feel responsible in some way."

"You aren't responsible. None of you are."

"I can take them to a hospital."

"No," I said firmly. "I'll take you to Permaisuri and then I'll take them to hospital."

In the end, we agreed that I should take the children first. We turned around and I went to the garage and drove the Land Rover all the way to the school.

We put the children in the back and made them as comfortable as possible. Safiya sat with her arms around them. She'd given them blankets because they were shivering, and it broke my heart to see their frail bodies and scared eyes.

I drove like a mad man to Terengganu, the sky getting lighter all the time. I'd not looked for a hospital before and not seen one. As soon as I entered the town, north of the river, I asked for directions and cursed that it was right over the other side, where Route Three turned inland through the hills.

"Hurry," Safiya said, and I did.

As we approached a boom barrier outside the hospital, I blared the horn again and again. Just in time, a security man jumped out of his hut and swung the barrier out of my path.

I ignored his protests and kept going all the way up to the entrance, then ran in shouting for assistance.

Within ten minutes, all four kids were in hospital beds with drips and people fussing over them. Safiya and I stood in the corridor and watched through the window.

"I wish I could do more," she said.

"They're in the best place," I said, and she looked at me with tears in her eyes.

"It's not the same thing."

I nodded. I guessed she was imagining these were hers and how she'd feel if they'd just been handed over to the authorities.

On the drive down, I'd been thinking about the remaining money in the vault underground and what to do with it. Now I decided.

I said, "See how you are. Give it a few days, maybe a few weeks. Recover and then come and see the children. You want to do something, then maybe you could give them a home."

It was probably too much for her to take in right then, but she nodded acceptance and we left the hospital and travelled back to Permaisuri.

At the café where her sister worked, I banged repeatedly on the door until the owner answered. He fetched the girl, and for three heartbeats, they stared at each other. Then they dived into each other's arms and hugged and cried and hugged some more.

I slipped away. I didn't want to intrude, and their joy was thanks enough.

When I came to the main road I saw a military police vehicle coming towards me. I stood up and waved to the driver. Twenty yards out, I realized it was Lieutenant Cole from 200 Provost in the passenger seat.

"We got your message," he said as a troop carrier pulled up behind him. Then another Land Rover and troop carrier arrived.

Captain Robshaw jumped out of the second jeep and swept back his unkempt blond hair.

"You're all right!" he said, jogging up and pumping my hand.

"And you're too late," I said. "The excitement has come and gone."

He shook his head. "Bugger! We left straight away. As soon as your Madam Chau confirmed, Ambrose mobilized us. We've been driving all bloody night."

I quickly summarized the situation and Robshaw sent the lieutenant in the direction of the post office to call the army. The MPs could help me with the commune but we needed the army to deal with the Chinese bandits and their gold mines.

"So Captain Harwood's really dead?" Robshaw asked as I directed his driver towards the commune.

"Twice," I said. "Once in the helicopter crash and now here."

Robshaw shook his head, not fully understanding.

"He faked it the first time and wasn't expecting to see me here," I explained. "He pretended he didn't know about it, and I should have challenged him."

"And Lieutenant Jenkins?" Robshaw asked. "I liked him."

"Looks like Harwood got him too. I think he must have guessed Harwood was the killer, but too late. We'll probably find his body up here somewhere. BlackJack wasn't one to hide his victims."

We were two miles away when I realized the smoke wasn't a single plume from the town hall. More places were burning.

SIXTY-EIGHT

I told the driver to put his foot down, worried that something had gone wrong. Worried that I'd been wrong. Had someone survived and set fire to the nursery?

We took the road to the upper gate and drove straight into the commune. My fears were unfounded. The fires came from the so-called school and the two treehouses. After going through the tunnel, I saw that the women had set fire to the bunkhouse, common room and the three huts.

The MPs were ordered to collect the bodies, and we added them to one of the fires. All that is except for Harwood's. His body had to be taken back and was bound tightly in the commune's green cloth so that the smell wouldn't be too bad.

Then the MPs used explosives to collapse the tunnel and underground lab.

"Get a specialist team out here, Robbo," I said on the other side of the hill, looking at the burnt wreckage of the town hall. "Cordon it off, and don't blow up the tunnel under there until they've been."

"What's there?"

"A big radioactive rock. Uranium, I think. I saw phantom light when it should have been pitch-black."

He agreed, and we discussed delaying the destruction of the tunnel under the bunker too.

"The money," Robshaw said to me. "What do we do with it?"

"Report that it was all taken," I said straight-faced.

"Who took it?"

That was a loose end. I'd believed Daniel when he'd told me that most had been taken. "Must have been Harwood," I said. "If not him, then one of the other ex-soldiers." Michael was the prime candidate. It was possible that he'd taken it—hidden it somewhere close by—before he was shot by Daniel.

We looked but we didn't find any more money or the missing suitcase. I'd also hoped we'd find the body of Jenkins out there, but we didn't.

I supervised the retrieval of Slugger's body from behind the garage.

"Get someone to take him home," I told Robshaw. "He was a hero." When his body was in the back of a Land Rover, I made sure the dirt had all been cleaned off before wrapping his body.

I didn't expect Cindy to invite me to the funeral. She'd blame me for this. So I put my hand on Slugger's chest and said, "Goodbye, old friend. And good luck." I knew he didn't believe in an afterlife, but if there were pearly gates on the other side then Scott "Slugger" Stevenson deserved admittance.

Most of the women said they were staying in the commune. They'd rebuild it and raise their babies. Only this time the gates would remain unlocked and no men would be allowed to join.

Eight of the women wanted to leave, and we arranged for a driver to take them wherever they wanted to go. He took the covered truck from the garage and I gave them money. I saved some for Safiya and gave the rest of the stash to the women who stayed behind.

It took us a whole day and everyone was exhausted at the end. Robshaw took me back to Permaisuri, where I left the money for Safiya and paid the owner of the lodging house. He was disappointed that he hadn't acquired the jeep, but I paid him well for his trouble.

Through the night, a corporal drove me home, and I slept the whole way, although my sleep was fitful. I'd been affected by what had been going on at Jeremiah's commune, and it would take many days before I could rid some of the images from my head.

I spent a large part of Sunday in Saint Andrews Cathedral, praying for my friend and the children of Shangri-La.

When I made it into the office on Monday, clean and refreshed, Madam Chau was excited to see me—although this was only evidenced by a brief smile and furtive glances. So at least I knew she was happy I was alive and well.

A pile of mail sat on my desk, but I refused to look at any cases, not for a while anyway.

Instead, I spent time thinking and drinking tea that Madam Chau made for me, and walking around the town. I didn't know why, I just figured it would help.

I also felt like I had unfinished business. I couldn't put my finger on it and kept wondering whether it was because I hadn't killed any of the main men. Harwood had killed Jeremiah, Daniel had despatched Harwood and then Safiya had dealt with the man who had raped her and taken her children away.

Or maybe there was something else that niggled me.

Harwood had been investigating the Chinese gold pipeline and suspected someone high up in the army.

Was that real or Harwood's smoke screen? I had no idea but was sure the Special Investigations Branch would probably continue the investigations without my involvement.

That wasn't the niggle. Something about Harwood troubled me but I couldn't put my finger on it.

That evening, I saw Sergeant Becks. More unfinished business. He didn't have a cricket bat with him this time. He was just about to go into Raffles for a drink with a couple of mates.

"Becks!" I shouted from across the road.

He swivelled, squinted at me and then laughed.

"Hey ho, it's the dog hunter," he bellowed, referring to Mrs Slone's ruse to get me into her house. "The little coward!"

"And you're Major Slone's puppy," I said.

He stepped away from the hotel and faced me across the road, showing his broad six foot five frame, biceps tense below his short sleeves.

His two cronies closed in behind, one on either side.

"Come on then!" I said, and walked away.

I glanced back and he was running to my side of the road. So I started running too.

I swung around the corner onto Bras Basah Road and went north towards the Cathay Building. I looked back and slowed a touch to ensure Becks was still coming. He was. All three of them were racing down the road, baying for my blood.

Not much further boys.

I stopped and doubled up, resting my hands on my knees as if exhausted. They were close now and I took off again.

Another few yards...

I turned sharp left and headed for a building, doors straight ahead.

I burst through and walked in. The YMCA Boxing Club was in session.

When Becks and his buddies charged in they pulled up sharply. Men closed in around them.

"What do you think you're doing?" Jack, the coach, yelled at them. He was ex-navy and as wide as he was tall—which was only about five foot seven, but no one messed with Jack. He looked tougher than old boots with hobnails.

"They're with me," I said as I slipped off my shoes and swung up over the ropes into the ring. "The big guy thinks I'm a coward."

Becks backed up, snarling. "We'll settle this another time, pussy Carter."

The doors to the gym were barred. Becks looked at them and then considered the guys in front of him.

Jack closed in. "Settle it now," he said. No argument. A command. "Or are *you* the coward?"

Becks snorted and rolled his neck, pushed his way towards the boxing ring and pulled himself in. He clenched his fists and stepped my way.

"Whoa!" Jack was suddenly there and between us. "You get in my ring, you fight by my rules. Gloves and faceguards."

"It's all right, Jack," I said, but he shook his head at me.

"My rules!"

The faceguards would be a problem. I wanted to knock this bozo out. Heavy gloves made it hard enough, since I'm more about speed than strength, but the head protection would make it especially hard. Unless he was a total novice in the ring.

He wasn't.

Becks started well with a good combination while protecting his chin. I moved around the ring and counterpunched. Becks tired quickly. A big guy with heavy muscles.

After thirty seconds, I started making contact. After a minute I was landing combinations, fast and hard, and then moving.

I thought about Slugger. He'd been my opponent once, a long time ago, before I respected him. Although Becks had nothing to do with him, I imagined I was fighting for Slugger.

Close to the two-minute mark, Jack looked at me.

"Keep going," I said. In other words this wasn't a series of two-minute rounds, but I doubt Becks would have made two rounds anyway. He was sweating and breathing hard. His punches no longer came close and then he became my punch bag. After three minutes I was calling my combinations as I delivered them. A training routine that got the other gym members cheering.

Becks staggered.

"Wish you had a cricket bat?" I asked.

He didn't answer.

I hit him with four more combinations and Becks sank to his knees.

Jack didn't step in, but he glanced at me wondering what I'd do.

A bigger man would have recognized the win. A bigger man would have realized I'd made my point. But I was not that man. Plus I had all the pent-up anger for Slugger.

I caught Becks with an uppercut that drove him to the canvas.

"Don't do someone else's job!" I shouted. He couldn't have heard me, but as I walked away I realized what I meant and why I was so angry.

I blamed myself for getting Slugger involved in my investigations in the past.

I blamed myself for Slugger's death.

SIXTY-NINE

The next morning, after a workout at the gym, I arrived at my office to find people spilling out of the door.

"What's going on?" I asked Madam Chau as she met me. There must have been twelve people inside and many more on the stairs and in the street.

She nodded towards my desk, and I recognized Mr Tharoor, the baker. He stepped forward with his hand out.

"Thank you," he said.

I shook his hand. "The problem—the extortion—it's over, right?"

"It is and I thank you. But I'm not the only one you helped."

He stepped aside and a little Chinese lady bowed and shook my hand.

"Thank you."

Then another and another. They walked up, bowed and thanked me. I think it was the most humbling moment of my life.

Mr Tharoor stood to one side as people filed in and out of the office.

Madam Chau sat at her desk and drank tea. She looked even more relaxed than when I'd returned from Malaya.

The phone rang and she picked it up, listened, and then held it in the air.

I mouthed, "Take a message," and continued receiving the visitors.

Finally, the hand-shaking was over, and Mr Tharoor said, "Sixty-two businesses. Each one of these people here today represents a business that paid extortion money to those thugs. Sixty-two individuals representing even more livelihoods. And not just that: we feel safe now. There is no better security than the confidence that extortion is unacceptable."

I nodded. "I'm gratified."

"And we would like to make this gesture." I hadn't noticed it before, but there had been a bag at his feet. He picked it up and handed it to me.

It was full of cash.

I could have taken money from the commune. I certainly needed it, and could have justified some as payment for what I'd done. But I hadn't. Madam Chau had told me I was wrong and she worried about our cash flow.

"It's very generous," I said, "but I can't accept this."

Madam Chau gave me the evil eye.

Tharoor said, "You can't refuse."

"But the whole point was to help you keep your hard-earned money."

He shook his head. "Those crooks took this each week. The least we can do is give you this last instalment—for what you did for us."

I started to complain, but he insisted. "Accept it, Mr Carter."

"Half," I said. "I'll take half."

He bowed and smiled before removing wads of cash and placing them on my desk. Finally he bowed again and I thanked everyone who was within earshot.

357

When they'd left, I asked Madam Chau to bank it immediately.

"We're saved," she said. "I always knew you'd come good."

"Thanks for your trust," I said with a touch of irony.

"Are we still in business?"

"What do you mean?"

"You have money, which is good, but I hope it doesn't mean you stop working."

I laughed. "Certainly not. Hand me the post I need to look at."

"Before that, there's a telephone message."

"Who was it?"

"Colonel Ambrose at Gillman Barracks," she said. "The message was that Captain Harwood was"—she checked her notes—"in deep cover. Does that make sense?"

"Yes," I said. But it didn't. The message meant that SIB knew that Harwood wouldn't report in. He'd said he was in deep cover because he believed there was someone else involved in the gold pipeline, someone senior in the army.

Madam Chau picked up the phone. "He said you'd want to call him back."

Two minutes later I was talking to Ambrose.

"It doesn't mean anything," I said when I got put through to the CO.

"Not on its own it doesn't," he said.

"There's something else?"

"A clerk screwed up."

I waited for more, heard him breathing and knew it was awkward.

"I've seen the yellow slips," he finally said. The yellow slips were the carbon copies of telephone

358

messages. They were kept as a record but rarely reviewed.

"And?" I prompted, and felt my chest tighten with anticipation.

"Captain Harwood called us on Thursday morning at oh four hundred."

I blew out air. "What did he say?"

"The message was to get the whole bloody army up to Permaisuri."

"Damn!"

"That was forty hours before your secretary called me. The message got lost." He explained what had happened but then said there was no excuse.

I ended the call with my head in a spin, returned to my desk and sank into the chair.

Madam Chau scuttled across to me with the pile of letters.

"Shall I read them out?" she asked.

"What? Yes, go ahead."

She started talking but my mind wasn't on it. I kept thinking about Harwood. He had really called for backup. I'd tagged him as guilty because the army hadn't been there.

I thought it through. The body in the helicopter crash was meant to be him. The guy at Tebrau Airfield remembered the Birmingham accent.

He was left-handed and evidence pointed to a left-handed killer. In Jeremiah's lab, he'd been holding the knife. He looked guilty as hell, but now I thought back, I remembered him struggling with something.

Had he been telling the truth. Did he recognize the knife?

Left-handedness was easily faked, the accent as well, In fact, he was recognized as having a Birmingham accent and yet I'd thought it was hardly noticeable.

Had someone exaggerated it? What if someone had wanted it to look like Harwood? What if this was all about luring me and Harwood to Jeremiah's commune?

Could the killer have been so conniving? Was this all about making it look like someone else was guilty?

Had I been deliberately deceived?

"Sorry, what did you say?" I asked Madam Chau as I realized she'd asked me a question.

She scowled at me.

"I didn't open the letter marked private. Do you want it?"

I held out my hand.

It was a small envelope with my name on it and "Hand delivered". Nothing more.

I sliced it open and my heart stopped.

A playing card fell onto my desk. The jack of spades.

BlackJack was still alive.

There was a note too.

It said, "Catch you later, Ash."

SEVENTY

Charles Balcombe stood on the balcony outside his cabin as the boat steamed into Hong Kong Harbour. They'd stopped briefly in Shanghai and he'd decided against it as a destination. The province had all the intensity of Singapore, without the British heritage. From the pier, he summed it up as busy and dirty.

Hong Kong, on the other hand, gleamed in the afternoon sunlight. Yes, he could see it was built up, but there were mountains behind and he breathed clean air.

The numerous Chinese junks with their curved wooden hulls and crimson sails looked like lizard's backs. It was like travelling back in time and he loved the sense of a new beginning. The old and the new.

And he had a huge amount of money—more wealth than he ever imagined. He could have bought this steamer, let alone travel in an upper-class cabin for the first time in his life.

His papers gave him a different identity. They were from the man he'd killed in the helicopter crash.

The helicopter crash.

It had been the most reckless thing he'd done in his life, and undoubtedly the most exhilarating. He wondered if he'd derived more pleasure from that one moment than from all the men he'd killed.

It had also been a stroke of genius. He'd thought of faking his own death, but this had been better. He'd set up Harwood as the patsy and planted the burned warrant card on the prisoner. That too had been clever. He'd picked up someone who looked like Harwood and wasn't in the military. No one would connect him to the murder, especially since he'd shot the pilot and let the prisoner burn to death. He'd longed to use his knife, but resisted. Just like he would now resist killing again.

A new life, a new attitude... for as long as he could last anyway.

It had taken three and a half days and he'd enjoyed the company of the other upper-class passengers. His fellow diners were either tourists or business owners. Balcombe had thought about pretending to own a business but feared being caught out. But he quickly learned that these people didn't talk shop. They preferred gossip and politics and a bit of flirting.

And the biggest flirt was Caroline, an attractive young woman who was joining her husband on the island. However, her marital status didn't stop her batting her eyelids at him. Last night she'd either been drunk or pretending to be, and insisted that he help her back to her cabin.

He'd intended to play the perfect gentleman. After all, these high society contacts would prove useful in his new home, and he didn't want to upset anyone. But she'd insisted again and practically dragged him into her cabin.

She saw his exposed right wrist. Three weeks later and the marks were still there.

"Handcuff," he'd said, and she'd laughed like he was joking. Then she'd torn off his shirt pretending to look for more scars.

Her embrace had been passionate, her hands all over him. But she'd abruptly stopped their love-making

362

before it went too far. And he knew she'd only been toying with him.

Now she came onto her balcony and acknowledged him with a coquettish smile. Last night, before he left, she'd made him promise to come to dinner with her and her husband. He'd agreed but had no intention of following through. Too awkward now.

The steamer came alongside a floating pier, a hundred little boats all around, calling out their services, offering transport and wares.

"Time to go," he said.

Porters carried luggage ashore and the passengers began to disembark by class. Balcombe and Caroline were at the front.

She had a floppy hat and held it on her head with one hand raised. It left a revealing gap under her arm. Standing behind her, he could see most of a white breast, small but firm.

She waved with her other hand and then turned. The cheeky smile on her face said that her pose had been deliberate.

"I'll introduce you to George, my husband," she said.

Balcombe nodded, but he wasn't thinking about the husband, he was thinking about Caroline's body. Then he shook the thought away.

"Ouch!" Caroline said as they went down the gangplank. She held up a finger and he saw a pinprick of blood. She sucked it and the blood returned.

At the bottom, Balcombe could see the husband wave and walk their way.

"Kiss it better," Caroline said. She held it up and Balcombe found his lips on her index finger.

"George," Caroline squealed with delight, flinging her arms around her husband. Then: "This is Charles. He's absolutely charming and I've invited him to dinner. I hope you don't mind."

George offered Balcombe a soft hand. "Of course! Where are you staying, dear chap?"

"The Peninsula," Balcombe said.

"Excellent, then I'll have my man pick you up at seven?"

Balcombe smiled and thanked them. A porter offered to take his two suitcases to the hotel but Jenkins waved the man away. He'd rapidly changed his appearance and bought appropriate clothes in Singapore, but most of the space in the cases was taken up by money. No way was he letting a porter carry his new wealth.

Caroline and her husband were walking away now. She looked back and gave him a knowing smile. He nodded.

Who was he kidding?

He could still taste her blood on his lips, and he found himself thinking of her white naked body. He imagined her looking at him as he slit her throat, understanding the power that he had over her, understanding that his face was the last thing she would see. But it wouldn't just be her. That's how he'd move on: he'd kill the husband too.

He'd been fooling himself. He could change his name from Jenkins to Balcombe, but he couldn't be someone he wasn't.

He was BlackJack and he was in Hong Kong.

Acknowledgements

Editors normally appear way down the list of people recognized, so I'm going to change that and thank Richard Sheehan for help and guidance. My wife, Kerry is my early barometer and I was relieved to hear her appreciation when she finished the book.

I'd also like to take the opportunity to recognize David Upshall and Doreen Lowe for your encouragement and enthusiasm. It's seriously appreciated! Early reviewers: Pete Tonkin, Alex Jones, Lauren Brabrook, Richard Lipscombe and Clinton Barrett deserve a mention and my gratitude for your help and guidance.

Thanks to my sister, Dr Kerry Bailey-Jones for answering my many and varied medical questions. I expect to receive your bill one day soon.

Finally, I always thank my father for inspiring the Singapore series, but I should also thank my mother, Maureen Bailey, for her support. I hope this one wasn't too "dark" for you!

IF YOU ENJOYED THIS BOOK

Feedback helps me understand what works, what doesn't and what readers want more of. It also brings a book to life.

Online reviews are also very important in encouraging others to try my books. I don't have the financial clout of a big publisher. I can't take out newspaper ads or run poster campaigns.

But what I do have is an enthusiastic and committed bunch of readers.

Honest reviews are a powerful tool. I'd be very grateful if you could spend a couple of minutes leaving a review, however short, on sites like Amazon and Goodreads.

Thank you
Murray

SINGAPORE 52

Ash Carter had to leave the Middle East in a hurry. But when he arrives in Singapore he finds himself in the middle of a much bigger problem.

No one knows where, or when, or who but someone is planning an attack. Carter is told to make sure it doesn't happen. With pressure from politicians and the army and with Chinese Secret Societies watching his every move, he has other plans.

He is more interested in finding out who killed his friend.

SINGAPORE GIRL

Ash Carter is asked to investigate a headless body.

Now working for the government, he needs to find out if this is just another drug-war punishment or something more.

When he suspects he's getting close to the truth. The investigation gets shut down.

But he knows it s not over. And it s not in his nature to quit.

SINGAPORE BOXER

Ash Carter goes undercover in central Malaya with a private militia providing protection against the Chinese terrorists.

One of the militia has disappeared and another is dead. And then someone tries to kill Carter. As things escalate, he finds himself drawn into a world of intrigue, disputes and deception.

Will Ash Carter uncover the truth before it's too late?

SINGAPORE GHOST

Ash Carter is in Penang babysitting a newspaper reporter. She's investigating ghost stories at the barracks but it's Carter's past that is back to haunt him.

Carter finds himself beholden to the leader of a Chinese Secret Society who wants to remove his big rival, Yipp without a turf war. However Yipp and Carter have so far had a good relationship.

But when investigations on behalf of the gorgeous Su Ling uncover Yipp's wicked actions, Carter's attitude changes.

Stuck between the two criminal organisations, Ash Carter must find a solution and put the ghosts to rest.

BLACK CREEK
WHITE LIES

One night, Jade Bridger takes a dead-end path by the creek,
and vanishes. Eighteen months after being wrongly
accused of her murder, Dan Searle returns to Cornwall to
rebuild his life and forget. But others won't let him forget.

He is quickly drawn back into the case and a dark and
violent mystery; one that involved another girl years before.
As the lies begin to unravel, Dan uncovers startling truths
about his family and the past.

With dangerous people trying to keep their secrets safe, he
must save those he loves - before time runs out...

I DARE YOU

Why was Kate's boyfriend snatched off the street?
People said she couldn't trust him. They said he was a liar.
But a year later she discovers a photograph that makes her
question everything she thought she knew.

As she investigates, people start to die and Kate is left
wondering who she can trust.

She follows clues from England to the Czech Republic and
finally to the US. All the while a killer is on her tail.

Kate just wants the truth.
But is the truth worth dying for?

DARE YOU TWICE

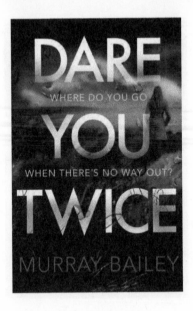

A teenage girl disappears from her locked bedroom. With no way out, and a trace of blood, the police conclude the worst. As Kate investigates the strange case, she finds her own life threatened.

She goes into hiding only to find herself drawn into another mysterious case. On the Dorset coast, a young man has vanished without trace. Except for a cryptic message he seems to have intended for Kate.

Accompanied by her friend and a British Detective, Kate follows the clues that take her to Paris, France. As the puzzle unfolds, Kate questions what she believes and has to work out what is really going on - or die trying.

MAP OF THE DEAD

Within days of solving a 3,000 year old puzzle, a researcher
dies in suspicious circumstances.

With only a few clues and a mysterious object Alex
MacLure follows a trail from London to Cairo.

He must crack the code and expose a shocking,
inconceivable truth before the secret is buried for ever.

SIGN OF THE DEAD

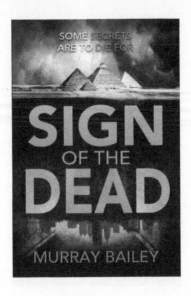

MacLure links up with Special Agent Reed to track down a serial killer.

As he decrypts an ancient story, MacLure realizes this is a race against time.

The Surgeon must be stopped before he completes his terrible and startling mission.